Chemically Insoluble

A Novel by
Rustyna Lynne

CCB Publishing
British Columbia, Canada

Chemically Insoluble

Copyright ©2015 by Rustyna Lynne
ISBN-13   978-1-77143-256-6
First Edition

Library and Archives Canada Cataloguing in Publication
Lynne, Rustyna, author
Chemically insoluble / by Rustyna Lynne. -- First edition.
Issued in print and electronic formats.
ISBN 978-1-77143-256-6 (pbk.).--ISBN 978-1-77143-257-3 (pdf)
Additional cataloguing data available from Library and Archives Canada

Cover artwork credit: Original cover design idea by Rustyna Lynne
Image: Pepper mill and salt photo © Stanislaff | Dreamstime.com

Disclaimer: This book is a work of fiction. Any names, places, events, characters or incidents portrayed in this book is through the author's imagination and have been used fictitiously. Any resemblance or similarity to actual events, locales or real persons, living or dead, is coincidental and not intended by the author.

Special Note: This novel contains intentionally misspelled words and uses incorrect grammar to capture the dialect, slang, slurring, etc. of the person(s) speaking.

Extreme care has been taken by the author to ensure that all information presented in this book is accurate and up to date at the time of publishing. Neither the author nor the publisher can be held responsible for any errors or omissions. Additionally, neither is any liability assumed for damages resulting from the use of the information contained herein.

Order this book online at:
Amazon.com, BarnesandNoble.com, or CCBPublishing.com

Publisher: CCB Publishing
             British Columbia, Canada
             www.ccbpublishing.com

Acknowledgements

Elaine: who edits out all my horrible habits, and miraculously makes my work blend. I especially enjoyed getting your curiosity aroused with this particular novel.

Mary, Diane and Cee: willing to take the patience to read *Chemically Insoluble*, the sequel to *Pepper and Salt*, and offer suggestions along the way.

Clarence—my love—for your patience and understanding.

Personal Note: Son—for you.

Books by Rustyna Lynne

Women's Fiction:
   Pepper and Salt
   Chemically Insoluble—Sequel

Science Fiction/Fantasy:
   Eftiam
     Trilogy in progress

Mystery:
   Liquid Gold (LG)

Children's Books:
   Derrick and Sierra Take Baths
   Tatiana's Shampoo
   Janel's Shampoo
   Giovanni's Pedicure
   Bella's Birthday Manicure
   Tyler Brushes His Teeth
   Chad's First Shave
   Another Sign of Chad Maturing
   *Scruffi Flies the Trees
    *=Soon to be published

Chemically Insoluble

Three women of similar backgrounds in business and lifestyles were combined to make-up the character of Susan. Currently, each woman has changed her life dramatically since the first writing of the novel ***Pepper and Salt.***

As the author, as time passed I wondered if I'd hear from them to possibly write their sequels. Much to my surprise they kept in touch. Why? In their words: 'We still want to further share our life stories, to possibly help other women to overcome mental and physical abuse.'

Another message of interest: writing ***Pepper and Salt***, I purposely never used the subtitle ***Chemically Insoluble*** within the text in anticipation of a sequel. I also felt as an Author this would reveal the characters' true transparencies no matter what. They truly are chemically insoluble, just as you can place certain solids and liquids together for only temporary mixture.

Prologue

Pepper and Salt exemplifies a relationship gone awry. Susan is a bright, talented businesswoman and is proud of her two daughters and son, who are torn between their parents during their separation and divorce. Frank's girlfriend Carol has her eye on the businesses and persuades him to legally wrest Susan of all business rights. The children sense this wedge Carol is driving and confide in their mom; Susan then retaliates to claim her children's rightful legacies. The strain is more than she realizes with caring for her businesses, Sister Staci coming out as a bisexual, and her family.

Susan becomes emotionally involved with Drew, a charismatic artist from Alaska who mysteriously comes on to Susan with a vengeance, concealing truths and cleverly manipulating her. After tricking her into marriage on a Las Vegas trip, suspense and dread grow. He takes long business trips, lies to Susan, hides her mail, arrives home most times drunk and drugged and is seen with other women, and also verbally abuses her children. Susan is a total victim: tied up, beaten and sexually abused. Drew cleverly dupes her ex-husband, family and friends into believing she has attempted suicide, isolating her more. She manages an escape to her brother's home. Drew hunts her down, forcing her back with him.

On the pivotal evening, Drew returns drunk with two friends, ordering Susan to make dinner for them although there is not a speck of food. Friends departing, Susan is left prey to a knife-wielding Drew. Attempting to stab her he falls on the bed passed out from drugs and liquor. Susan escapes, hiding out for months, keeping in touch with children, family and friends from various locales until convinced a return is safe. Susan finds courage to start a new life, winning back her family and friends in the process.

Now many years later, Susan is still in the recovery process after losing her businesses and children, and after her horrible trickster marriage to Drew and his spousal abuses. Heavy scars are left on both her and her children. Will they ever recover in this lifetime?

¿NIGHTMARES?

"HELP ME! ... HELP! ... HELP ME PLEASE!"... Running the stairs two at a time ..."CALL THE POLICE ... HE'S KILLING MY SON ... PLEASE, CALL THE POLICE"... reaching the bottom stair, still screaming banging on the manager's door ... screaming, making sure everyone hears *Someone has to hear in this complex.* Finally the outside light comes on...

Opening the door, the manager stands in Levis, no shirt. "Now what the hell is going on? God you guys sure do cost me sleep. You..."

"CALL THE POLICE NOW, HE'S KILLING MY SON!" turning Susan runs up the stairs,

"WHAT ARE YOU DOING WITH YOUR KIDS THERE IN THE FIRST PLACE? HE'S NOT SUPPOSED TO BE LIVING..."

"SHUT UP AND CALL THE COPS ASSHOLE!" reaching the stair landing, "IT'LL BE ON YOUR HEAD IF YOU DON'T." He could not see her smile. "IT'LL COST YOU YOUR JOB." sirens were now heard entering the parking lot... *Someone else must have called them, thank God.*

The first policeman rounded the corner, gun ready ..."UP HERE!" He looked up, seeing a woman dressed in a nightgown. Immediately he scaled the stairs to the landing. "HE'S LOCKED HIMSELF IN MY SON'S ROOM. HE'S GOING TO KILL MY CHILD! I CAN'T GET IN, HELP HIM PLEASE. PLEASE DON'T LET HIM HURT MY CHILD!"

"Ma'am, please calm down. You will be able to think more clearly." The policeman waited to see her focus her attention on him. "Now, I need you to tell your manager to call for an ambulance. Also I need you to wait out here." Turning, he moved cautiously into the apartment. Susan instead entered the apartment about twenty steps behind the officer.

Ron the manager had already dialed for the ambulance, overhearing the officer's request as he mounted the stairs behind them.

Pounding on the bedroom door, "Sir, this is the Police, please open this door, now. You don't want to hurt your son. Just unlock the door and let the boy out. Then we can talk."

"TALK? I HAVE TAH TEACH THIS BOY A LESS … ON." Crack went the sound … A SCREAM! "HE DOESN'T LISS … EN YOU KNOW…"

"GOD NO … MY SON …"

A SCREAM… again from the room … SCREAMING … her eyes flew open; she was sitting in her bed, finding her gown and bedding soaked with perspiration. She realized she'd been crying; *the nightmares never go away. Will they ever? Why can't I remember? Even shrinks can't give me an answer. Normally I have one a week, but since all the kids will now be with me, I'm averaging two to three a week. I don't want the children to see and hear this. Will there be more, like every night? I've got to get answers somehow. Dream amnesia? What a concept.* Getting out of bed, she moved to the bathroom to shower and change her gown.

SAFETY

As Susan was passing the next door neighbor's apartment, Benita opened her door, "Another one, eh?" Benita stood with her robe of blue wrapped tightly.

"Sorry I woke you again." Embarrassed, "I must be going, I'm late for work."

"I make dinner. Jus come when ready, Sí?"

"Thanks Benita. Saves me from cooking, can I bring anything?"

"Sí … yourself, if I find I need, I phone. Need some-ting to keep busy. Bambinos gone, you eat no, so it's best way."

* * *

"Good Morning lovely lady."

Turning from the file drawer and looking toward the door, she spied an exquisitely dressed female with a small frame, white hair, in her late 80's and a beautiful smile. "Well, to what do I owe this surprise and so early in the morning Ms. Percy?"

"Just thought I'd drop by and see how things are running. Not with the schools, I know that's in order, but with you? I do miss our daily lunches. We must change that, so we can see each other more. You know I hate emails and phones; they just don't have quite the same effect."

"I've missed you also." She moved in and gave the woman a great hug, "Coffee?"

"Lord yes, I could use a cup." She handed Susan a small white bag, "To add to the bulk of our thighs I brought nasty pastry." Automatically Percy rounded the desk, dropping herself into her old office chair.

Like old times, you still desire to be sitting there in charge. Susan took a seat on the guest side of the desk.

"Little one, you're still having those nightmares?"

"It shows? Thought the cosmetics could cover, but I guess they don't," Susan replied.

"Possibly, for someone else, yes. Not for me. Since we're already on the subject of the freak, I got a call yesterday. He's back in the area. Did he ever get served?"

So that's why you're here. "I haven't heard from the lawyer, so I guess not. Every time they try to serve him he skips out. Where exactly did they see him?"

"Drew checked out the school on Main. He'll try them all. He isn't sure where you're living, so I think you best watch your back. Why don't you stay with us?"

"Put you two in jeopardy?" Uncrossing and re-crossing her legs, "I don't think so. No, no matter where I am he'll try to hunt me down. Wonder where he got wheels or do you know if he may be on foot? I just don't want the kids harmed. They're with Frank this weekend."

"Don't know about the car, guess we could check; no information really. I just assumed he still had your car. You remember the one you left behind this school; seems so long ago now. Have you decided to tell the kids what their dear Father; what's his name? Let's see, oh yes his name is Frank. You know like what he's pulling?"

"No, the kids need to find out about their father on their own. They may not see it now, but they will when they're older. Oh, and I heard Drew sold my car for drugs."

"You're too nice, Susan. I would've let them know Frank isn't paying his share to help raise them. And I suppose they don't know he's the one who cheated." Holding up her hand, and taking a drink, "No, I know the answer, so I'll leave it alone. But it may be wise not to stay at your apartment right now."

"I can't keep running; and that's also the advice from the shrink. You know she doesn't remember what I say one visit to the next. She has way too many patients; I doubt she ever reads files."

"Like so many she's overworked these days. It's time to quit going; you're far beyond her, but giving you advice to not run from Drew, well you're right, she doesn't read her files. If she did read them, she'd know that was not the right advice. However, the real reason I'm here is I'm having a get together for that honey of mine tomorrow night and I want you there. Since the kids aren't home yet, you can come without offering an excuse."

Adjusting her sweater, Susan laughed, "Well I guess I better be there. Is it his birthday?"

"No, his book got published, so we want to celebrate. Nowadays any excuse to have some fun is a good thing."

"Will your new investor be there?"

This caused Percy to fidget in her seat, answering without looking at Susan, "Not if I have anything to say about it. Offering to sell the schools to the Cohens, just for me to retire was wrong. No, Jim and I made a great mistake not offering the schools to you; by rights they should be yours. However, you were going through so many trials and tribulations at the time with Frank, the divorce and the freak, it all got too crazy. And now this Ferris gal is definitely the worst decision I've ever made. I should have discussed it with you first, but you know hindsight..."

"I wasn't in a good state then to help, but I do agree, you could have taken a different avenue."

"You know she wants to come in and check out the schools again, and during school hours."

"Well I'll speak to her. She's an investor only. Ferris doesn't know the first thing about running schools of this type. It's one thing for her to come in for services, that's fine, but by law she's not to divulge she's an investor or act like she owns the place. Charges can be brought up on her then."

"She's looking out for her investment. Although I think someone is advising her as to what to look for."

"Yeah and I'm still the main shareholder, that's the prize she's really after. This year I should be able to have her out of our hair. You know you make a great cup of java, can I get another?"

Smiling to herself, *change of subject;* Susan got up and poured Percy another cup, "I've got some great news. Missy has decided she wants to come back and live with us."

"Wow, really? What, her Daddy isn't giving her everything she wants? We do know that's why she went with him in the first place. Plus thinking you were the cause of the divorce."

"I think it's more to do with wife number two; she feels Missy is competition. Also, Missy sees what Carol gets into. Guess she reports all to her father. At least that's the story I get from Tara and FJ."

"Well holy heaven, Frank should never have married Carol.

Everyone knows that. The kids sure didn't lie to him about her cheating when they lived with him. He just put the blinders on. What goes around does come around. He deserves what he asked for. I'd like to give him a lot more of my mind. Anyway that means you need a bigger place. Maybe you should get a house. Are you in a position to buy yet?"

"Actually I am; do you think you can help us find a compatible home?"

"I'll check with Maggie and see if she has anything available. If she doesn't one of her friends might. Before I leave this morning, can one of the seniors give me a shampoo and blow dry?"

"Now why're you asking me? I'm sure you checked the roster walking through the clinic on your way here."

"Right you are, but no one is available. I'd have to wait."

"Peter usually comes in early, so I'll get you shampooed for him and have you in his chair before his first client arrives."

"Well let's go," Getting out of the chair Percy beat a path to the shampoo area of the clinic.

BENITA

"Hey, dinner almost ready; wine on de table, you pour for us."

No sound came from the outer room. Cautiously Benita took a large knife from the block, hiding it in her skirt. Slowly she rounded the corner into her living room; a man with very curly hair, about six feet tall, light chocolate skin possibly from the sun, in Levis and t-shirt, stood before her. His eyes were piercing and dark, she knew this had to be Susan's ex! She could feel the cold emanating from this man and the color of his aura was black. Benita felt cold. Goose-bumps erupted on her skin. She waited for him to speak or make a move … at the same time she prayed Susan would not come up the stairs. She noticed the apartment door remained open.

Seeing this woman of Spanish descent, added a curve. After a few seconds he spoke, "Ah, excuse me, I guess I have the wrong apartment, I'll leave." The man said this as he quickly turned leaving her apartment, not bothering to close her door.

Benita slowly proceeded to the door. "Who you look for?" she called out.

Not stopping, descending the stairs, "I don't rightly know her name; I saw her on the street and thought her striking."

"And you ti'nk jus' enter without knock? You no wait to be invite? No name? You lie! No come again! I tell manager and policía! ADIÓS!" SLAM … went her door, as she quickly turned both locks. Benita walked straight to her window and looked out, cell phone in hand so he could see her dialing. She called manager Ron immediately and rapidly explained what occurred and this man was still on the stairs, daringly taking out a cigarette and lighting it.

Ron looked out his office window as he dialed 911, giving the description of the man who used to live in the complex. Ron knew the man well. He would stay inside. He was not going to mess with this one. His thoughts were for Susan to move out of the complex immediately.

* * *

Benita was hanging over the rail, watching as Susan ascended the stairs. "Sorry I'm late; we had such a heavy day. I saw police out in the parking lot, did something happen?"

Benita did not answer, but grabbed Susan quickly by the arm pushing her into her apartment. "We go to your place; you get clothes now. You sleep my place."

"Wait a minute, Benita, what ... oh ... oh no ..." Susan leaned against the door..."Drew... he was here?"

"Jes and he enter into this apartment, t'inking it yours."

"Oh? Benita ... I ... I'm so sorry ..." *Well that ruins the surprise and my hopes of having her live with us.* "I don't know what to say."

"You no worry; I had knife in skirt. I unlocked door for you. I t'ink you come, but no, I round corner, stand bold, tell'n me he looking for striking woman he saw. He lies to me. Tell heem to get out, I call Ron and cops, hurry lock door, run to window, let him see me dial. You know that bastard ... he, he ... stands on stairs take out cigarette, light it, like nut'ing wrong."

Her accent gets heavy when she's upset. She wants to speak Spanish. Normal I guess.

"Now we go your place, get clothes, I no take no for answer... Susan followed without question, doing as Benita asked. *It'll help her feel better.* Suddenly Susan felt a cold chill.

* * *

Susan poured wine wishing they could still have the blinds open, but took it in stride. Taking out her phone, she called Frank to see how they were managing. Meanwhile Benita was busy finishing dinner preparations, but she made sure to speak with the children before they hung up.

"You no tell Frank about Drew," as they sat down to dinner.

"I just didn't want to get into it with Frank tonight, didn't want to spoil our evening." Benita smiled as she dished the enchiladas onto Susan's plate. "These look and smell marvelous."

"Sí, you need good food in your body. You get t'in again. No sleep can do that."

"Oh, gosh, these are to die for. I must have the recipe."

"Nut'ing special, just love."

"Percy came in today. She's giving a party tomorrow night; I want you to come. You'll just love them."

"No, I not belong in such en… en…oh how you say?

"Environment?" Benita nodded her head. "Guess what? You're wrong, you do belong and I insist. Anyway, I already told Percy you were coming, so you put on your best dress, you're going to a party tomorrow night. And there is no getting out of this, I know where you live."

* * *

Lying on the bed in Benita's guest room, she reflected back on her day. *Well I don't have to notify the cops. They're now patrolling the area. Good thing I asked Percy to check into housing, because Ron will want me to check out of here; can't blame him. I'll have to tell the kids when they get home. That means telling Frank. He'll want the kids with him, but Carol won't. I also know he won't put his foot down. Wonder if Drew found out where we are living by checking the schools? That would make sense. Yes, I must think more as to the way he might. Probably how he knew I was still here, but didn't know I moved into a different apartment. Benita can't believe he just boldly walked into her apartment. Means he's been watching; most times I do come to Benita's first; can't put her in jeopardy. He'll do anything to get at me. I must remember to think like him once again in order to help us survive. That foils my idea of having her live with us. It sure would have helped though. I'll come up with something else. Must try and rest … funny I have felt like someone has been in my apartment … Was I just being paranoid? … Maybe…*

* * *

Susan climbed the stairs. *Kids must be late coming home. Usually Frank Jr. runs out to greet me. Benita's light is on, but the drapes are drawn. Maybe she has someone there.* Turning the lock … *door unlocked?* "Hey kids, I'm home."

"Hello my fire of beauty."

Susan jumped inches off the floor... adjusting to where his voice came from ... *far left corner... close enough to grab me if I try to run...* "Drew... how the hell did you get in?" *I can't show my fear. I must stay strong. Where are my kids?* ... Susan did not take her hand from the doorknob; *think, think don't let him get to you.* She was ready to run ... *drapes drawn ... signal ... Benita has kids with her... I'm sure she called Ron; he will definitely call the cops.*

"You know I have my ways. You look wonderful! I guess your brats stayed after school. I've missed you. But I'm here now; we can pick up where we left off."

"No!" ... this was said all too quick for Drew. "Ah, we can't! I suggest you leave and go back to your new love interest." Turning, Susan proceeded to turn the knob...

"Darling, I wouldn't do that if I were you." Speaking, he moved like silk. He was beside her. He grabbed her around the waist with one hand, holding her hair with the other, now firmly pulling, forcing her head to drop backward; he planted a firm hard kiss on her lips. *God please help me get out of this! Think* ... she dropped her briefcase. *I should have used it to hit him. Come on girl think...* Again he turned her, quickly pitching her onto the couch head first. Remembering past experiences seemed to clear her mind. She dodged his ploy by rolling quickly to her side, ducking her head, using her purse for protection she avoided diving and hitting head into the block wall. "Do you know it took me three days to figure out exactly which place was yours? Why did you move from ours? I expected you to be there when I got back." He yelled loud enough for it to carry out the unopened window.

Righting herself she sat on the couch ... *He's talking as if we're still together. God ... I must start again to think like him. It's the only way to get rid of him. It takes so much energy. He seems sicker than before. Is he? Maybe he's on something* ... sirens sounded in the distance...

Glaring at her... a low growl came from his throat ... he looked as if he was going to continue coming for her... "What the?"... "Cops?"... His fists doubled by his hips. "Damn we were just getting back to old times" ... a sneer... "I will be back! YOU best make no mistake about that! Do you hear me?" He turned, hit the door with his fist, leaving a slight dent … while the rest of him flew out the door … he seemed to literally fly descending the stairs.

Susan let out a scream; Benita was there in seconds shaking her awake. "Susan, you dream again," picking Susan up, she held her in her arms tightly rocking her, "Its ok, ju safe, ju safe."

"Oh God, it …. It was so real, when I went to get clothes this evening, it felt like someone had been in the apartment, I think that's what caused this nightmare." She wiped the sweat from her forehead. "I've got to get over these horrible dreams."

Letting Susan go, Benita looked at her. "You no go see that shrink no more. She bad for ju. I no like."

This made Susan laugh through her tears, as she threw her feet over the side of the bed, "Don't worry, I already stopped and you know what? Percy said the same thing."

"This Percy, she sound like a buena person."

"She is and you will get to meet her tomorrow, no, I guess tonight," looking at her watch.

FAVOR

Opening the door, "Susan, what the ... you know Carol won't like this, she'll think we're trying to get back together or something."

"Don't flatter yourself Frank, I wouldn't be here if I didn't need your help," Susan said forcefully, stepping inside. "I was hoping you'd be here."

"Don't tell me lover boy's back?"

"How did you know?" A surprised look crossed her face as he closed the door, noticing he was still putting on his shirt.

"Oh shit, I was joking. When did they let him out?"

"Let him out, what are you talking about? Do you have information about him you haven't shared?"

"Ah, no, I guess I assumed he was in jail, since he hasn't been around."

"Oh? Well anyway he's been seen around the schools and my complex, trying to figure out which one is mine. So I need to find a new place." *Don't dare talk about him entering Benita's apartment. This place sure is dreary. No sunlight getting in. That's depressing.*

Frank motioned for her to sit; she took the closest chair, making sure there was no room for him to sit near her. *Don't want dear Carol, to think I'm here to take her man.* Susan almost laughed out loud at her private joke, "The kid's better stay with me then for a while. I think you best get out of that complex, ASAP."

Just then Carol rounded the corner coming into the living room. "What the hell are you doing here?"

"Honey, ah ... Drew has been seen in the area."

"So what! That has nothing to do with us."

"Carol, in case you forgot, Frank and I do have children together. So it has everything to do with Frank and you, since you do live with Frank." *She's so stupid!*

"The kids are going to be here a while longer until Susan can get a new place." Frank patted the seat next to him on the couch.

"What? I don't have a say in this? I really don't think they should

12

be here. This puts us in jeopardy." Sitting next to Frank she made sure to cover his knee with her hand, running it up higher in a playful way. Frank turned brilliant red; the room fell silent for a second or two. *Slut! Your outfit has the same look.*

"No Carol, they'll stay with us." Frank was not budging on his decision. *Well you finally got some balls Frank.* Carol, now pissed off, stopped playing and moved as far to the end of the couch as possible without climbing over it.

"It seems to me you don't mind if the children are put in harm's way." *Some step-mother you're making.* Susan rose to leave. "Thanks Frank; do you want me here when the kids are told?"

"Are you going to let her speak to me like that?"

Frank ignored Carol, "I don't think so; they're looking forward to being in one house again. Do you have a location in mind?" sitting in his usual lazy position not bothering to get up and see her to the door.

"Well I hope I hear something from Maggie tonight. I'm looking for a house and I asked her to make sure it was closer to you and Carol, so we could both have better access to the kids, plus it's in an area I think Drew wouldn't think to look," Susan divulged this information with a huge catlike smile.

"Great, we'd like that, wouldn't we Carol?" Frank was smiling, but Carol's brows furrowed as she glared at them.

"I'll call later tonight to talk with the kids. Hopefully we can get moved somewhere before the end of the week or first of next week. I just don't want to inconvenience you for long, ya know." Susan turned the knob and was out the door before anymore was said. *Frank, Carol will now start a fight. Man I guess you did choose with what's between your legs, and not with your head.*

RIGHT CHOICES

"This is just the right amount of people, Percy. I was hesitant on coming, but I'm glad I did. And wow, what you've done with this townhome is fantastic."

"Susan, I told you it would be a small party, only choice friends. I'm so glad to finally meet Benita; she's lovely and Harold really seems taken with her. He's followed her around all night. I think he'll ask her out. It would be wonderful. He's been alone a very long time. Do you think she would go out with him?"

"I don't know. But you're right; Harold seems to be right there with her every second." Susan took a sip of her wine. "The reading was sensational; I can't wait to read the book."

"Jim is so glad to have finally written the book." Taking a small step away from Susan, "Dinner is served, everyone," Percy called to the roomful of guests. *What a beautiful blue gown she's wearing.*

Crossing into the dining area Maggie spoke, "Hi Susan, I'm so glad you're here; I have some houses for you to look at. Our office has four, and if you don't like those we can look through some of my friends' listings."

"I'm sure Percy told you of our situation. I need to make a move rather quickly. Could we meet tomorrow?" Susan asked. *Oh dear me, Benita is overhearing this conversation with Maggie.*

"Of course; I'll call first thing in the morning, we can discuss it then. I just can't get over what Percy has done with this townhouse. I think she should go into decorating as her second career."

"I agree, but with kids, I sure couldn't do whites," Susan smiled, throwing out her arms to encompass all the white in the room as she spoke.

"I heard that. And no you sure couldn't with those rug rats of yours, but when you get old like us you can, but if you have grandchildren you can't." Jim offered.

* * *

"Percy's house so bonito, I afraid to sit. I might spill somet'ing." Benita said admiringly. "It cost plenty money you can be sure."

"The house is gorgeous and Percy did the decorating herself. She's very talented. You looked as if you were enjoying yourself," Susan smiled, keeping her eyes on the road.

"Señor Harold, he seems a muy nice man. But I'm single many years." Benita was glad it was dark; she was blushing.

"Benita, he's a very good man and good looking. I think he really likes you," glancing at her passenger, looking back to the road. "He will call and ask you out. I think you should go out with him. You deserve someone special. You are special, you know."

Benita smiled. "He already did," now laughing out loud.

"Well great! Did you accept?"

"Jes," giggling like a school girl.

Susan was excited for her friend. "Oh boy, wait until Percy hears, she'll be ecstatic."

"No, give it little muy time; see how t'ings go, before anyt'ing said. We ... we from mucho different worlds. It ... may no work. We too long without spouses."

"Ok, but I think it will work out. Enjoy what you've been given and run with it. Don't let anyone stand in your way."

They enjoyed the peace for a few minutes. "Mija, I hear you talk with Maggie. You moving?"

"I think I have to since all three of my kids are coming back home to live." Susan said with a smile. *Oh my friend I so want you with us.*

"That's so wonderful, oh jes, you have no room left. Oh jes, see de reason. But did you not t'ink about that snake that lurks after you?"

"Well, I'm looking in an area where I don't think he will come, and I will place court orders again wherever we are. I hope to find a place within the week."

"Oh ... Oh mija ... You are like mi daughter and mi grandkids, I will miss you terribly. I be muy lonely."

"Well you don't have to be.*" I sure blurted that out quick. This is your chance; don't let it pass you by.* "I've been thinking would you consider moving with us?" *Dear Lord let her say yes...*

Benita reached across to Susan hanging on to her with a huge hug causing her to swerve, "Oh jes... jes... I get ready qui'k."

15

Giggling, "I thought you might be afraid to come." Still through giggles, "Tomorrow morning be ready bright and early. We'll go looking for our house!"

"I muy 'fraid for ju. Kids need protect. It best I with ju. I help with payment; we get house together, no?"

I know you want to help; I'll take your money and put it toward the kids' education. I will tell you later on what we did together. "Jes, jes, jes!"

* * *

The very first house they came upon Susan and Benita fell in love with. It was like looking at a storybook territorial cottage. A walled-in yard, five bedrooms, a great room living area, with four bathrooms and huge patio in the back yard, already landscaped. Not many changes would be needed to make it comfortable. The colors were light and also the wood; sky lighting also gave tremendous light coming into the home. Not the least bit dreary.

* * *

Maggie stressed they were not to make any decisions until they saw all the homes she had on the list. It was now close to noon. "Well you've seen them all. Would you like to go back to any, or do you want lunch? We could discuss the houses you've looked at. Also if you aren't sure of these, we can look for other listings after lunch."

Benita immediately said, "Let's do lunch." Susan smiled knowing Benita already had her mind made up just as she had. It was the first home they saw.

Getting seated in the nearest restaurant, taking a sip of her drink Susan mentioned, "I like the first house, in the older neighborhood. I believe it suits our lifestyle and it's in our price range. Frankly I'm surprised it's so reasonable. How do you feel Benita?"

"Jes, perfecto! You get suite, I get room next to yours. Kids can fight over others."

Laughing heartily, "You two sure are an easy sell. I've showed that house so many times, but I knew the right buyers would come along.

You noted of course that it's in the old prestige neighborhood of Phoenix, off Central Avenue. That makes it even better for resale."

"Maggie, that's why I couldn't believe the house, is so reasonably priced."

"The woman who owns it wants to make sure it goes to a younger family, so they too can enjoy that area of the city to raise kids. She's quite a woman. Don't be surprised if she wants to meet you before she agrees to an offer."

"I would love to meet her, wouldn't you Benita?"

Nodding her head, asking, "This house not listed online?"

"No, Benita, this woman said she wanted me to decide who should buy her home. It's extremely special to her. After her husband passed, she couldn't live in it anymore, too many memories. But she doesn't want to sell it to just anybody."

"Sound like Buena woman, want to meet her."

"Ok then, I'll see if we can't get with her right after lunch. She's down the street from here living in her daughter's guest house."

* * *

"Oh Mom, this house is beautiful, don't you think so too Benita?" Missy enthused, turning in a circle.

"Jes, we t'ink so too," Benita grinning from ear to ear.

"Did you see how big the bedrooms are?" FJ asked. "I like the one down at the end of the hall."

Tara was the first to ask, "Mom can we afford something like this? And gee since there are five bedrooms, Benita maybe could come live with us too?"

"In answer to your first query child, yes, I saved up the money and we can afford it. Did you like the other houses we looked at?"

"No," came in unison.

"This one is the coolest ever," FJ proclaimed.

"It sounds like we've got a vote then, right Benita?" Benita nodded her head in pleasure. "Now in answer to your second query, Benita will be living with us since she and I have just signed the papers. We now own this house!" The screams of pleasure came out! They ran to both women hugging and kissing. "There is one thing that you must do before we can move in. You three have to meet the lady who is selling the house to us. You better put on your best 'yes ma'am' attitudes."

"Wait until Aunt Staci sees this place," Tara commented.

"Yes, my sister will love helping us decorate this house with Percy. We just have to make sure it's what we want in our home along with some of their ideas. She sometimes gets carried away," Susan replied with a cheesy smile, looking to Benita.

SLY VISITATION

Susan's excitement over her new home made it hard to go into the office, let alone early. *Possibly I can get home early to help Benita pack.* Trying to put her mind into her paperwork made her more anxious. Picking up her coffee cup, she engrossed herself with the papers before her; *maybe if I get everything done, I can possibly leave early. I really must be careful to hide the boxes, in case Drew tries to come around again. Benita's right, sleeping in her apartment is safer. Ron sure got a curve thrown his way with us both moving. I'm more scared about Drew being here in the area than I've been letting on. Why does he want to have me back; stupid question; he's sick! I guess with him ownership is the only thing in the mind. At least the police are finally taking this seriously...Get back to work ... I sure like the quiet, let's me get more done this time of day.* Again she bent to her paperwork.

Ten minutes later a sound came from the back clinic door. *I didn't unlock that door...*looking to her watch, *it's not quite time for everyone to start coming in.* Susan automatically reached for her top left drawer, listening for any other odd sound ... she started to rise ...*You're just being paranoid* ... she sat back down ... *It's hard not to be paranoid with him in the area* ... listening again ... *Just a noise ... settling?... Must have been* ... again she went to paperwork. Within the hour she had most of her work caught up. Again looking to her watch ... *Well time to unlock the doors for the students; staff's also late this morning* ... grabbing her keys to make the rounds, she walked to the back door... the hallway was semi dark ... but she knew someone was there, she could feel it ... "Who's there?"

"Hello my Queen of Fire. You look amazing in that sheath." He stood against the wall, his arms across his chest. "I've enjoyed watching you."

Susan stopped moving; squinting, she could now see him against the wall. The blast of Drew being there in front of her hit hard ... *I should have listened to my instinct and with the sounds* ... "How did

19

you get in? You aren't to be near or on the premises."

"You never changed locks; I made keys to your schools a long while ago. One never knows when a need arises. Can't be too careful now can I? Darling, now why would I let a little court order scare me off? You knew I'd come for you anyway."

I should've known he would have a key made. Why didn't I change the locks? I wasn't thorough enough ... A banging came from the door next to Drew. Susan jumped at the sound but loved the fact someone was there wanting in. "I must open the door, students and staff are here." *Will he remember staff has keys?*

He never said a word, but casually sauntered up to her, leaning his head down to her neck and ear; inhaling her scent ... he then grabbed her strongly around the waist pulling her to him, sliding his hand down her lower back and buttocks and pushing, so she could feel his erection through his Levis. He kissed her ear and licked her neck. "See you soon, my fire."

Susan closed her eyes tight. *Why'd I do that? Control?* The memory of the kiss and lick made her to start to regurgitate. She had to control herself, swallowing hard to push back the bile in her throat. Sounds came from outside, which jolted her to run to the door. Throwing it open quickly, she bent over holding her stomach.

"Ms. Susan? Are you ok?"

"Yes ... yes Jeremy, I'm fine," shaking as she spoke. "Ah...I forgot the time while running ah... I seem to have acquired a chill."

She hurried back to her office, picked up the phone, and dialing her locksmith, she left a message asking him to come to the Main Street School ASAP if he could. She then proceeded to dial the police, letting them know Drew had violated court orders. Still shaking, she called Percy, then Staci. Both would be there at lunch, time to talk. Finally she sank back into her chair letting emotional exhaustion takeover.

FEAR

Benita was waiting on the stairs, a security guard near but not alongside. "Scum here today. We must hurry with everyt'ing. You look awful, he show up there too?"

"Yes, let's talk inside." Without another word they moved into Benita's apartment.

"I no get your packing started, but mine packed already, except for last minute. I no much to pack, nor you." Benita moved into the kitchen area, pouring glasses of wine for them, and then seated herself at the set table. "T'is a psycho man."

"Yes he is; do you still want to move with us?" Susan asked as she removed her heels, throwing them to the side. *Please say yes...*

"Jes, he jes make me so angry, need to be in nut house."

"Well the nut houses are full and he's conned them out of it in some way. He does it well, even when he violates court orders, he seems to be able to talk his way out of jail. Anyway Drew showed up at the main school this morning. He let me know today he had made a key awhile back. This I didn't know and stupidly neither I nor any of my staff thought to change the school locks. Anyway he was inside. Good thing a student banged on the back door almost immediately. Who knows what would have happened? I got hold of our locksmith and he will change all the school locks in the middle of the night. I had to pay extra for it, but I think it's worth it. I called the cops. They're now taking us seriously and will patrol the schools, kids' schools, and the complex, then our new home.

"Wow, quite a day, now see why you no home to help pack. It's ok, I no mind."

"I'm very sorry I didn't call. Oh and Percy and Staci came by for lunch. We think it's best to move in the middle of the night. He won't expect that from me. Um ...we aren't going to move in a normal way. Trust me on this one, I can't say how yet, but with my brother-in-law and Frank, we are getting the help we need. You, the kids and I are going to go visit Val and her new hubby for the weekend. We just won't return here, we'll go straight to our new home."

"But what if he follows us from schools?"

"I've been able to get away from him before, with the help of others, it will be done. Just hang in there with our packing. Neither of us really has much, so we're easy to get moved. You know manager Ron is even being helpful. He's glad to be rid of me, but he sure didn't count on you moving too."

Laughing, "Jes, he make funny face when he find out. But I not tell him I'm moving with you. He no need know."

Both laughing heartily, "I didn't tell him either."

"Why you no tell me plan? You no trust?"

"No, no nothing like that. I trust you implicitly. It's Drew I will never trust. This way, if he would happen to try to ask too many questions to trip you up or anyone else you'd have no idea and you wouldn't be able to divulge a thing, because you actually don't know. He has only a partial idea, and I only gave others part of the planto get us moved. Otherwise I would not have consulted with anyone." *I'm afraid he'd hurt all of you. Yes, I do think he will do anything now to get his way.*

"Ok, let's eat."

"I'm surprised you made dinner. I thought you would be so tired you'd want to go out."

"No, make less for us to take and is healthy. We need our strength. We have furniture to buy for our home. Kids need to help pick out too. So save money, no restaurant."

"Good thinking, bet you already have a long list for furniture. The kids are looking online for their rooms. I already have an idea for mine; how about you?"

"I already bought mine for bedroom, pictures in cabinet there; holding in storage until I call for, also ideas for living area of house, but we should agree."

Susan smiled, happy to have a friend she could count on. "Girl you're way ahead of me."

* * *

Getting out of her car... reaching inside the mailbox at the north school, she found an envelope from the locksmith ... *This will throw Drew a curve* ... with the new keys for her and her staff. It *seems odd to arrive at this school so early in the morning. It'll give the staff a head's-up. This was Tracy's favorite school. Wonder how her and Nick like Florida? Wonder if she's still happy? So odd I don't hear from her. We've been the best of friends as well as working partners for so many years. Not to write or call, doesn't make sense and to not return any? It has to be Nick's doing. I know it is. The kids really miss her, too. It'll be nice to have Benita and the kids and me all under one roof. Not sure I'm happy with the new director of this school, but I have to give him a trial run for at least three months* ... turning on the lights, she noticed some of the clean-up chores had not been done last eve.

Just as she was about to enter the office, a student came into the school. "Wow Margaret, you're really early."

Margaret stopped short, "Ah, Ms. Susan I ... where's Mr. Freed?"

This student looks petrified ..."He's not in yet. Is there something I can help you with? You're on the high school program, so why are you here so early, you aren't due until one this afternoon."

"Oh, Ms. Susan ... Ah .... My key ... wha... ah ... is there something wrong?" Mr. Freed stopped short as he breezed in, looking from Margaret to Susan.

"I was about to ask you the same question and waiting for an answer from Margaret here." Looking over to Margaret then back to Mr. Freed, realizing something was amiss.

"You best go on to school Margaret; we'll discuss the problem later." Mr. Freed directed. Margaret did not answer as she flew out of the building.

"What is going on with Margaret?"

"She failed an exam and I was going to give her some counseling." His explanation did not match his body language. He was an attractive middle-aged man, but she did not like his beady eyes darting around, not meeting hers.

"I'm sure it could've waited until it was her time here at school. The program is very strict and I don't need the school district hassling us about taking them away from their regular curriculum."

"I didn't realize it would cause a problem. But why are you here so early?"

"No reason, just felt a change would be nice for me to see how things are running." *He's extremely nervous. I will get to the bottom of this.* "So, what exam did she fail? Can I see it?"

Quickly entering the office, he sat in his chair, "Ah ... anatomy, I think it was." still not looking at Susan while speaking. "I threw the exam out."

"So it's already on the terminal?" *He's lying to me.*

"I believe Goldie already posted them."

Let it pass for now. "So, do you want to bring me up to date on things here? Oh and I notice some of the clean-ups weren't done last night. Is there a reason for that?"

"Absentees probably, they'll get caught up this morning."

"Quite a lot of absentees, don't you think?" I know I won't get an answer and you're definitely lying.

By the time they finished the school was buzzing with students and staff. It was time for first class. On her way out Susan stopped and spoke with students and staff. Many were requesting to see her privately. Something was definitely amiss at this school, she felt it. At the receptionist's desk, "Goldie, did you post student exams?"

"I always do, you know that."

"What was Margaret's failing grade on anatomy?"

"Failing grade? Margaret is a straight "A" student. But she does have some problems on clinic floor." Goldie looked to the student at the desk and asked her to come back after her morning class. The student left. Goldie turned back, "Ms. Susan, something is very wrong here at this school. I planned to call you this morning. Here are some student names to talk to." Handing her the list, "I'd rather you spoke with them, but not without their parents present."

"Thanks." *I should definitely listen to my instincts; I knew there was something very wrong.* Leaving, Susan called the main school and got the information she needed, and then called to ask Margaret and her mother to meet her at 1:00 PM at the main school.

After a two-hour session with Margaret and her mother, and speaking with other female students from the north school, Mr. Freed was escorted from the school by the police with sexual assault charges from more than one student and a temporary director was in place. Susan also notified the State Board to have his license revoked. *This was sure an odd way to come back to work, especially after what my family and I have been through. Goes to show one never knows what lies ahead.*

*   *   *

"Hi Mom," came in unison from Susan's office door. Benita was standing behind all three children.

Susan jumped up to greet them with huge hugs and kisses. "Mom, I'm too big for that," FJ squirmed, embarrassed, looking out the window to see if anyone was watching from the clinic floor.

"You're not that big, my man, and I will cool it in front of the public, but not at home, ok?"

"Yeah," he smiled. "I missed you too."

"It's been a long three days," Tara commented, rolling her eyes to Missy and FJ. "Can we get a service? I'd like a manicure, how about you Missy?"

"Not today, Benita and I have a surprise for you." Looking to Benita, "Did you park the car in its place?"

"Jes, we go now?"

"Where are we going?" Missy looked concerned. "Like, I had plans made, Mom. It's Friday night!" Looking to her Mother as if she should have known it was date night, even if this would be her first day back living with them.

Today's normal teen... "Well, cancel your plans, girls; we definitely will not be around."

"Aren't we going to..." looking around to see if anyone was in earshot, and dropping her voice... "The new house?" Tara asked.

"In due time, but we have something else to do first. Let me get my things." Walking back to her desk, she moved papers, closed files and drawers, grabbed her coat and purse. "Let's scoot out the back way."

A black limousine awaited them in the back of the building, "Mom? Really; like, we can afford this?" Missy asked.

"No we can't, but it's your uncle's. He's letting us use it this weekend."

"Wow, really?" Not waiting for an answer Tara opened the door and crawled inside, running her hands over the leather. "This is going to be

25

fun, it's fun already!"

"Are you driving, Mom?"

"No, when you get in, your driver will open the intercom and say Hi. I think you'll be very pleased to see who it is."

Once arranged in the limo, a sexy deep male voice announced, "Hello, sit back and relax, there's drinks and snacks in the bar. It will be about a two hour drive. Oh and by the way my name is Harold!"

"The kids started giggling and clapping. "Señor Harold, it really you?" Benita asked her face now flushed red with shock.

"You know Harold, Benita?" FJ asked, "He's so nice to us, he's always over at Ms. Percy's."

"Yes, Ms. Benita, I am your driver." His smile could be heard through the intercom.

* * *

Harold drove north. Once on the highway he opened the connecting window so they could all converse freely. "Can I come up front, Harold?" FJ queried.

"No, son, its better you don't, it's only allowed if the back is completely full."

"Will you teach me to drive the limo when I'm older? Then I can earn money while in school."

"Of course I will."

Missy and Tara texted with their friends, while Susan and Benita enjoyed a glass of red and the relaxation of the drive. "Why you no tell me?"

"I wanted to surprise you and he suggested it. I had no idea he drove a limo. He made a good living at it while in college from what I gather. Enjoy it Benita, don't let this blessing pass you by."

Missy slid over next to Benita, "We don't mind having Harold with us, he treats us like real ladies and he's so-o-o handsome. He likes you don't he? Where'd you meet him?"

"I met him at Ms. Percy's party." Again she blushed, but smiled looking into his rearview mirror, "Jes, he handsome and nice."

"We're happy for you Benita. Mom, are we going to Aunt Val's?"

Susan smiled, *my girls figured things out.* "Yes, but you can't let anyone know where we're going, and you the reason why."

Looking over to Tara, Missy said, "I was right."

Tara wore a stole-the-cookie-jar smile. "It's ok Mom, we're glad we're going to Aunt Val's. We really didn't have such a great weekend planned. This's better and anything's better than dealing with Carol. She told me I was not to call my Dad 'Dad' cause he's not my real father. Can you believe her?" giggling, "Then when I tried to not do it, Dad asked why I was calling him Frank. They got into an argument. And you know I'm not supposed to tell you but she's down right mean to Missy too and you already know about FJ, but I can't figure why Missy stayed there so long and put up with it. FJ and I were surprised she didn't give Dad a bad time about us staying an extra week. But we did see her mark the days off on the calendar," Tara whispered explosively, as though she had to get everything out all at once.

Susan looked to Missy. Missy did not see this as she was too busy giving her sister a mean glare. She knew they would soon have their quiet time. She could see it in Missy's eyes. *Guess they don't know I spoke with their father personally. Now that's extremely interesting.* "Well we have a grand weekend to enjoy with Aunt Val, and your new Uncle Matt, so let's begin."

Harold started singing, "A hundred bottles of beer on the wall" and they all joined in.

* * *

"I really like your new place Val. How do you like living here in the North Country?"

"I didn't believe I would care for Flagstaff, but if it makes Matt happy, then I'll adjust." *Not sure about that answer.* "So, Drew's back in your area?"

Short, but sweet change of subject, "Yes. Our lives were finally starting to go well and now he shows up. I worry for the kids and Benita." She took another sip of tea. "Oh, you best come down soon. You're in need of a weave in those grey and whites of yours."

"I do know I need a retouch." Val almost seemed to snarl, and then she got a serious look. "Susan, you knew he would show up sooner or later. You can't time anything, it just happens when it's supposed to.

Drew will be showing up to find you the rest of your life, unless you can somehow get someone to see how screwed up his head is and put him away for life."

"You're right; I made one hell of a mistake in my life and it will haunt me the rest of it. I just worry it will wear on into the children's' futures."

"It already has! I can see the changes in them now that I've been away from those scruffy rug rats. They'll be altered when it comes to future relationships. Speaking of altered relationships how's Staci?"

"Everything seems to be fine with the changes in their household. The kids love Irma and have adjusted to their odd ménage relationship. I say this because Sid's still living with them too. However, I truly never felt my sister would end up gay. Sometimes it seems like a fiction novel, but it's here in our world. Irma truly loves her and those kids. One can't fault that. Sid isn't much when it comes to fathering, but he does love his family.

She and Irma have been a godsend in helping with the kids. You know, I really miss our female gang times together, but life goes on."

"Those kids of hers are definitely going to have relationship problems also."

"Maybe, Val, but it doesn't seem to have affected them right now. Chelle seems calmer now there is more security in the home. The girlie clubs are thriving, too."

"So, Carol does benefit! Maybe you and Frank splitting is best." Val held her hand up so she could finish, she knew Susan would balk at her statement. "You seem happier with yourself; you're not killing yourself running all the businesses. You're spending more time with the kids and now you're looking to move into a new house. No, through all this, you're blessed. Selling the restaurant did help you get the house and is giving you more peace; it's wonderful."

Susan was quiet for a few moments, "I guess I never looked at it that way. If I'm calmer, then I sure haven't noticed it with all the nightmares, but more time with the kids has been great. If it wasn't for them I doubt I would be here."

"I agree with Benita about you not seeing the shrink. She was the most unfit I've ever seen. Didn't like her when I met her; she was always fidgety, like she would jump out of her own skin."

"Everyone seems to agree about the shrink. It was nice of Matt to give us time together."

"Yeah, he's thoughtful that way. I think I picked a great man. I truly never thought it would happen. He and the rug rats should be back from the soda shop soon. Can't believe they have one of those old time places here. But I should, everything here seems old time. Guess we better set up sleeping arrangements." *Now what makes you say this? You live in an old historical town. You really don't like it here, so maybe there's going to be problems for you two. I pray not, he's so right for you.*

SISTERS

"Hard to believe this is the same home you moved into a little over three months ago. Damn, we sure have made it into a magazine layout."

"Staci dear, are you congratulating yourself or all of us?"

"I guess a little of both," looking around with a huge smile on her face. "Come on; let's walk through, so I can take everything in."

"Sis, you're on your own, I see this place daily. Besides you'll change your mind as soon as you see the teenagers' rooms. Instead I'm going to the patio with a cup of coffee and enjoy some relaxation. Not often I get to." Pouring her coffee, "Can you believe Matt and Val taking all the kids to the movies?"

"How can you drink coffee in the heat of the day? No, but I think he loves kids and is trying to get Val to agree to a baby. We're all aware she's against having babies come into this world," Staci followed behind with a soda in hand, closing the screen. "Only thing lacking in this back yard is a pool. We do have to change that."

"You know that's out of the question. I did good to get the house and still have some money left. The rest has to go for college educations."

"If you really want the pool, then you know there are ways to get there. Just say the word. You know I don't think either of my two will go to college. It doesn't really make me unhappy, but in some ways it does, because I couldn't. I wouldn't have got through school if it hadn't been for you and Dad. But today there are so many more programs to assist with learning problems like mine. My kids just don't have the desire."

"I'm not sure mine will either Staci, but I want to have the money there for them if they choose; although both my girls are trying for scholarships and they do talk about going. Missy needs to start looking into colleges this year, so we have to sit down together and talk about it. Maybe if you discussed it more with your kids, they'd get more interested, you know like you have a desire for them to go. You really must tell them."

Adjusting her bra strap, "I did speak with them. Frankly I'm not sure if they are interested in a profession, period. Seems they just want to stay home forever. Maybe we should have your girls talk it up in front of them. But knowing your two they already have. Is Frank still not paying his share? Never mind. Sorry I brought it up. I know the answer. You know he's thinking of splitting with Carol."

"No! Really? The kids never mentioned it. Wonder if they know?"

"I doubt it. Hubby told me. Frank confided in him. He found Carol with another man in their bed. So all those so called lies your kids kept telling him came back to bite him and her in the butt."

"Well I do hope he comes to his senses and divorces her. She does have a way of entangling him right back in." Susan noticed how Staci seemed to drop her eyes at her comment. *Something's troubling her.*

"Sus, do you have any idea when Tracy might come home to visit?"

"I don't have any idea. Trying to get through to her by phone, emails, and or snail is still a problem. She must be very busy. Or maybe she wants a new life without us in it. That does happen when people move away."

"Susan, you aren't serious? I don't believe that for a minute."

"Well sometimes people do weird things for love. Look at Val, she moved to cold country for Matt. She's always made it clear; on the job that she refuses to go to cold country. She goes so far as to place the wording in her contracts. Not many can get away with it, but she has for years."

"Well, maybe with her only going to work in warm climates, she thinks she can better manage living in the cold climate for him. But this is Tracy we're supposedly talking about, not Val."

"What about Nick?" the doorbell interrupted.

"Don't get up, it's Irma, she has the key."

"Why would she ring the bell then?" Susan rose, going to the door, looking into one of the cameras along the way. "Oh my God"... running back to the sliding door... "Get in here quick Staci," Susan stated in a high whisper, "And be quiet about it." Blazer came from the side of the couch; Susan quickly gave him hand signals. Blazer returned to the side of the couch and crouched down with a low growl.

Staci jumped from her chair, started for the patio door, then turned back for her glass, holding it tightly she scooted into the house. Susan closed the door as she came in, pushing Staci into the hall so he could not see them. Staci could see him in the mirror above the cupboards. "Oh God, its Drew"... shaking ... "He's found us!" Pulling the phone from her pocket Staci dialed 911, and then she dialed Irma, leaving a message about what was coming down. "I was going to tell you he's been seen in the area."

Drew's shadow reflected off the ceramic tile; he found the sliding door open ... *God I thought we locked it* ... Susan pushed Staci behind her.

Staci backed away into one of the bedrooms to see if there was something she could use for a weapon.

I can't let him think he's frightened me. Leaning against the wall crossing her arms, *talk to him or try until the cops get here.*

Drew stood in the doorway with his hand on the slider, taking in the great room. "This is exquisite," he whispered to himself.

Susan could only imagine the shock on his face ... *Cat got your tongue? What's he going to do next? ...*

He moved forward then stopped to listen. Moving further into the room, he reached across the bar to the coffee pot ... his hand touched for its warmth ... *if he turns he'll see us...*

A very deep low growl came from the other side of the room. Sitting beside the peach colored contemporary couch was a Red Merle Australian shepherd. Drew froze in his tracks ... again a very low growl.

Should I let Blazer have him? Nothing would please me more, it would serve him right. Oh shit, I better take pictures of everything in this house in case he tries this again. I would need to know for insurance purposes. He didn't leave me many home furnishings when we lived together. Why can't they get to this man to serve him divorce papers? I'll speak to the cops about that. He'll still keep trying to have me pay his bills, to keep himself attached. There has got to be a way to get this man permanently out of my life. Man, he's making me angry. "I should allow my dog to take a good chomp out of you. You just couldn't help yourself, could you?"

Drew's head spun quickly spying Susan leaning against the wall with her arms crossed. He started to take a step toward her when one hundred-fifty pounds, on contact felt more like three hundred pounds of dog muscle knocked him hard to the floor. Blazer's teeth showed in his face. "Ah ... nice dog, Susan, call this mutt off."

"Why? You broke into my home. And he's not a mutt and he's far from ordinary. He can just keep you there until the cops arrive." Susan found herself enjoying this altered scenario, and for a change in his presence, she didn't feel afraid.

"My dear beauty of fire ... come on ... don't do this. It took me so long to find you. We have much to discuss. I miss you. And ... you've done ... ah ... remarkable things with this home of ours."

"Good Lord, this man never stops. He's really a sick puppy, isn't he?" Staci showing herself from behind Susan, a baseball bat in hand. *God ... almost forgot Staci was here.*

A sneer came to Drew's face as his mind raced; wondering if the cops would arrive or if she really called them. Maybe he should assume she was bluffing? Would this dog jump for his throat and make mincemeat of him "Susan, please call the mutt off. You know I hate dogs and I don't like the fact he's breathing in my face and ah and this floor's cold."

"The way you're sweating I think you'd enjoy the coolness."

Drew wanted her to call the dog off so he could win the dog over if not this time, the next time. Susan was ignoring his request. "Ah, what's his or her name?"

"Sorry Drew, you lose on all counts." A knock sounded on the front door.

Staci went straight away to open it. She really didn't worry about Drew reaching for her. Blazer was handling Drew quite nicely. "Please come in officers, he's right there on the floor. He broke into my sister's home."

* * *

"We should've put on the alarm system as soon as we got in the house, and locked the back door too. But I guess I was too scared to think, I just wanted to hide," Susan remarked.

"Ditto." Staci said.

Irma asked, "Did you tell him Blazer's name?"

"No, thank goodness. Guess we were thinking pretty straight then." the two women high fived each other. Staci frowned, adding, "Sis, you sure didn't show you were afraid."

Crossing her arms across her breasts, hugging herself, "I ... I truly never expected him to find us in this area of the city. It's been three years ... and when I realized he was at the door, I panicked." Still sitting with her arms braced, "Ya know I really felt I would be better at dealing with this, but I guess I'm not. Boy old Blazer kept him pinned down. I didn't let him see me signal Blazer off either. I ruffled into his coat with my fingers and gave him the signals, if that's your question Irma. Well at least he's in jail for a few days for breaking court orders."

"That's all they'll do to him?"

"Pretty much, Staci, but if I were to go to court against him anytime, then the restraining orders would hold more weight." *Of injury or death ...* "At least that's what I'm told."

"I think it's just a way for the court to get more money and not a damn thing people can do about it," Irma spouted. "He's never paid one ounce of support to my cousin. Get this, she still allows him to see his son."

I'm surprised he wants to see him; has to be another motive. "Maybe she still has feelings for him."

"You're right Susan; she's never gotten over him. Drew knows it and uses it. She still gives him money when he asks for a loan." Staci said. *Hit a nerve there...* "Let's get going Staci."

Irma was out the door. Staci commented, "I think that put her in a mood. She has a hard time talking things out. Maybe one day... Sorry must run."

"Well I sure can't say anything. She bottles it up, and I have nightmares and can't remember them. One day she may talk. At least that's what the shrink told me."

Looking back from the door, "Yeah and they can't seem to hypnotize you to find out about your dreams."

* * *

"Mom, are we going to move again? I don't want to," FJ expressed from the couch, ruffling Blazer's ears.

"I'm not moving," Tara blurted out, looking over to her sister. "He has no right to come here. What about having police protection? Aren't they supposed to keep an eye on things?"

Missy sat with arms across her chest, looking to the floor simulating absolute unconcern, but all within the room knew her ears were perked.

"You don't seem to be thinking straight right now, and you're shocked this occurred. No, we aren't moving again. And as far as police protection goes, they can only do so much. They have a very large city to look out for and our problem is maybe not as complex as others. I want y'all to make sure Benita or I are home with you always, but that's probably impossible, isn't it. Try to make sure you are with friends when we aren't around. Also, before opening the door check the peep hole and also the cameras to see who's there. When you get home make sure to reset the alarm and keep it on constantly, and keep checking the cameras. Ask your friends to call if they can before coming over. Oh, and we need to try and not have the same routine when we leave the house. Maybe I'm repeating myself I don't know, but I think you get the point."

"He's never going to give up is he; he'll just keep making our lives miserable," a near-whisper came from Missy.

"Your Mama can't say for him, only God knows what in store for us. She just wants we make reminder in our cabeza. Harold could come and stay with us, but he's no place to sleep, but heem only a block n'half away."

"Ok, Mom, we know what to do, are we done? I have homework to do and I've got to help FJ with his math," Tara said.

"Aw do I have to?"

"Yes!" all four women said unanimously. Everyone smiled.

"I also make special dinner," Benita stated, rising, "Tonight enchiladas. I t'ink Bueno time."

"Yum, do you need help?"

"No, I 'tink you need time with Mom, Missy, no?"

Missy smiled at Benita, giving thanks with her eyes. "Sí Benita."

"What's going on?"

"Ok, I guess I will tell all of you now. I've made my decision about which college I want to try for. I spoke with my counselor and did a lot of soul searching." Again smiling, moving forward in her chair, "I want to go to the U of A!" Every one of them started clapping, to her surprise. "You aren't surprised?"

"Sissy, we were all hoping it would be the U of A instead of ASU," Tara announced. This made Blazer get excited from the commotion. He made the rounds for everyone to pet him. "Have you written them yet?"

"Matter of fact I did," pulling a letter from her pocket, unfolding it dramatically and readying to read it aloud for all to hear.

"Oh, no, just the facts"... Tara could not take any more ... "Have you been accepted?"

Looking stoic for a few minutes, Missy then jumped up from her chair screaming and jumping, "YES ... YES ... YES!" at the top of her lungs, "and with full scholarship all four years!"

Everyone was so happy they joined in the jumping and hugging.

After all calmed down, Benita went back to the kitchen to get dinner going, Tara and FJ went to their rooms for homework. Missy and Susan remained with Blazer in the living room. "I am so very proud of you and what you have accomplished so far in your life. Have you decided on a major yet?"

"Before I go into that Mom, I need to speak with you about something." Missy was silent for a few minutes. *What does she want to say? Should I prompt her?* "Remember all those times you had me doing the bill paying? Well this made me think about a scholarship. Thanks to Harold, he helped me do the paperwork. I think you should do this with Tara and FJ also. It helped me understand, a lot more about what you go through for us.

"At Dad's, Carol was very mean to me. She never had a kind word to say. She never even tried to hug me or kiss me. Oh she took me shopping, to put on a good show for Dad, but when we'd get to the mall, she'd give me five dollars and give a certain time to meet her back at the car, so I would call a friend or two and have them meet me there." *Oh my God, does this woman have no warm blood?*

"In all the time I was at Dad's he hugged me one time. He never spoke with me alone either. And to think I was so upset with you divorcing him. I can't believe I was so ignorant. I thought you were at fault on the break-up and I just wouldn't give in and call to come home. I know you're asking why in your head. I guess I went into a depressive state and thought I wasn't worth anything and could never be anyone or smart enough."

"Oh honey…"

"Tara would keep telling me how great it was back with you, FJ and Benita and that I should come home. She told me you had time to spend with them since we no longer had the restaurant and salon. And now with only Percy's schools you're more relaxed. I got so jealous; I wouldn't let myself come home. Not until Tara and FJ were given the very same horrible treatment from Carol. FJ got it worse than I did, but I guess I just never really saw the complete picture until then.

"Then coming home and having you hug me, and kiss me, like I never left, even though I know I hurt you …" Missy choked up … "it was so wonderful. I …" Missy now let tears flow … "and then having someone like Benita for an extra grandmother …" choking with tears … Benita brought over the box of tissues and immediately returned to the kitchen. Susan grabbed her out of her chair and brought her to the couch. Blazer laid his snout on her knee … Susan hugged her like never before, letting her cry … Susan cried too, unable to get a word to come, knowing this was hard for Missy. *She's not one to show much emotion or admit her wrongs. She's learning* … "Mom" … choking sob … another… "How can Dad do what he's doing?"

"Like what? What's he doing?"

"Maaawm …" pulling away … "Ah, I just talked about you having me pay the bills. Why hasn't Dad given you child support? Doesn't he love us?"

Mothering Missy, Susan picked up a Kleenex and wiped her child's eyes … Missy pulled away … "Of course your Father loves you, don't you ever doubt that. But when it comes to paying his fair share, you'll just have to ask him."

"Damn it, take my father to court and get it. This isn't right."

Whoa! "Did you say anything to your brother and sister about this?"

Blowing and wiping her nose, "No, Tara would get stomping mad and tell him off and FJ would just pout about it blaming himself," looking down to Blazer, she scratched his ear.

Astute, "I've been too busy taking care of you all and working and recently getting us a new home, decorated and settled. There hasn't been time for much else. Don't let it worry you; it will catch up with him. But never forget, your father does love you."

Missy rolled her eyes, "It makes it … very difficult to believe."

Susan just nodded her head. "Yes it does, doesn't it? I know he does in his own weird way. "

¿FOLLOWED?

"Do you really think you're being followed?"

"Yes, I do, Brody, so could you please act like my credit card won't go through and call the police?"

"Sure if you want me to," automatically looking peripherally out the window of his store.

"Yes, please. I also want to be sure not to have this person show up at my home. Here's the details of the car this person is driving, and I do believe it's a male."

"Wow, Susan you're serious." He looked down at the piece of paper she had with the color, make and model of the car, as she moved the loaf of bread toward him.

Susan handed Brody her credit card. Brody pretended to run the card, talking back and forth giving the impression they were passing the time of day waiting for the transaction. Susan always paid cash, but tonight she purposely used the card. He pretended to run the card again … they laughed as though neither of them could figure why it would not go through. Brody picked up the phone and dialed 911 instead of the credit card company. Talks with the police, hung up, talks with her and gives her back her card. She talked a few more minutes, handing him cash. He then bagged the groceries. Susan turned and walked out of the store. Brody went to the window, looking out into the parking lot. The car she described was sitting off to the side in shadow. Susan got into her car and drove off as though she was going home. She got one block down the street and made a U-turn as if she had forgotten something, and headed back the way she came.

Again turning into the One Stop parking lot, Susan found a police car in the lot. She parked, looking into the rearview mirror; the car following her proceeded on. As she got out of her car, the police officer came out of the store and spoke with her.

Susan got back in her car, circled the block a few times, and then turned toward home, always checking around her for headlights and the same car. *The officer said he'd be close by. I don't see him anywhere.*

Maybe he's good at hiding. Know he went to look for the car, but... I feel it's Drew ... must be extremely careful. Makes me remember when he looked for me in the parking lot and in the supermarket aisles. Eventually he did find me, tied me up and drove around until dusk, giving him a better advantage to hide from the cops.

Once in the drive she readied her keys. Susan looked around to see if she could see anyone nearby or in the shadows. Just then she saw the police car slowly turning the corner. Quickly she jumped from her car running toward the front door. As she went to unlock the door... *it's already unlocked?* ... opening the door ... *that's odd, the alarm didn't signal her intruding* ... quickly she ran out to see if the cop was still there ... *he's gone, what if Drew's inside?* ... Susan started to shake ...

"Mom, are you ok?" Missy asked from the doorway.

Susan about jumped out of her skin, turning, "You scared the bee-gees-us out of me. Why didn't the alarm come on?"

"Oh ... I took the garbage out. Guess I forgot to turn it back on. Let me help with those groceries." taking the groceries, "Don't start Mom, it was a mistake, ok? You're getting paranoid." Susan didn't say a word, just gave her a look, making her daughter quickly look the other way. "Benita went over to Harold's so it's just the four of us tonight. Oh I need to get to Tucson sometime in August and get everything ready for my classes. Can we make a trip down there and look around?"

"Sure, do you want to go this weekend? We could make it a family outing."

"Ah, Mom can it just be you and me?" Missy did not look over to her mother; instead she opened a cupboard to place a box of cereal.

Looking to Missy, she could see and feel this was a turning point for all of them. *Things are changing in your life; no longer will they be the same. This one is leaving the nest to be on her own; soon the others will leave in succession. Are you ready? Not at all; is any mother?* "Sure, let me check with Benita and see how her schedule is." *Things are very serious with her and Harold; marriage there?*

Susan sighed out loud, causing Missy to turn abruptly. "Are you ok Mom?"

"Yes, just trying to deal with some things running through my mind; a real un-inspiring blocking mode."

"Do you need to talk about it?"

"Thanks, but no, this is something I have to accept and deal with as a mother."

Missy smiled, "Yes, Mom, it's time for me to start my own journey in life. But I'm not in a super big hurry ya know."

Susan reached out and grabbed her daughter, hugging her close, tears in her eyes. "I know, baby, I know." *One never knows.*

* * *

What the hell is this? I'm sitting here crying my eyes out. You and your kids had a great evening doing homework, playing games, sharing, why am I crying like this? I didn't have the heart to put a damper on the evening by telling about Drew following me. Jumping out of her bed, Susan went to the kitchen and made herself a cup of hot mint- chamomile tea. Going to the refrigerator, she chose to take out one of her buried frozen snicker bars. *This is desperate measures.* Returning to her bedroom, going into the bathroom to refresh, she then climbed back into bed. She couldn't tear off the wrapper fast enough. Taking a bite she chomped with utmost pleasure. *That's odd Blazer is usually here for a hand-out. Guess he didn't need a treat with me tonight.* Reading awhile, and with the tea and candy she felt more relaxed. *I've got this undercurrent feeling like I used to have when I knew Drew was close by and things were getting messy. The alarms on, got the phone by the bed and of course my gun under the pillow. So calm down girl and try to sleep.* Reading about ten minutes more, Susan did feel the urge to sleep...

* * *

Val, Staci, Irma, Percy, Benita and Susan were lunching together. "This is so great, all of us together. My Percy, you've done wonders with this home. Will you come and design mine?" Val asked. *Tracy you are missing out. This is like old times. First we've all been together in a long time and a few new added to the gal buds. Drew took away a lot of ways to make good memories, possessions, love and...oh well, don't ponder about the past this is a new life.*

41

"If you need my help darlin', I'll be there. I only do it for close friends."

"Did you help Susan?" Val asked with a huge smile.

Susan laughed heartily, "Val you're a trip. Staci and Percy both helped along with Benita and me, and of course the kids added their advice so we all ah you know collaborated and voila we made the cottage great."

"Well then we all have to do Matt and I's place. It sure needs it and it may help me. I don't enjoy such an old fashioned-looking house and the furnishings remind me of old folks and I'm in cold country."

It got slightly uncomfortable around the table ... "What does Matt like in the way of home comfort?" Irma asked, keeping her head down eating salad. *Go for the gusto Irma.*

Val looked to Irma, and then to the others, "He... says it doesn't matter to him, but he does remark about all the great cherry woods, or other wood types I have no appreciation for. You know he's grown up in the mountain country and outdoor sports are his world being a ski instructor. He grew up with all that old fashioned furniture, heavy ugly drapes and dreary dark houses." Sighing before she went on, "It's very difficult when I try to broach the subject."

"Maybe not," Staci piped in. "I'm sure Percy and I can come up with some ideas to satisfy you both."

Val smiled widely, "Really?" That would be awesome!"

"We definitely can," Percy smiled over to Staci, then Val, "Just send us pictures of the house from all angles inside and out. Also if you have architectural drawings, send those. Then, we can make some drawings ourselves, and find colors and fabrics. After that we will all make a trip up to go over everything and go shopping within your budget."

"Gee, do the rest of us get to play?" Susan inquired.

"Sort of, yes, but we all know who the best decorators are at this table," Staci blurted giving her sister a 'gotcha'.

"Know a few t'ings you no get right, Staci."

"Darn it Benita, you always come to her defense, but I guess you have to since you do live with my sister, you poor thing, but I still love ya."

"I hate to eat and run, Percy, but I do have to get to work." Irma confessed.

"Before you leave, there is an announcement you should hear," Susan said. Looking to Benita, "Well?"

Fidgeting in her chair, Benita blushed and giggled at the same time. This made all of them laugh with her, "Well Señor Harold … we gonna get married."

Clapping, along with, "Fantastic, wonderful, "Knew it"… "When?" came from all directions of the table.

"Now we have a wedding to plan, shower to plan, wow, we'll be extremely busy." Percy stated, rising and going to the liquor cabinet. "This calls for a special bottle of wine. Irma you should call into work; having car trouble."

"Thanks Percy, but I must get to work. I'll take a rain check." Irma looked to Susan, making an eye motion for her to follow; *she needs to talk.*

When they arrived at the door, Susan gave Irma a hug, "What's up?"

"My gal Staci says you're still having those horrible nightmares. I spoke with a friend of mine and asked her about you. If you're interested she can give you memory-regression sessions to help you remember. That's if you want to. You know, like if you decide you want to, here's her card, just call, she'd like to help."

"Thanks Irma, I've thought about it, but I must admit I'm not sure I want to remember those dreams. This is also a form of hypnosis isn't it?"

"Yes, but a little different the way it's done. It's worth a try. She did say having the type of nightmares you're having ages a person quickly."

Giggling, "Well one sure doesn't want that to happen. I'll give it some thought. Thanks again."

Irma was out the door, Susan stood there watching her leave, her thoughts achingly many…

SOFT ENTRY

"Ms. Susan, all the doors are locked. Are you sure you don't want me to wait? We can go out together."

"No, I still have mountains of paperwork here that needs to be caught up by tomorrow, with all the financial aid, for the newest batch of students coming this next semester. Cindy, you go on ahead. It'll probably be a good two hours before I can get out of here. I've already parked my car out under the street light in front of the building."

"Ok, I called Benita to tell her you're working late. I just don't like leaving you here alone with that psycho running loose."

I don't like being here alone either, but I don't want to keep her from her family. Susan smiled, "I can't keep living in constant fear now can I? So you go on ahead. I'll be fine, just make sure the back door is locked and the evening lights are on, ok?" *I can't let anyone know the constant fear I live with.*

"Ok then, goodnight."

* * *

Two hours later, Susan took the stack of folders and carried them into Fran's office for processing the next day. *I'm so tired; feel I could sleep for a week. Guess I'll try to get some extra sleep over the weekend.*

Back in her office, Susan grabbed her purse, doused the light ... *I guess Cindy forgot to turn on the evening lights.* She walked toward the alarm system, "God, I wish I didn' luf you." Jumping a good foot from the floor... her heart pounded and her entire body went into spasms. Quickly her hand went to the doorknob to run... "No, you bes' not do that! Ev'yone tells me I sh'ld forget you; go on without you, but they don't know how it hurts to be wit ou you. The pain is unbear'ble. Wa'ching every secon of day, jus to get a goo look at you, wann'ng you. I's on the both of us. I know you wan' me too, but no one wans us together. Can you e'splain why?" now sipping from his bottle.

44

He's drunk; think fast ... where's a cop when you need one? Slowly she turned the knob hoping he would not see her do it.

Like grease lightening, dropping the bottle, it splattered into pieces as he banged her up against the door, "I tol' you not to do that! God you smell good," *his breath is sickening* ... she gagged from the smell, "So'ry, been cel'brating, come to take you ho'm."

Home? Turning her head sideways, trying to keep from upchucking, "Home? What do you mean home?"

"My dh'r I sp'nt aw day get'ng ready for you. Brh'ng you home."

A knock on the door, "Hello Ms. Susan, this is Officer Reed, are you ready to go?"

"God damn you!" Drew whispered, letting her go he headed for the back of the school.

Susan quickly turned the lock, "He ... he's here ... going to the back of the clinic." Speaking, she was shaking so hard her teeth were chattering.

The officer drew his gun and took off in pursuit, "Call 911, for back up." He disappeared into the darkness.

Quickly closing the front door, resting against the door, she punched the numbers into her cell phone with both hands, still shaking. "Officer Reed ..."rubbing her forehead ... "ah, needs back up at the American Academy of Beauty on Main Street." She seated herself in the closest chair, and then punched up Benita's image. "Hey ... ah ... I'm still here, Drew got into the school ... No ... I'm fine." Rubbing her forehead, then her eyes, "No really ... I'm fine. Ah ... Officer Reed's in pursuit, so I'll be a little longer, they'll need a report." Closing the phone she bent over hugging herself spastically crying.

* * *

Four hours later, Benita met Susan at the door, giving her one huge hug, "You look a wreck. We watch for you. All here; tea ready, I get, sit." The kids ran to Susan the minute she entered while Benita re-set the alarm. No one said a thing; they just hugged in a group.

Staci, her kids, Irma, and Harold, were also waiting as she entered the living area. *I'm still shaken and this has shaken all of them too.*

Benita took over, bringing tea for all, "Ok, now you tell."

"Well ..."moving to sit on the arm of the couch, her kids clustered at her feet ... "I was working on financial aid papers for the new students. All went well. I delivered them to Fran's office and got my things to leave. I noticed ... the clinic night lights weren't on." Looking off down the hall toward her bedroom door, "I just thought Cindy forgot to turn them on. But now I don't think she forgot." Taking a breath, "I think he came into the school during hours, hid in an obscure place, turned the lights off after Cindy left, and waited for me to come from my office. Like his intentions were mapped out. As I went to turn them on, his exact words, 'I wouldn't do that if I were you'... I ran for the front door, as y'all know I park my car under the street light around front to let officers know I'm working late. He jumped me then. The stench on his breath was so bad, I knew he was drunk." Susan started shaking again from the memory.

"Did he hurt you?" Tara asked.

"No, but he did give me a scare this time. Just the odd way he was speaking, but he was full of alcohol, so he was hard to understand; you know, like a lot of gibberish out of the past." *I can't tell them about his saying he wanted to take me home. They'll really freak out.*

* * *

A half hour later, the kids, in their rooms, playing games on their cell phones, trying to take their minds off the unknown things possibly to come.

"I no like what is happn'ng. He going to do somet'ing loco," Benita offered.

"She's right!" The adults all said in unison.

Everyone seemed to mull this over, stretching the silence out into minutes. Irma moved about, fetching more tea and coffee, then resettled. "I know Drew better than any of you, besides what Susan went through with him. He's definitely not a man to be trusted. I don't think you should work at the school in the evenings anymore, Susan, and also make sure you leave when everyone else does, with lots of people around you. From all that you said, I do think he's planning something or trying to." She said. Again, all agreed in unison.

Harold looked over to Susan, "This may sound like an odd time to

46

bring up this matter, but I believe it relevant to the situation at hand." Looking to Benita, she moved from the other side of the bar, coming behind him and placing her hand on his shoulder. *They really make a lovely couple.* "As you all know Benita and I are to be married; the sooner the better in my point of view. But this then takes into the fact the kids would be here alone sometimes without any supervision and not any of us here wants that."

"Well Irma and I can take over for you guys, this wedding doesn't have to wait, Harold." Staci answered.

"I'm not finished madam, so please just wait, ok?" Fidgeting with his shirt, smiling wryly he looked to all of them and then placed his hand over Benita's. "Well, I have a big home and there is more than enough room for all of us. So Susan, we're asking you and the kids to come and live with us."

Everyone's mouths gaped, eyes as big as marbles … no one knew what to say. "We have too small space here, to all live in dis house." Benita finally offered.

"That's such a huge offer Harold." Susan stated, re-adjusting herself in the chair, "I … I don't know what to say. I … I'll give it serious thought. I do believe though you and Benita need time together to adjust as a married couple before something like you suggested happens."

"Susan we love those kids as if they were our own, we feel like their grandparents. No, matter of fact we are, even though your folks are alive. They don't even try to give them attention."

He's right. Staci and Susan gave each other a knowing look.

"Your kids come to us to talk more than you know. They're the kids we've never had. And besides, we're in a position that this cannot wait."

"You do have a good point. Can I sleep on it? I'm very tired. Tomorrow we will sit and go over all this again, ok?"

"Fair enough."

"Well we need to get home, but we'll come back tomorrow to hear all about this. Things are getting to be more like a good novel or movie." Staci stated.

* * *

Missy popped from her room, leaning against the door jam in her pj's, as Susan made her way to her room "Mom, how are you really feeling?"

"Extremely tired right now; I was really shaken."

I've been doing some thinking; I don't think I should go away right now."

"Missy, no; you're going to college, this is important for you. He's not going to stop us from living. No matter what happens, promise me you will not change your plans.

"But what about Tara and FJ?"

"Benita, Harold, Staci, Irma and I will make sure they're cared for. Oh and don't forget Percy and James. You're not to worry about that, do you hear me?"

Smiling, she hugged her Mother deeply, "I love you Mom."

"I love you and am very proud to have a daughter as wonderful and thoughtful as you. Now off to bed." *She's worried, that Drew's going to do something rash. She's thinking she's going to have to care for her siblings. Can't let her think this way; it's ... morbid...*

* * *

Susan woke abruptly, reality setting in with sweaty nightshirt and wringing wet hair. *First time I didn't wake up screaming.* Confused still, it took her a few seconds to adjust to her surroundings. *Benita is definitely back home and in a cooking mood. Coffee, huevos rancheros and who knows what else.* Looking to her clock ... *I didn't expect to sleep in. But with the shakeup from this mad man, I still feel drained. Best get showered to help Benita.* Once showered and dressed in t-shirt and shorts, opening her door, "Morning Benita. I thought you and Harold were at his place.

"Buenos Dias, Mija. Sí, after mass he bring me here. He go to change."

"You've already been to mass? Glad it's the weekend, I sure needed the rest." Pouring coffee, "What can I do to help?"

"No, just wake kids."

"Why don't we let them sleep in, so we can have some time together; seems like we never see each other anymore. And I miss our gab sessions."

Benita turned with a huge smile. "Sí, Harold takes lot of time."

"That's why I think you and he need time alone in your marriage, and not have all of us under the same roof," kissing Benita on the cheek, she walked around sitting on the end bar stool.

"I tell Harold you no do this, so he has backup plan. I like backup plan better. No like grande casa, but you no tell him."

"Wow, you just said a mouthful. His house is beautiful. Yes, it's very large but…

"No cozy."

"Does Harold know how you feel?"

Benita shook her head, and turning her midi length colorful skirt swayed. Showing tears in her eyes, Susan went to Benita, hugging her close. "I no want to hurt him, he so wond'ful, but house mucho grande and old wife there."

Susan reached out and shut down the burners, then got Benita coffee, leading them to the bar. Sitting, Susan also grabbed the Kleenex box and handed it to Benita. "Here; I do think you need to tell Harold how you feel. He'll understand. Does he still have pictures of his wife around the house?"

"Sí, it many years, but everyt'ng the same."

"So, you think he's still in love with her ghost?"

"Sí," now the tears really started to flow down her face.

Susan held her, letting her cry it out. Once she seemed calmer, "You must let Harold know how you feel. This is not a good way to start a marriage. Believe me, Percy is his best friend since childhood and she knew he loved you the minute he saw you. She said she never saw him like that with his wife. Harold would never intentionally hurt you. Now he's coming back here for breakfast, so you best go splash water on your face. But you must tell him before the day is out. I'll get the three of us set up for breakfast."

The key turned in the latch, and in bopped Staci, Irma, their kids and Harold, who in turn reset the alarm. "You did expect us for breakfast didn't you?" Staci questioned, noticing only three place settings.

Benita coming down the hall, "Sí knew you want huevos rancheros. Susan no knows; let's set buffet style." Chelle and Sid Jr. gleefully hurried down the hall to the other bedrooms to wake their cousins.

Harold moved into the kitchen giving Benita a kiss on the cheek, "You ok honey?"

Susan's ears were perked and she couldn't help but notice how Benita shook her head and turned to get things moving faster in the kitchen. Also she spied Harold holding rolled architectural papers in one hand, now placing them on top of the refrigerator out of the way.

"You're up rather early aren't you, Sis?"

"Didn't want to miss anything; you know I'm just down right nosy."

"We know!" came in unison with smiles and giggles.

* * *

A few hours later all were sitting around playing games and enjoying the day. Harold went to the refrigerator and pulled down the rolled papers, returning, "Can we all come over here to the back patio table, I want to speak to all of you about something and also show you something." Without waiting for answers he went to the back patio table and rolled out his papers.

"Mom, do we have to?" Chelle asked from her favorite chair.

"Yes, I think so; it seems he wants to speak with all of us." Staci said with a grin, heading to the patio, almost sprinting, "This is getting exciting."

Once gathered around the table, "After we left here last night I got to thinking about a lot of things. Well um, ah" … fidgeting … especially about you all coming to live with Benita and I in my home."

"Move again?" Tara asked, with surprise.

"Wow, Harold your house is huge and has a pool, which I know we'd really enjoy. But you know this house is cozy and we all really love this place." Missy stated."

"I know girls, and that's something I got to thinking about. So give me a chance to say everything before you all complain, ok?" Harold looked to Benita. "The most important person in my life deserves to have her own home. I really don't like the big house I live in. Benita dear, I'm sorry for not thinking of whether you would want to live there, but when you didn't get excited last evening when I suggested it,

I knew something was wrong. It doesn't matter where I live as long as I live with you for the rest of my life." As soon as Harold and Benita looked to the other they shed tears, kissed and held each other … everyone clapped. Smiling, he composed himself. "Now, Susan and Benita have a very good piece of prime land here, so I got to thinking, look here … every one of them bent to look on.

"It's a drawing," FJ said.

"Is that a swimming pool?" Staci asked.

"Yes it is. Exercise is important, you know." Harold added a huge smile.

"Harold, this is the house we live in now isn't it?" Susan asked.

"I'm so glad you noticed. You see I remembered you saying Benita and I should live in our own place. Well I got to thinking, we could have our own home and you keep yours and we can still live together. So, this house in the back can be for Benita and me and if much later we decided to sell this place, we can then sell it as a guest house, off the main house with a pool."

"Whoopie, we're getting a pool, like when we lived at the old house!" FJ yelled.

"What a smashing idea." came from Irma.

"Great resale value," came from Staci.

"Susan?"

Everyone looked her way. *My God, it's gorgeous and we'd still have plenty of land left. He took the time to draw almost every detail. What an unbelievable man. Benita you are one blessed woman.* Susan looked to Benita, acknowledging … *Benita and I really don't want to be separated now or after the kids are grown and gone. This has been hard on both of us, more than I realized.* "It's beautiful Harold, I … I see why you love the backup plan, Benita. It's so well thought out … I … love it, but Benita and I can't afford this."

"We can sit and work things out together, and with the sale of my house that will give us more than enough to build all this. Oh, and you females must tell me all the stuff that needs to go in it. How about you kids?" All were smiling and shaking their heads yes, and jumping and clapping. "Well then I guess we're doing some heavy renovation."

"Looks like we have another decorating project besides Val's place," Staci commented.

Susan's cell rang. "Excuse me." She went into the living area to answer the phone, "Hey Percy, on a weekend, what's up?"

"Just wondering how you like the plans for your new addition?"

"How do you know?"

"Well shoot, he woke us up in the wee hours of the morning. We were over to Harold's all night drawing up those plans. He's sure in love with Benita. It's so wonderful to see and he really loves you and those kids of yours we're all partial to; seems we are growing leaps and bounds as a family."

"You really said a mouthful. I couldn't believe it when I saw them; we just finished looking at them. We'll sit down and study them more thoroughly later when it's calmer around here. I was surprised when Harold said he would sell his place."

"I'm not. He hates it. Susan, his marriage was only for convenience to save his parents financially. That's what the rich do to protect assets and keep the money flowing, so he was sacrificed. I was blessed my parents didn't do it to me and I married the man I love. To see my BF-Harold in love is wonderful."

Interesting, very interesting indeed, wait until I tell Benita. Susan looked out to see Harold and Benita off to the side, hugging, laughing, kissing and enjoying each other. "To be able to find that sort of relationship is rare and it looks like we'll be having this wedding very soon. I guess we'll be moving the wedding to your back yard, we may be under renovation."

"No problem, and to think we'll be decorating another place."

"Staci spoke those same words. The kids are excited about it, especially having a pool. You know, the best thing for me was to hear how my kids really love our home. It was music to my ears."

"Yes, best investment after the divorce, and with happiness. Enjoy the rest of your day; I'll be into the schools tomorrow. That so called new partner is giving us problems again. She's trying to make it legal; we'll speak more about it tomorrow. Now I'm going to take a nap. I definitely need it!"

Looking around her home, as she closed her phone, *I'm truly blessed. With this addition, we'll be increasing the value. Tara will most likely go to college also. Almost a sure thing, but that's if she wants to. The only worry to be sure, is crazy Drew. I must make sure from now on to keep one step ahead of him.* Walking down the hall, looking at Benita's room, *hmmm, now this I can turn into an office.*

* * *

"Hello?"

"Harold? ... Ah its Missy... is ... is Mom there?"

Quickly he threw his feet to the side of the bed, trying to put clothes on as he spoke. "No, we're still in bed. What is it honey?" Now he was motioning for Benita to do the same, as he spoke he looked straight at Benita. "No, your mother isn't here; maybe she went into the office early."

Benita made the sign of the cross on herself, running for the bathroom as she heard Harold say they'd be there in five minutes. Hollering from the bathroom, "God, he take her, my heart tells me. How he get in?"

"Her phone is beside her bed, and the car is still in the garage. Maybe she went for a walk. We'll find out honey, now let's get to the car."

"She walk, she take phone, no, he take her! I jes know..."

* * *

Coming in the door like lightning, "What do you mean your mom wasn't in her room this morning?" Harold immediately asked.

Shaking and tears flowing down Missy's cheeks, "Mom is always up before us making sure breakfast is ready, when Benita's with you. I couldn't smell the coffee from my room. She wasn't in the kitchen and..." Missy moved to the sliding door in the back, "I haven't touched this door yet; it was open when I came out here this morning. I ... I already called the police, but they probably won't do anything since it hasn't been twenty-four hours."

The couple looked to each other assuming Benita's hunch was right. "Maybe somet'ing happened at schools and she leave early, you know like Percy come get her."

"No, you know mom wouldn't do things that way, she'd wake me to give me instructions."

"How'd he get in?" Harold asked. Running his hand through his silver hair, then over his mouth, "Where's Blazer?" Harold moved to the couch and looked in back of the huge philodendron in the corner. "He's not there." Looking wary he called out for Blazer. Immediately he went down the hall checking all the rooms. Returning, "He's not in here." Harold carefully went out the back patio door, trying not to disturb evidence.

Now Missy cried uncontrollably ... Benita held her firmly in her arms, and pushed hair from Missy's face. "Policia will ask too."

Tara sleepily dragged into the living area. "Mornin ..." rubbing her eyes, and then she looked around, frowning, "What's going on? Where's Mom? Not like her to sleep in. Why didn't someone wake me, I'm going to be late for school," plopping herself down on a barstool.

Harold quietly entered without anyone noticing. Swiftly he moved beside Tara, "Honey it seems ... it seems..."

"Seems what?"... Fear showed on her face as she slid from the stool backing away from the three ..."What the hell is going on?" Looking more closely around to each and every one, "Oh God, I..." Panic now in her voice and getting louder. Harold grabbed her in his arms. She struggled to get away, but eventually hugged him close and released painful tears.

"Before we say more, we best wake FJ." Missy commented.

A knock sounded on the door. "Tara and Missy, go get some other clothes on right now," Harold called on his way to the front door. "Good morning Officers, thank you for coming so promptly."

Benita went down the hall with the girls, going straight into FJ's room.

* * *

Benita fixed coffee for everyone after she was allowed into the kitchen. Everyone had been fingerprinted, the living area dusted and now individual questioning started. Other police were in Susan's room looking for evidence, as well as the patio door area. Also, Blazer had been found. Slowly he was coming around from a sedative that had been placed in meat.

The front door flew open and in breezed Percy. FJ ran to her, she stooped down and scooped him into her arms. "Thanks for coming."

"Little man, did you think I wouldn't? You should know better. But since your Mother isn't coming to the school this morning, I will have to go straight there. I think you kids deserve a day out of school, don't you?" Not waiting an answer, she looked over to one of the officers. "Why Andy, I'm glad you're assigned to this case. Have you put out an all-points bulletin yet?"

"No ma'am, it hasn't been…"

"Don't give me that crap." she opened her phone with one hand still holding FJ's with her other as he clung to her hip for dear life. "Captain Berry, please; tell him it's Percy." Seconds passed. "Berry, Percy here; I'm at my School Director's house, I'm sure you're aware she's been kidnapped. It's imperative we find her immediately. Yes, it's Susan, and thanks for the promptness. Come by the main school in about an hour, coffee will be ready." She closed her phone. "Andy, it's now an all-point."

Shaking his head, Andy smiled wryly, "Yes ma'am."

Questioning went on for another hour. Everyone was totally exhausted. Percy had gone to the schools about ten minutes before the police finished. It was suddenly very quiet in the house. All sat staring into space, wondering who was going to speak first.

Missy repositioned herself in her chair, "It's my fault, you know."

Tara asked, "What are you talking about?"

Now staring out the windows, "I took the garbage out and…"

"You freak'n forgot to put on the alarm, again!" Tara stood up screaming at the top of her lungs. Missy sat quietly taking Tara's abuse, as tears began to fall. "You always do this, you know. You didn't think it serious enough to put the alarm on and off all the time." Tara stood in front of her sister, gripping her fists by her sides. "Now you went and let that ugly person take our mother. I … I will never forgive you for this!" With that Tara ran to her bedroom.

Benita started to go down the hall. "No, let her go." Harold said. "She will think over what she said and regret it later. Give her time to come to grips with all this. We're all in shock. And no, Missy, you aren't at fault. Anyone of us could've forgotten to set the alarm. Don't blame yourself. It was an honest mistake and I'm sure your mother scolded you about it already."

"But Tara didn't let me finish. When Mom came in from going down to the mart for a few things last night she re-set the alarm. So yes, he had to have come in when I was outside at the garbage can."

"That could happen to any of us. No blame yourself. Tara will t'ink through. She jes 'fraid e' losing more familia."

"How are we going to get her home?" FJ quietly asked.

"You know son, that's a very good question. I'm sure it will be on TV soon and many people are going to be looking for her. They will back track and investigate every step that your Mom made. Tell you what, I'll come and stay with you until your Mother comes home. That is if you'll have me. We'll set up some kind of sleeping arrangements, ok?"

"You can sleep with me, Uncle Harold. I have a very big bed."

"Why thank you, Frank."

Benita beamed with pride at his handling of the kids, and FJ beamed because someone finally spoke to him as a man. Missy quietly cried, slouching in the chair.

* * *

Susan stirred, feeling disturbed and cold.... *Ow... my head...* slowly she opened her eyelids... it was dark and felt musty, dank, but with the scent of a cleaning solvent, this disturbed her stomach ... *Where the hell am I?* Trying to move, she seemed confined as if wrapped cocoon style, tightly in sheets and blankets. A hint of light came from underneath a door. *My head's killing me, like I was out drinking with the girls...This definitely isn't home. Where the hell am I? ...* Again she tried moving, to no avail. ... *Backtrack, we played games, all went to bed, I had a good cry ... Ow my head ... tea, I had tea and a snickers...*

A ceiling light flipped on! The glare of light was blinding. Slowly adjusting, looking around, the confinement of the sheets and blanket made removing her hands from the bindings almost impossible. Determined, with more struggles, she managed to free them; they were separately bound with plastic ties as used in gardening. This helped shade her eyes from the glare. Looking around she realized her confinement was complete. It was a small room, definitely concrete with no windows. The only escape route was the door. This door was metal with no knob on the inside ... *This is a fruit cellar or was* ...the door flew open, "Good afternoon, my red fire. Are you hungry?"

A whimper escaped Susan, as she realized her dilemma. *Oh God no, please don't let this be happening. I must be dreaming... I should have realized ... I guess the fog in my hurting head... Did I think it was a nightmare?* Drew *set* the tray of food down on a table at the end of the bed. *You're not dreaming! Oh dear Lord give me strength... will I ever see my kids again?*

"If your head's hurting a little, I think I gave you a little more sedative than I should have, but it will pass. I had to make sure we got out of there quietly. My, my, you and your children, the maid and her boyfriend sure had a great time together last night. Sorry I couldn't join in, but it would've changed everything. Now that so called Mexican maid-grandmother staying with you can have your brats forever in that house and we can live here. You can redecorate this place any way you like. It will be wonderful."

"You can't be serious? I ... I must get home to my kids, they'll be getting up soon and... and they'll need their breakfast before school..." Susan tried getting up as she spoke, but found she was really bound tight.

He blankly stared at her. Again, she tried to maneuver completely from the sheets and blankets cocooning her. Admiring his handiwork, he blurted, "Obviously, I'm good at everything," he said as if to himself. Hands on his hips, his usual Levis and t-shirt, "I guess the shock of seeing me so soon again was too much for you. You didn't hear me say good afternoon. Your kids have been up for hours and I know the police have been to your home. Your boss must have a lot of clout in this city, because an all-points bulletin came across the TV before twenty-four hours lapsed. Oh yes, they're hoping for your safe return, even offering a reward. They should know I would never hurt you, my fire queen." Drew came over to where she lay. "I'll untie you only if you promise not to try to leave. However, if you make one mistake you'll be bundled up again, do you understand?"

Understand? Those words are embedded in my mind. God, how am I to get out of this? "Yes... please... I ... feel like I can't breathe. It ... it must be getting warm outside." *Talk sweet to this lunatic.*

Reaching across, he quickly zipped off the tape, holding the sheets. "Yes, it's warm this morning." Picking Susan up ...*I forgot how strong he is...* he laid her on the cool cement floor, rolling her across the floor as he unwound her wrapping. She realized she was still in her nightshirt, now feeling exposed; she tried to hide her private places, as she landed against the opposite wall. Laughing, "I've seen every inch of you Susan, there is no need to be embarrassed; and I've enjoyed the fruits of you. Tonight will be very special for us to start anew, but I must make preparations. I have a special dinner planned for us, and renewing our vows per say."

Susan was non- responsive to his need for conversation. She felt sick to her stomach; bile so close her throat burned enough for her to vomit; she tried to gulp the bile back down. *I can't let him get the slightest inkling of anything out of the ordinary. I can't be sure when he'll fly off the handle. No, I once again must try to think like a criminal. This is not going to be easy but if I want to ever see my family again...*her lower lip quivered, almost crying out loud... *I MUST!*

Crossing the room he, picked her up once again and carried her to the bed, sitting her upright on the edge. She realized her hands and feet were still bound. She pushed her hands out in front, thinking he would untie them. He turned away, ignoring the suggestive move. *Well that's not going to come about.* Picking up the tray he came alongside her. *He's going to feed me. Is there something in it to keep me from running?* He sat on the bed, laid the tray next to him, and taking a napkin he placed it on her lap. He picked up a bowl of broth and a spoon; bringing it to her mouth ... *Smells like chicken.* Susan did not open her mouth. Smiling, he took a sip of the broth. She then took the broth. *I'll play your cat and mouse game, but man you better be ready for me to get out of here. Then I'll have you put in jail for kidnapping and into a psych ward.*

BLAME

"No, I'm not apologizing when it's her fault!" Tara stamped her foot, hand on her hip to dramatize, making sure to get her point across.

"Are you sure it's her fault? Did you ever think Drew may have figured a way to get the alarm code?" Harold casually asked, still looking at his newspaper, drinking his coffee.

"Hunh?"… Silence… slowly she made her way over to the bar, looking at him straight on. "How would he be able to do that?"

Harold looked up from his reading, took a sip of his coffee and looked at her, "I don't rightly know, but this Drew seems to be a pretty shrewd character. I just threw that out there, to show you things aren't always black and white. He did get in once before when your Mother and Staci were right here. So I think you need to give your sister some leeway, don't you?"

Tara looked around the room before she could look Harold in the eye. "Yeah, you've made your point. Besides she knows I can't go long being mad. I … I was just so angry, she's always forgetting to do the simplest things and not any of us can get her to change."

"I think she's more conscious of the alarm system now. She's punished herself enough; she doesn't need the rest of us helping."

Tara reached over and kissed Harold on the cheek. "I love you. Benita has found a gem."

"No, I'm the one who found the gem. Isn't she wonderful?"

"Sure wish Mom…." Tara stopped, tears coming into her eyes…

Harold reached out and grabbed her hand. "Don't worry, they'll find your Mom. She'll have a chance to find some real love soon."

Tears glistened on her cheeks, attempting to run into the corners of her mouth as she shook her head uncertainly. "I best go speak with my Sis. Thanks for making me come to my senses." Harold watched her go down the hall to Missy's room and knock.

The satisfaction Howard felt was more than fatherly, it was downright Godly.

* * *

"What do you want?" Obviously from the knock Missy knew who was there.

Opening the door, "I need to talk to you."

"Well I don't want to talk to you."

Tara stood close to the door, not attempting to leave. Missy did not move from her bed. "I ... I'm sorry for what I said. I was wrong." Missy remained silent. Tara crossed the room, lay on Missy's bed and positioned her feet on the wall, looking up at the ceiling, mimicking her sister's position. "We used to do this almost every night. What happened?"

"We grew up."

"Not sure I like it."

"Well it can be a bore, nerve wracking, scary and many other things all at the same time."... Silence between them... "You're right, it's my fault."

"No, you were wrong not resetting the alarm. It's the small stuff that ticks me off, that you shouldn't forget. I needed to yell and it was you I did it to. Harold made me see another side to the situation. He said Drew could've gotten the code somehow. He says the cops will find her, but it's been a week and..." she could not finish the sentence. "Anyway, if it's true, you know, about him getting the alarm code, well then I wonder if he's been into Mother's jewelry and other stuff and selling stuff again to have money. He does have a big habit to feed."

Missy's head turned toward Tara, "Oh! You could be right. Let's go check Mom's room right now. Wait, we can't, Harold's sleeping in her room. We'll have to talk with Benita and Harold so we can check out the room." Both girls back-flipped off the bed, landing on their feet, giving each other high fives and adding a hug they needed. In unison, "I'm sorry." They laughed.

FJ and Benita had just returned from the store. Harold joined in to help unload and put away the groceries. The two girls sprinted down the hall. "Can we talk to you guys a minute?" Missy inquired.

"Sure, help us finish unloading the car; we can talk while we put groceries away," Harold commanded. "Before you head out the door, you may want to check over by the couch. Someone's back from the vet and really needs attention. Gleefully they ran to see Blazer lying on the floor wagging his tail, but not moving otherwise.

"The vet let Blazer come home early he's doing so well." FJ said to his sisters.

Missy looked to Benita and Harold, "Is he going to be all right?"

He's one very strong dog. I don't know how he survived that amount of poison he was given, but he has. We are very blessed," Harold said.

When the two adults and kids were rejoined back in the house, "What's up?" Benita and FJ looked on while the two sisters stood together.

"Well Harold, when you and Tara talked about Drew maybe figuring a way to get the alarm code, this actually got her brain to work."

"Hey, it's a great brain, I'll have you know. If Drew somehow got the code, then just maybe he took some of the stuff here in the house and started selling it.

"He did before, jes?" Benita asked, shock showing in her expression.

"What? You've got to be serious? He actually did that and no one did anything about him then?" Harold asked disbelievingly.

"No one noticed until long after the fact, because of the way he did it. He would clean and rearrange furniture, then put some of the stuff in storage, then slowly sell the things without us knowing, and the storage unit was always so full no one ever could stand the thought of getting in there to find things. You know, I now believe he coded the boxes and not one of us figured he might have done that. Later we found many empty boxes in the storage. Ask Aunt Staci, she's furious, because he sold most of the family heirlooms. Also, you know like Aunt Staci was the first to realize he took Mom's cosmetics because he couldn't stand to look at her without having make-up on twenty-four seven."

"You have got to be kidding. This man is definitely criminally insane. But proving it is a problem. That seems to be the main factor."

"I tell you he no bueno!" Benita spat out.

FJ stated, "He sold my guitar."

"So let's go into Mom's room and get the photos she took of everything, then we can go from there, but in this short a period most likely it's been Mom's jewelry or what's left that he hadn't sold before." Missy said.

Harold shook his head in disbelief. "Wow, yes, I think that's the place to begin. Let's go." Halfway down the hall, he stopped, "Tara and Missy, why didn't you tell this to the police?"

"I guess we didn't think of it until you jarred my brain," Tara admitted.

* * *

Two hours later, Harold was calling the police giving them a complete description of the ten missing pieces of Susan's jewelry.

Benita was in the kitchen making tea for her and Harold as she listened. Finally, he returned to sit at his favorite spot at the bar, close to the front door as though he was on guard. "My mijas, they are so wond'ful."

"I've been meaning to ask you honey, what does mija mean?"

"Ju' know, eh babies, special, ah...."

"I get it, like a special nickname in English. That explains it. Pretty soon I'll be as fluent as you in Spanish."

"Je..." she corrected herself ... "You speak better Englesa."

"I can teach you."

Giving him his tea, "Jes fair when calm, but .... I speak dos when ... you know, excite."

"True, but you know what; I love you just the way you are." He gave her a pat on the behind as she sat down beside him, "You know I'm proud of our mijas too."

"Oh, mijo-boy, mija-girl, but still same."

UNEXPECTED

How many days has it been? Susan rechecked the scratching's she had made on the wall. *Two; seems an eternity. How many more without food or water? Will anyone ever find me if he doesn't return?* Susan was growing more fearful by the minute. There seemed no route of escape. *He was supposedly fixing us a dinner, but ...* her hands and feet were still bound. Struggling she turned on her side. *I'm afraid of getting bed sores, especially lying in my urine. I smell and feel horrible. Why would he just leave me like this? He was speaking of reviving our marriage. I knew what that meant; I experienced enough of that before both good and bad. Thank goodness there are no rats. At least he cleaned the place thoroughly before my arrival which is truly his nature. And it seems airtight. I don't know if I'm in the country, city or what, it's so damn quiet almost like a bunker, I can't hear the outside. Think ...* minutes passed *... I really don't think he brought me far. This type of cellar would only be in the neighborhood we live in. It's the oldest part of the city, where farming used to be a huge part of life. More patience and time was put into building strong solid homes. Not like the pre-fab sticks of today. But where would he get the money to rent a place like this? He sold most of my furniture and things to keep his habits going. It doesn't make sense. Maybe he has another woman caring for him and I 'm just a passing fancy again. Wonder if my kids think about me? I don't know what time it is. Is it day or night, what? God help me get through this. If I ever get out of here, I don't think I'll ever let my kids from my sight. Missy and I were going to Tucson so she could check out her campus. Wonder if she'll go on to school as I requested and major in law?* Her stomach made a huge growl. *Yes I'm hungry, but I'm sure not going to eat very soon. At least that seems to be the case. What if he leaves me here to die? It could happen. I'm not afraid of dying; I came close to it before, because of you Drew. Poor Benita, she wasn't expecting to be a mother, just a grandma. And she's getting married. Will her and Harold go and do it anyway, even though I can't be there? They should. They should not wait on anyone; it's wonderful they're so in love. I never checked into* *those regression treatments Irma spoke of. If I stay in here long enough without anyone to talk to, starve and who knows what else, there won't be any kind of treatments. I'm getting tired ... must be night time...*

* * *

The door swung wide with a jolt. "Darling I'm home!"

Susan jumped, rolled over rather swiftly despite her bindings; awakening from a long hard sleep ... trying to adjust to the light now blinding her eyes and the loud voice ... not realizing where she was for a second ... soon it came flooding back.

"God it smells something horribly fierce in here. Why, it smells of human excrement." Drew said this as though it should never be, "Did you wet yourself? Now why would you do that?" speaking, standing over her.

"Ah ... well when one has no way of walking to a bathroom for a couple of days it makes it rather hard. Did you expect me to hold it for that long?"

Slap ... the sound echoed within the cell ... "You should never talk to me disrespectfully. I am your husband." Tears welled with the excruciating pain, her face reddened, and her lip was swelling with blood trickling down the corner of her mouth to her chin. *I will not cry ... I will not cry ... he will not break me down ever again.* "You know, that makes me angry. I was so looking forward to coming home, finally having our dinner and getting back to a normal routine of life for us." *This is almost the same routine I remember. Not drunk, but on some kind of drug. This is your normal.* With the slap and his statement he walked out closing the door behind him.

Oh God that hurt ... she let her tears fall ... *No, he hasn't changed he is still the same. Goes off quickly... I will have to watch exactly what I say and do ... please Dear Lord let me get home to my family and get him locked away so he doesn't hurt anyone else.* Her tears flowed for a good while ... exhausted, sleep returned...

* * *

The door opened, Drew walked in with a tray of food and drink.

64

"It's time to wake, my love." He set down the tray, "And I think you should eat before you soak in a bath. After all you want to smell and look nice for our most special evening." The ray of light hurt her eyes. He didn't seem to notice. He took her by both arms and pulled her into a sitting position. Again Susan raised her hands to him, hoping he would remove the bindings. "I'll be removing them soon enough, everything will be fine." *You're on something, can tell, you're way too congenial.* He placed the tray in his lap and fed her like a baby. She didn't care what the breakfast was: eggs, bacon, potatoes, biscuits, coffee and juice. If drugs were added, she didn't care she was famished and he had remembered exactly how she liked it made.

Susan finished every morsel and really wanted more, but did not say a word. Drew stood, tray in hand and walked out the door leaving it open. This shocked her. *Did he purposely do that? Oh yes, learn to re-think ... He definitely did.* Almost immediately she heard him coming down the steps, there were four she counted. *Guess the kitchen is close to this cellar; makes sense, after all it's a fruit cellar.*

"Now about that bath, you smell so foul." Bending down to her feet, he took a pair of shears and cut the binding around her ankles. *Never saw them in his hand, how did he hide them so well?* "Come on, get up." Bending forward, she tried standing. She was weak; her legs gave out from under her. He caught her by the arms, and held her there giving her time to get her balance. "I'm so sorry, my fire, but I was called away. I had a job to do."

Since when did you ever have a job? "Oh?" Again she tried moving, but her legs were much too weak.

Drew picked her up and threw her over his shoulder like a sack of potatoes. *This brings back horrible memories from a grocery store scene when I tried to hide from you. A most horrible unpleasant memory, but I almost got away that time.* He walked the four stairs as though there was nothing to it. They were going through a well-maintained garden of bougainvillea, roses, and natural plants with lawn furniture, barbecue grill station, tables and chairs ... *he's using someone else's home. He could definitely not afford a place like this. Not with his habits. Maybe he's house sitting. Can't believe someone trusts him. But he talked as if this was a house for us to live in always. At least that's what he made it sound like.* He stopped, she could hear a door opening, *and this must lead to the kitchen. It's a real door, not a slider.* He took her through a hallway to the right. *Linoleum? It's an adobe house. I can almost picture the full layout without having to think about it. Wow, didn't expect an outdated kitchen. Every appliance is an antique. There's no table, so that archway leads to a dining room. He must have just purchased the lawn furniture, because this house really needs work. Oh I'm getting dizzy, is it from hanging over his shoulder or is it drugs he put in my foods?* The bathroom was straight ahead down the hall; *ancient just like the kitchen.* He sat her on the commode seat. *Wonder if there's a pull chain for the toilet?*

"Don't you just love the antiques in this house?"

"I've never liked antiques." Surprised at how hoarse her voice sounded.

"Oh? I was sure you did. Maybe you'll change your mind. I looked so hard for a home that would make you happy. Please, think it through. You will change your mind won't you?" His eyes bored into hers, but there were now two of him sitting on the edge of the tub which had ugly animal legs. *I ... I know what you're saying, but right now... I can't really give a shit ...* "Now I can undo your wrists." He cut the cording. He smiled, as he started to delicately undress her. He seemed to avoid touching her most intimate parts. *You ... you... really got weirder...*finishing, he picked her up placing her into the bath. *Heavenly water ... can't think, very... tired...*

* * *

Where ... oh, guess this is the bedroom. How long have I been asleep? ... Rethinking ... I guess ... I should say, drugged? Looking down at her body ... *well, I do have clothes on. It must be near dusk, it's sort of dark in here; can't make out too much about this room.* Rising on one elbow, she decided to throw her legs to the side of the bed, a chain rattling on her ankle ... *Damn ... here we go again. Talk about deja-vù ... definitely not going far.* Listening, she could hear Drew in the kitchen. *I may as well find out how far the lead is.* Standing up cautiously, staying close to the bed rail, she picked the chain up, holding it close so it would not catch on anything. She walked to the doorway of the room. Sure enough, it stopped her just before exiting. Now she followed the lead to its stationary beginning. It was bracketed into the concrete floor. *He cemented it into the floor. Well getting out is not viable without a useful tool.* Not giving up hope, she picked up the chain again, walking the room holding on to different pieces of furniture for support as she checked the lay of the land. She was surprised to find a piano, dressing table, and two dressers. She was able to access all pieces. *He has to be using someone else's home; neither of us plays piano. Maybe he had a girlfriend before deciding to bring me here and everything's hers. Wonder what he did with her. No Susan, don't go there ...* going back to the bed, she sat down ... *so this is to be my domain, like forever? I refuse! ... if I can get to a phone, they'll believe me this time when I say I'm chained, plus I was kidnapped, it's been on TV...*

"Hello sleeping beauty. I guess you were very tired." Jumping, Susan made no comment out loud ... *You definitely know why I slept, did you enjoy yourself? I know you didn't insert yourself into me, I would have felt the remains, and it's been so many years.* "How do you like your gown?" he asked, coming into the room and standing before her. She could tell he had showered for the occasion and put on fresh Levis and white dress shirt with cuffs rolled to the elbows. He even smelled good. He truly looked quite handsome.

Oh you are planning a long sexy evening aren't you? Looking down to her dressing gown, "Yes, it's nice; you remembered my size."

"I never forget anything." He reached over the headboard of the bed and turned on the reading lamp. *I didn't notice that.* "Why don't you apply some make-up and do your hair before dinner." Susan knew it was a demand not a request. Obediently she rose and went to the dressing table. All of her cosmetics were there from her home. *I wonder if any of my family realized my cosmetics are not in my bathroom. How did he get into the house? How did he get me out without anyone waking? How did he get me out without Blazer taking him down?* Reluctantly she sat and started working quietly. As he left the room, she knew he was pleased she had obeyed his command.

Twenty minutes later he was back. "I'll make sure you have better lighting in this room. It's not conducive for cosmetic application." *It's a bad application. I knew you were watching me.* "You look lovely, shall we?"

Susan looked down at her feet, stuck out her foot, showing the ankle brace and chain, "I don't think I can travel far."

Smiling, he took a key from a chain around his neck, reached down and unlocked the bracelet. *Doesn't seem afraid I'll try to run.* He stood bending his arm for her to take it. Realizing she did need help, allowing him to escort her into the dining room. It was a pleasing scene, candle light and complete settings with fine china. The table itself was of a very beautiful highly polished cherry wood. The living room was very austere. It had old Victorian couches and chairs; *definitely no place to sit comfortably.* The walls of both rooms were painted a dark green, making the place dark. *Unhappy people must have lived here; negative colors everywhere.*

"Please sit here." Susan sat; he then moved to a corner and brought another chain with a bracelet. "Your ankle please," holding out his hand he bent over ... *can I kick him hard enough to knock him over and get out the door?* Susan looked to the door, but could not see locks from where she sat. "Don't think I'd make it that simple for you, did you Susan? Now give me your ankle." Reluctantly she gave him her ankle, knowing from his comment he had somehow rigged the doors and windows so she could not escape. *I can only watch and wait.*

* * *

"Dinner was very good, thank you."

"You're welcome, but I think it was beyond good, don't you?"

Susan did not answer his query, but made another. "Where are you getting all the money? A fine lobster dinner, this house, it doesn't go along with what I've experienced with you in the past."

He smiled slyly, "Things have changed dramatically. I told you I would soon be coming into money."

No I don't recall him ever telling me that. "Ok, I'll bite, how or when or where did you get money? Remember I was the one who worked, you just took all my things and sold them for your habits."

His face abruptly changed; he quickly slid his chair back from the table, the legs screeching on the flooring. *Will he come to my side of the table and hit me? Maybe this will get me out of having sex tonight.* Instead he reached down and picked up his plate, placing the utensils on it. Then he reached across and did the same with hers. Turning without a word, he walked into the kitchen, returning to fully clear the table, ending with pinching out the candles. "It's time my fire, I've waited five long years for this. Come..." rounding the table, he reached down and unlocked her ankle bracelet. *Well the key around his neck must fit all the ankle bracelets.* Taking her hand he pulled her toward the bedroom.

In the bedroom he lit all four candles. Pulling back the linens he turned to her to unzip the front of her gown. Automatically she reached up to stop him, tears forming in her eyes. *God, I don't want this. Dear Lord, help me get through this.* He misinterpreted her tears. "It's all right. I know you're nervous. I'm not going to hurt you." *No you won't, because it's been so long since you've had me, but give it time if I have to keep bearing this intrusion. You will not have me like you think. I will never give myself to you. Never!*

Her gown now completely removed, he picked her up and gently placed her on the bed. Now he moved so she could watch him slide his Levis down to the floor. Already he was showing his manhood at full attention. *He still doesn't wear underwear. I forgot how blessed you are. Probably ruined me for other men in the future, but I haven't been trying to find out either. Wonder how many other women you've been with since me. Probably no protection either. You made that quite clear some time ago. Your mind does not think for others, only your satisfaction.* Slowly he removed his shirt, letting it fall to the floor. *Wow, he still has a six pack too. Hard not to get excited, but I can't allow myself...* He lay down beside her, not taking his eyes off hers. Again his penis was growing more subtly. Reaching out he started to slowly fondle her breasts. "They are still so beautiful and full, like no other woman I've encountered." *Sure, give that story to someone else...* his hands now traveling, taking in all contours and crevices of her body. He apparently wanted her to feel good, but she was still not succumbing to his advances.

He wants me to give in, I know it. Damn this is harder than I thought it would be. I just have to keep thinking about all the horrible things you've done to me and my family, which will keep me from giving myself to you. Oh shit ... no, no don't do that, don't go there ... he slid down her body placing his head into her vaginal crevice enjoying the spices he knew she could offer ... "You will give yourself to me, maybe not tonight, but you eventually will." *As long as you keep telling yourself that, it will keep me from giving in to your so called great lovemaking. So take advantage, have a good time, I'll just lay here while you play.* Eventually he placed his rock hard penis into her and satisfied himself.

ACTION

"What do you mean the teacher said he was not teachable?" Harold inquired.

"She says he no got enough brain to learn. He need repeat grade."

"He has a wonderful brain and he learns very well. I think it's more to do with his mother not being here than his brain power."

"Sí, I tell this, she no care, says she no want him in her class." Benita waved her arms everywhere while explaining herself, causing her skirt to dance around.

"Whoa, since when does a teacher tell a grandparent or parent she doesn't want the child in their class?"

From the hallway entrance FJ stood listening, "She told me she didn't want me in her class."

Harold and Benita turned to find FJ standing before them. Immediately Harold motioned with his hand for FJ to come and sit beside him on the arm of the chair, where he seemed to have most of his conversations with FJ of late. He noticed how despondent his adopted grandson had become and wanted desperately to help in any way possible. "Son, you mean she actually said those very words to you?

"Yes," Frank Junior stated, looking to the floor, embarrassment written all over him. "I'm not like the other kids in my class."

"No, Frank you aren't. Do you remember why you were placed into this class?"

"Yes, I'm smarter than most Special Ed students like me in my school. I don't have much trouble with my class, but Ms. Phelps doesn't like me."

"Has she said this to you?"

"Yes. She says I disrupt her class because I've said she doesn't give us a chance to explain things to her. She thinks we cannot think."

"I see. Well I don't want you to stress over this. We have other worries right now and I'm sure that's what's bothering you the most."

"When is Mom, coming home?" tears trickling down his cheeks.

"Son, I wish I could give you some good news, but I can't." Harold pulled FJ from the arm of his chair onto his lap, encircling his arms; he hugged and rocked FJ. "I'll bet our Benita has a good treat for you in that kitchen somewhere."

Bouncing up, "Yeah, Benita, can I have a cherry popsicle?"

"Sí Mijo, si, come…"

Harold jumped up too, but headed for the door. "I'll be back in a little while. Something very important just came up."

Benita knew where he was off to; concern was written all over her face. Shortly after Harold left, Tara breezed in, "Hey everyone, how is? Benita you look upset. And hey bud, have you saved any popsicles for me?" Tara moved to kiss each one as she asked questions, laying down her backpack.

"I'll get you one." FJ said, heading for the fridge.

"Where's Harold?" Tara inquired, reaching for her Popsicle, "Thanks."

Benita looked at Tara, "I t'ink he go see friend about Mijo's teacher."

"Old Phelps is at it again, huh?"

"What ju mean?"

"Causing trouble over Frank? Mom, Missy and I went and met with the principle over her, but they wouldn't do anything to help the situation. So, Mom decided to give it some time before she went further up the ladder with it." Tara explained this while she dialed her cell. "Harold, here's something to tell your friend about Ms. Phelps. I can bring him the re …." entering her bedroom, she closed the door. Nothing more could be overheard.

Benita did sit, astounded.

* * *

"Yes!" Missy jumped up and danced around her dorm room, as she closed her phone.

"What?" Sophie asked, from her bed, books piled all around.

"Ms. Phelps is gone for good, thanks to Harold."

"Really, that's great."

"Who's Phelps?" Kent asked.

"Oh, she's FJ's teacher, or was." Missy said.

"Oh, she's the one that didn't want him in her class, right?" Sophie asked.

"Yeah, well she's the one who's now no longer there. Harold and my sister Tara met with the board and she's no longer there. My sister was smart enough to record a conversation we had with the principal… anyway, it's a long story, but FJ will now have better teaching. Mom will be happy about that. I've got to run to my next class, talk with ya later." Out the door Missy flew.

"What?" Kent asked, not quite understanding.

"The teacher was a real scab; she didn't want FJ in her class."

"Soph, I got that much, but what's the big deal?"

"Her brother FJ is a Special Ed kid, but he's high functioning."

"Ah, is that why she goes home every weekend?"

"Yep. Says she helps with FJ's studies. Both sisters tutor him. Their mom used to help, but with her not being there it's just the two of them."

"Not there? What happened, did she die?"

"In a way, Kent … her mom is the one you hear about on the news who was kidnapped."

"Oh wow, she's … she's been gone a long time now. You know they probably stopped looking for her mom. I don't think they'll find her and if they do, I doubt she'll…

"Kent! Let's get back to our studies, ok?"

"Sophie, now I understand why she's like she is. That chick is definitely afraid of men. If she gets a man it will have to be one she completely controls."

* * *

Why'd I have to wake up? God all I want is to at least say good-bye to my kids. I'm going to die … I know. I guess talking about seeing my kids is too much for him to take. That seems to be what sets him off the fastest. She tried moving … *Beatings daily. I … I can't even remember when it started. How long have I been here?* Susan tried moving again, the pain was too much, and she fell back onto the bed. *At least he'll be gone a few days … some reprieve.* He left food in the room, and added extra chain so she could get to the bathroom. Again she struggled to rise; getting to one elbow, looking around the room ... *it's so stuffy ... can hardly breathe ... must be very hot out ... no window cracked.*

Susan was giving up, no longer looking for a way to get out. Ever since the first night she knew this time he had outsmarted her. The first night he made love to her, he forgot to replace the ankle chain. He fell asleep. With her heart in her mouth she crept from the bed. Getting to the door she realized, she would need metal cutters to get all the different locks off the door. Two were taller than she, but she had tried desperately to reach them. Going into the kitchen, she searched every drawer for tools; there were none. Eating utensils wouldn't do. Quickly she moved to the windows, finding bars on the outside. She was unable to open the windows from the inside. Looking closely she found he had nailed them shut. He had done this to every window she could reach. Also she thought she may be in a ghetto and the only reason this house was in good condition was that someone had refurbished it and had a security wall and gate. But being night time she couldn't be sure.

Since that night, she saw a wall definitely surrounded the property. The house sat on a very small lot. She could not see over the wall. Nor did she know if they had neighbors, but she did assume that if so they were not friendly. So the thought of a ghetto was out of the scenario. *Usually he made friends with all his neighbors, just to get booze or drugs.* She could see palm trees above the wall and assumed she was near her own neighborhood for the amount of palms around. It was the only area of the city that still had large amounts of date palms. When Drew opened the doors for air she could smell orange blossoms. This caused her allergies to flare up. *One night I had an asthma attack and thought I'd get to the hospital, but he wouldn't even give me that.* He remembered and had bought a machine and inhalers for her, through his medical buddies. She was down for three days before she could get out of bed.

I feel I've been here forever. What day is it? What month? He said I would get to see my kids ... guess that's out of his picture. I did have to open my mouth letting him know he'd never really have me. Guess that's why he's beating me. Susan looked in the mirror... *don't know who that person is. Hair is knotted with blood, can't see from one eye* ... staring at her reflection ... *oh I don't give a damn. I want to die...*

The front door opened, and then slammed. Susan jumped. She slid into the bed, turned on her side facing the wall and pretended to sleep; praying he would not bother her. Listening, she waited to hear him approach the door of the bedroom. Something was off, he was talking to someone. *No .... He's talking to himself ...* "Why now? ... I ... I've done everything he's wanted. I can't go to Mexico ... I just can't." As he talked she could tell he was pacing between the living room, dining room and hall... "I can't leave her... it's too long a period of time ... I can't let them know ... Why now? Why me? ..." *Shit he's now into the liquor cabinet. I don't think I can take another beating!* Susan began to shake uncontrollably. *Maybe he'll fall asleep. He's coming ... got to get control ... act asleep.*

Stopping in the archway, he looked in thinking he would see her sitting up. To his surprise she was in bed asleep. Why, he wondered? It was afternoon, she should be up. He turned on the lamp over the headboard; he saw blood in her hair. "Oh God, did I do that? I must've really hurt her this time," he whispered. "God, please forgive me, I do love her. Damn, she just makes me so angry. I ... I don't even remember hitting her." Turning out the light he tiptoed from the room.

Susan sighed with relief. She almost cried. She knew he would not bother her for at least two to three hours. It took some doing, but she calmed herself. *How can he expect someone to love him? ...* She did sleep.

THE SCARE

"Wow, Aunt Staci, that looks fantastic. Did you design the layout or did Percy and or both?" Tara asked

"Oh honey, y'all helped. We listened to what everyone suggested and then Percy and I sat down and drew it all out. We made sure to use color so you could all relate to it easier. We also brought the design for Val's house too. They're coming today aren't they?"

"They say jes," Benita stated.

"Well they better hurry or we'll have all the tamales gone before they get here." Harold announced, in between his bites and huge smile.

"That'll be their loss," Percy said, "More for us. These are fantastic Benita. You should open a restaurant."

"No, jus family fine."

"When do we start the interior designing of the additions?" Missy asked.

"About another month if all goes well," Harold answered.

"Mom will be so surprised to see how much it's changed." FJ commented.

"Yes, honey, she will." Percy said, love overflowing in her voice.

The doorbell rang. Tara strolled over to the monitor. "Aunt Val and her gorgeous hunk are here." The hellos and hugs were handed out plenty before they could move to get their plates for the tamale feast.

Val and Matt seated themselves at the bar, not wanting to be far from the food. "Staci, how's the designing coming on our home?" Val asked without realizing what she had asked.

"Designing? Is there something you need to tell me?" Matt inquired forcefully.

The room went silent. Val did not look up from her food, but closed her eyes, realizing she unknowingly validated herself. "I ... I was saving it as a surprise," still unable to bring herself to look Matt in the eyes.

"Well, I'm surprised." Matt said flatly.

"Matt, when we were up there visiting, all these women went crazy

76

over your rustic historical home, and how it needed to have some modernization along with its wonderful antiques," Irma kindly offered, trying to soften the blow.

Tara immediately picked up on it. "Yes, Uncle Matt, you know how Aunt Staci and Percy love to decorate. Well, you know... we all started offering different suggestions, and of course decided those two should make some designs to help improve the value of your home. I must say it's sure an improvement over what you have now. Wait until you see them."

Harold busted out laughing. "Hey man" ... laughing ... "you ...you may as well learn when women are together they're going to make changes to your life as well as your home," still laughing ... "Why do you think we're adding on here? I couldn't get Benita to move, so I'm coming to her. I don't plan on ever living without her. And if you want to have Val happy, you better think differently than you've been doing. And I mean right now. I've noticed how you want nothing to change, but that just can't be. She married you because she loves you, and I believe you her. But there are now two opinions to consider. I'll bet it still looks like a bachelor pad. I don't know any woman that would want to live comfortably under those conditions. So Val's opinion should matter to you. Consult one another and make changes together in everything you do, and believe me you'll have a happy marriage. That's the only way a marriage can work. Grow up, kid." The room was silent; a few minutes went by. "Benita, when we became grandparents I sure didn't realize we'd have so many grandchildren so soon."

"Jes, dear, we gather rather queeck, but we do like it."

Matt set down his fork, looked at Val, then to the entire room, "Ah, twenty minutes here and I've been really put in my place." He fidgeted in his seat, contemplating what to say next and just how to say it. "I ... I deserved that, Harold. Val, I owe you an apology. You've been unhappy and I just thought it because it was colder weather, but you've said many times our house has no light and is very depressing. When you come into this home you seem much happier. I'm sorry also for taking you from your friends, but I promise to make sure we see them and talk with them as much as possible. Thank you for giving up all this here and coming to me." Matt reached over and hugged his wife and kissed her passionately. Everyone applauded and gave oohs and aahs. Still holding Val, "As soon as we're done eating, let's have a look at those plans Harold drew."

"This man learns swiftly." Harold said smiling.

* * *

Entering the room at high speed, Drew switched on the overhead light as he stepped by the side of the bed, "What is the matter with you? Why are you still ..." his words stopped as he turned Susan over. **"Oh God! Oh my God! Oh Susan darling!** ...." Dropping to his knees, he checked for a pulse in her neck, he could barely feel one. "Oh God, don't let her die." Moving quickly he took the key and unlocked the bracelet on her ankle.

He picked Susan up in one full sweep, rushing her out to the car. Once placed into the car, he noticed blood clotted in her hair and all over her gown. Fastening her seat belt, he rushed to the other side of the car. Getting in he started the car before he had the door shut, closing it as he pulled out of the drive. "I can't let them know at ER, who she is or who I am. I'll be hauled in. Damn, Joyce, why are you off duty this weekend? Now I've got no cover protection." Thinking seriously how to handle his dilemma, he drove at high speed. His mind kept trying to play back how on earth he had beaten her so badly. Drew honestly didn't remember beating her at all. "Maybe she did it to herself while I was gone. But why would she do that; to run from me? Why?" he beat the steering wheel with both hands, "No, no she loves me as much as I love her. Maybe she tripped over the chain and fell. She couldn't get up, but kept trying and hurt herself more. Yes, that's it, I'm sure that's it. She wouldn't try to leave me." This conclusion was satisfactory to him. "I'll tell them I found her along the road."

Arriving at the ER, he yelled for someone to help as he rounded from his side of the car to open the passenger door. A man came out with a wheelchair. "I think this woman needs a gurney, not a wheelchair." He ran past the old man with the wheelchair, and found a nurse leading him to a gurney for Susan.

"What's wrong with her?" the nurse asked.

"Hell I don't know. I found her along the road. I brought her here right away, she hardly has a pulse. I sure hope she's going to be all right."

"Was there any ID on her?"

"I … no … I really don't know. Like I said, I found her on the side of the road." Drew answered.

"Well, don't leave. Wait out there." At the same time she motioned to a man standing along the wall. He was a huge man, likely security, and he started talking into an earpiece immediately. Another woman came with papers.

"Sir, you will have to wait in the waiting room, so we can do our job," trying to guide Drew to the waiting room. He was most reluctant. The woman found this odd, "So, in the meantime, how about filling out these papers for me. At least maybe you can give us the location where you found her. This way we can have the police check the area for some information."

Looking back, Drew could see a doctor entering the area, going straight to Susan on the gurney. He checked her vitals; the nurse stood next to the doctor quietly conversing.

Drew wanted out before the police came, but the guy who was standing along the wall now stood near the ER entrance. Papers in hand, he moved toward the restrooms, knowing they were watching him. Joyce and Caroline had told him about the guys who would bring in their girlfriends or wives and then try to make it out of the hospital, so they wouldn't have to face charges for what they did. After stopping at the water fountain, he moved to a chair. Drew decided to fill out the papers to throw them off. They would then forget about him.

The security man slowly moved to another area of the waiting room. As soon as he was looking the other way, Drew headed straight out the door. Reaching his car, he quickly pulled out, noticing a policeman entering the hospital from his rearview mirror. "That was a close call. God, don't die my darling, I'll return for you." Drew said this as he tore the papers into bits and let them fly from the open window.

His cell phone trilled out his favorite great Marvin Gaye tune, the screen reading *'Yuri'*. He laid the phone back on the seat, allowing it to go to voice mail. He then picked it up and played the message. "The plane is waiting. You better have your ass here in less than one hour.

Like twenty minutes. Otherwise…" The message ended, he clicked off and stepped on the gas pedal. "Does Yuri know I'm the one who has Susan? Bet he suspects, that's why he's trying to keep me under tabs. This is an unexpected blessing I'm given. It will certainly help me out. I can go out of the country, Yuri will be thrown off, and Susan can get rest in the hospital, and I do the job and come back, get my beloved and take her home again." He smiled as he drove on.

THE CALL

"You two women sure know what you're doin'. I really thought I would hate these drawings after Harold's tongue-lashing. I was prepared to like them for Val. But to my surprise they're really beautiful. You sure represent Professionalism. There aren't many changes to our place, just total improvement."

"Matt, we listened carefully and everyone did have great ideas on how to help the both of you." Percy commented.

"Yeah, even the kids have started learning from us, and sometimes give better ideas than we do. Now when can we get started on the place?" Staci asked, moving forward in her chair as she salivated with desire.

The phone rang; "I'll get it" Harold called out, since he was the closest to it.

Everyone seemed to be talking at once with the excitement of redecorating Val and Matt's home, except for Missy; she seemed to see the uncharacteristic change in Harold's expression and the odd tone of his voice. She found herself holding up her hands. "Shush everyone..." no one seemed to pay attention ... finally she got Benita's attention, "Benita, something's going on."

Benita turned to look toward Harold on the phone near the bar. She too noticed the change. "Sí, Harold business like." Once this was said, they all stopped to watch and listen.

"Yes, we'll be there right away." Harold answered, hanging up the phone. His face was pale and his eyes serious. Clearing his throat, looking over to the others, "It seems they found Susan."

FJ jumped up, "WOW! Let's go get her!"

"She's in the hospital." The room went still as everyone anticipated the worst. "It seems someone brought her to the hospital. She's in pretty rough condition."

Missy stood, "Let's go! We must go now! Irma and Matt, please drive. We'll have to take two cars. I don't think the rest of us can handle driving right now. Harold, you can fill us in on the way." Before anyone could put a word in Tara stood and grabbed FJ's hand, Missy his other; the kids led the parade out the door.

* * *

"If she's in a coma, then no one knows what happened to her?" Tara asked.

"Well they did say she was in very rough shape." Harold avoided sharing the cause of the coma.

"In other words, she was badly beaten," Missy stated looking out the car window. "We've seen this before, Harold. It's not new for any of us. You don't have to go around the subject."

"What's a coma?" FJ inquired.

"It's like Mom's sleeping but can't wake up." Tara answered.

"Is this from the beatings?" as he prodded to know more.

"Most likely," Missy answered eyes still out the window.

"Are we there yet?" FJ asked.

"Almost, FJ, but I must remind you, they may not allow you in to see your Mom because of your age," Harold said.

"But I want to see my Mom," FJ now about to cry.

"We all want to see Mom, but they have certain rules in hospitals, Frank. Don't get upset, we don't know for sure," Tara trying to soften Harold's statement.

Irma was driving her car.

"I don't like not knowing what else Harold had to tell." Staci brooded. "Not knowing anything drives me nuts."

"Well you're just going to have to wait until we get there to find out more. Susan's in a coma, it's not like she's going to be waking soon. At the most we will just find out how bad her injuries are, and they'll send us home," Irma said.

"Who brought Aunt Susan into the hospital?" Sid Jr. asked.

"Harold said, they didn't know." Irma said.

Everyone stayed quiet after the brief exchange.

* * *

Missy and Harold went to the desk, "We were given a call to come to this hospital for Susan Hentlemen. "She's in the intensive care unit."

Missy grabbed Harold's arm for support. "Could you give us directions?" Harold asked. Missy did not even hear the directions, she stared straight ahead. Before turning, he looked at her. "Missy you must be very strong. Your brother and sister need you."

She looked at Harold as her tears made her vision blur. "You're right, I can't break down now. Give me a sec before we turn around." The entourage was given directions to the intensive care unit.

At another desk, Staci, Harold and Missy stopped. The nurse looked at all three in front of her, "Yes?"

"We're here to see Susan Hentleman," Harold managed to get out. His legs felt as though they would give out from under him. But he knew he would have to be the strongest of all of them and keep his head clear for decision-making.

"Only family members can see her, but I will have to get permission from her doctor, to see if she's allowed visitors. Please wait over there with the others."

Staci wasn't backing down, "We're all family members."

"I mean blood relations dear, and I can tell you are not all related by blood." Without further conversation the nurse picked up the phone, pressed the intercom button and paged Susan's doctor over the system.

Half an hour later a tall thin man with a dark balding head and black-rimmed glasses came through the double doors. He spoke with the nurse at the desk; she followed him to the group of nine waiting to hear his words. As the doctor approached, he commented "Well, Harold, I sure didn't expect you to be here; how are you doing?"

"Not so well right now Ernest. What can you tell us about Susan? Oh, kids, this is Dr. Ernest Cohen."

"Hello." All spoke at once.

"This is all family?" Ernest started to laugh, knowing this wasn't quite true.

"It's a long story, but yes, we're all family, some adoptees."

Ernest Cohen looked at Harold and then the complete crew before him. "Ms. Hentleman is not doing well. She's in a coma, therefore it may be tomorrow before anyone can visit her, but truly we don't know when she will awaken. She has extensive internal injuries and it will be some months before she is up and around."

"Was our Mom beaten by Drew?" FJ inquired.

Cohen's mouth dropped open at FJ's query. He was without words.

"Why don't you sit down, Ernest, this may take a few minutes to explain," Harold suggested.

Cohen dismissed the nurse and quickly sat while the others brought chairs to make a circle.

BLESSING

A nurse was taking Susan's vitals. Susan moaned, slowly opening her eyes. The light seemed to be blinding. *A window? Must be daytime, the light is so bright. It's coming through the window. Not same window with bars.* Her eyes closed again, another moan. *Where am I?* She spoke with a hoarse voice, sounding as if a whisper.

"Good morning, Ms. Hentleman, I'm your nurse Mandy. Give yourself a few minutes to adjust your eyes to the light. You're in Banner Hospital." She pressed the call button, "Page Dr. Cohen to Ms. Hentleman's room, she's awake."

It felt as though the nurse was shouting. *My head hurts.* Susan again tried to open her eyes. This time they adjusted better to the light. Within minutes a doctor entered. "Good morning, glad you're awake. It's been three days since you were brought in. I'm Doctor Ernest Cohen. Do you remember anything?"

Susan's mouth was dry and as she tried to converse, she realized how raspy her voice was. Nurse Mandy came alongside her bed, offering her ice chips. She then noticed the IV. "The"... came out extremely hoarse ... again she took more ice chips. "I ... I was in a house, chained, and in a bed." Tears were now leaking down her cheeks. "I remember everything. Where are my kids and family? Are they alright? How did I get here? How do you know my name?"

"I understand you were kidnapped. Is this true?"

"Yes, Drew, soon to be ex. I've been trying to serve papers for a divorce; diagnosed as a sociopath. He's also an alcoholic and drug addict."

"Do you know where he was keeping you?"

"I believe somewhere near my home, I'm not really sure. Shouldn't I be telling this to the police? Weird for a doctor to ask these types of questions, isn't it?"

Dr. Cohen laughed heartily. "Yes, we made sure to give them a call. Also some of your family is waiting for you. They've been here day and night taking turns. I'll allow them in, but you need rest. You've been through a lot. I want to make sure you're able to understand what you've been through and mentally able to handle everything. You seem to be doing well."

"Oh, I know exactly what happened and why. I'm sure my kids and the rest of my family are frantic. We'll have changes to make in our lives once again. He'll never give up trying to get at me. I'm worried for my kids. He's not to be trusted. Believe me he'll be here soon to try and take me out of here."

"Then I believe we'll have to post guards for you."

"It's never stopped him before." Susan looked to the ceiling, closed her eyes trying desperately not to cry. She was shaking now just from the thought of Drew possibly coming into the hospital to get her or her kids for his own satisfaction. *He'll use the kids as bait.*

* * *

Cohen seems too inquisitive about my kids and me and family. The kids say he's a good friend of Harold's. Fine but what does that have to do with us? Why does he want to know so much? My kids want me home now. I want to go home now! He acts like he wants to keep me here forever. I've been here well over a week. I can go home now. I'll insist on it. Why hasn't Drew made a move to contact me? Did he bring me here, as everyone seems to think he did? He must have thought I was dying; wouldn't have been long if he kept on abusing me. What is Yuri making him do? I know that's who his boss is. It's got to be drug dealing. It sure isn't his art ... snickering to herself...

Dr. Cohen and his nurse were at the door, "Good morning, Susan, how do you feel?"

"Ready to go home and I insist on it." Susan left no room for contradiction.

Cohen smiled, "Good to hear, because I am releasing you this very day."

"Thank you!" *Bet you weren't, but reality is you can't keep me here any longer.*

WORK

Two months later

Delving into work is the only way to help me get past all this, and of course the kids and the home renovations. The changes that occurred while I was away blew my mind. The pool mostly constructed and now the new cottage for Benita and Howard almost completed. Soon they'll be decorating the inside. Soon we'll have a wedding. Val and Matt's new changes for their home are stunning. Yes, this is all helping to keep me occupied, but I feel lost and out of place from the aftermath.

"Honey, it looks so good to see you back at your desk."

Looking to the door, "Percy, I was just going to call you!"

"As deep in thought as you were, I doubt that. Now get up and move from my chair." Hugging and kissing, Susan happily moved from the chair, getting Percy coffee and taking one of the guest chairs. This made her feel that things were more normal. "What did you think of the renovations at home?"

"Fantastic ... all the surprises still have me somewhat bewildered."

"Shoot, Harold wants to get married to Benita, that's the rush. He's paying them extra if they finish in less time. Just hope the work is as superb despite his hurry."

Susan laughed, "Oh I've seen him standing out there and having them redo areas he felt needed improving. He's a go-getter, that's for sure. Should be more men like him, and the babe you married. Then maybe I'd find someone too."

"Speaking of good men, I hear you have an interested party."

"I do?"

"Oh my, I spoke out of turn. I just figured he finally got up the nerve to ask you out."

"Percy. Who? Don't keep me in the dark."

"Why, Ernest Cohen, of course."

"Oh."

"Now, that was not a good sound. No chemistry, eh? Well maybe you should just give it time. He's a very intelligent, hardworking man and he's very taken with you."

"Intelligent, yes … hardworking, probably, but dating him, I don't know. He knows so much about me now and he's seen my body and…."

"Come on Susan, what is it? This isn't like you."

I can't explain this to her. She wouldn't understand the complexity. "I can't put my finger on it, but I find him kinda creepy."

Percy did not comment immediately. She twirled her old desk chair around as though she was not listening, then, "Does this have something to do with Drew taking you away from us?"

Hell yes, it does, it has everything to do with it. This doctor looked at me the same way Drew does, with that can't wait to take you sexual look. He gets excited just thinking about it. The man hates women. "Ah … I'm not saying that exactly, but close." Susan could not say more, she started to shake. "Can we change the subject? It brings back too much."

"I'm sorry. If you don't feel comfortable about him forget I brought Cohen up. When you're ready to talk you will." Percy jumped out of her chair. "Come on, we're going shopping and to lunch. This place can manage on its own for a few hours. You need some girl time and I'm not taking no for an answer."

Smiling, Susan grabbed her purse, then stopping. "Percy, is he related to the Cohens who tried to buy the schools years ago?"

"He's their son. Why?"

"No reason, just curious." *It explains more than you know.*

LOCKED OUT

Drew walked back and forth in front of the door of the fourth beauty school showing open frustration. After trying his key in every school door, "Huh … she changed all the locks to these schools. I can't believe she did this to me! Probably her boss had it done. Susan wouldn't keep us apart; no, no not my fire beauty."

He was so upset he did not see the police car patrolling in front of the school. The car stopped shining a spotlight on him. The officer used his speaker, "Are you alright sir? Do you have a reason to be here?"

Stopping, he noticed that someone was addressing him. He looked toward the car, using his hand to shield the light from his eyes. He thought quickly on his feet, "Ah, I think I was given a wrong address."

"Is there a certain business you're hunting?

"I was led to believe this was a residential address," laughing sarcastically. "I guess she didn't want me to find her. Is there any place near here where I can call for a taxi?"

"Yes, there's a restaurant on the next block. Just take a right at the end of this block."

Drew smiled broadly watching the cop move on down the street. "He never even asked for my ID; takes all types. Cops are so stupid." Little did Drew know the police officer knew who he was, called in for back-up, and gave the location of his vehicle down the block from the school. The plan now was to follow him to his home base location.

Pretending he was walking to the restaurant, he turned the corner. "Don't worry darling, soon you'll be in my arms again." As soon as he turned right, he ran down the alley to get his car.

LUNCH

"Dr. Cohen…"

"Susan, please call me Ernest. It's not like I haven't been talking with you on the phone this past month, trying to get you to have lunch with me."

As she was being seated, "Ernest…I…I finally agreed to have lunch with you, to let you know I'm just not ready for any kind of relationship. Too much has happened in my life. I don't know if I'll ever be ready after everything that's happened."

"I understand your fears, Susan, and I would never push you. I've seen many a patient in your circumstance, but you are the first woman, I've taken an interest in since med school. You appear to be such a strong woman. I do believe we can overcome this together and we can have a grand relationship."

Whoa, wasn't expecting that, "Really?"

"Don't get me wrong, my career was more important, but I did almost marry. We were in med school together. I hope you don't mind, my ordering for us, but I'm due back at the hospital rather quickly." Ernest took a bite of his tuna steak.

He spoke like getting married was just business. "Sorry it didn't work for you."

"I'm ok with it. We wouldn't have lasted. We are both too career oriented. But now that I'm older and in a better place I am finally ready for a lasting relationship. Beth and I are still very good friends, but neither of us would move for the other and long-distance relationships just don't work; at least in my experience."

"You make it sound like a marriage is to be a business deal." *I shouldn't have blurted that out. Stick your head in your plate for that blunder.*

"Well it can be to help each other career wise, easier for politics, that sort of thing. Love can come if the two really want it."

Susan set down her fork, folded her napkin, picked up her purse, opened it, and put enough cash on the table to cover her side of the bill.

"Ernest, I came to let you know I am not interested in pursuing a relationship with you or anyone else. Already I can see we would never work. So, please don't call me anymore." She rose from her chair to make her escape, before she lost her composure.

Cohen reached out grabbing her wrist, "Call me when you're ready. You and I are an item made to be together."

"Let go of my wrist, now. You don't want me to make a scene." As he did, he gave her a look Drew often did, just before he had his way, jolting her to the point of feeling inner panic. His smile was hateful. Quickly she left the restaurant. *I never want to see that person ever again!*

* * *

"This Doctor, sound like he loco in the cabeza."

"I told Percy I wasn't interested in him. He gives me the creeps. I went to lunch to let him know I wasn't interested. It was like he never heard what I said." Susan shivered remembering the lunch date.

"You tell staff you no want to take his calls; he not a bueno person. You did right to get away."

"Benita," Fidgeting in her chair, looking around the room, Susan went on... "Do you think I have something in me that attracts psychotic men?"

"No Mija, no, you just in weird place right now. God will help, he has his ways. You like me, hopeless romantic." Smiling, "But you will find good man one day when time right." Benita reached over and hugged Susan, letting her know it was alright to doubt, but to have faith. "This Doctor, he not know love, raised different. Feel sorry for him. Look at Señor Harold's marriage, had to just to save family dinero."

"You're right, I'm not taking the time to look at the big picture," still hugging Benita. *I can't tell her what he said when he grabbed my wrist or the way he looked. It's been two months and we haven't seen anything of Drew. I know he's wondering why there wasn't an all-points bulletin out for his arrest. Now possibly I have Ernest to worry about. I just can't afford to turn my back...*

91

¿NABBED AGAIN?

"Goldie, is Susan still there?"

"Hello, Ms. Percy. Nice to hear your voice, I don't get to speak with you often. How is that grand looking man of yours?"

"Gorgeous as ever, how are you?" *God help me, enough with this small talk.*

"Just fine, just fine. Ms. Susan hasn't arrived yet today."

"Never arrived? Didn't she have an appointment there?" Percy now annoyed and her voice sounded so.

"Yes and they went out to get breakfast since Ms. Susan called and said her car broke down and would get here as soon as she got her car towed and had a rental. That was about two hours ago. I don't know if I…"

"Goldie, call 911 right now, I'm on my way. I will try to get hold of Betty and Terry at the auto place. Somehow I don't think that was Susan you spoke with."

"Oh dear, dialing right now." Cutting off, Goldie switched to her second line, dialing…

* * *

The police inquiry of staff members, mainly Goldie, was held in the school office. Percy handled the appointment Susan missed in the nearby restaurant.

A few hours later, Percy and the Chief sat quietly together in the office, digesting what had occurred. "You know she's the daughter we never had?" Percy stated.

"Yes, Jim and I've discussed it at length." The chief answered. "You know, I just couldn't keep a guard on him. He didn't try to make any sort of contact in the last two months." The Chief got out of the guest chair, starting to pace back and forth in front of the desk, "Also, the night he tried to get into the school, we had five following him, but he never went home, he got on a private plane instead. It's that

92

nightclub owner's plane."

"I know Pierce, you're doing your best," tears welled in her eyes, as she rocked back and forth in her chair. "I keep getting this feeling in my gut like we'll never see her again, or if we do, she'll be mentally inept to function normally. Her children need her, I need her, and damn it, we all need her. We're all brain mess from this schizoid, especially the kids!"

"That's why I want to put it out to the media as a kidnapping. This time it's the only way to get her back faster, if at all. Maybe we can save her from your gut feelings. I don't think it will hurt the schools."

"Well, to hell with the schools!" Realizing she was nearly shouting, she softened her tone. "If this is what it takes, let's do it. I'll go straight over to the kids and talk with them and call Missy. I'm sure she'll want to come home. Thank you for your help." Percy stood, looking much older than her age at this point. Rounding the desk she walked the chief to the door.

"You're still my only gal," Smiling, he stooped down to kiss her cheek and give her a hug.

* * *

Susan could not believe she had a flat tire on her six-month-old, almost new car. Terry said he'd come and change her tire. He too was surprised she had a flat. He figured she'd picked up a nail.

Tired of sitting in the car on such a nice morning, she got out of the car and tried phoning Goldie, but the line was busy. While this was going on she saw Terry's tow truck pull up. She could not make out the driver. *He must be new, dark clothes and hat.*

As soon as the driver got out and started walking toward her Susan knew who it was. *Oh god no!* Susan turned and ran in the opposite direction. It took Drew only seconds to catch her. Arms and feet flailing, a couple cars blew horns but kept on whizzing by. Drew never spoke, but she felt the pinch of a needle in her neck. *Don't let me die, my kids need me...*

* * *

"Only one Prof gave me a hard time about taking my exams early, but the administrator stepped in to help." Missy said. "Passed all my exams; I think that really has Bertonelli pissed."

"I'm just glad you were able to come home," Percy commented.

"Sí, family now together helps all." Benita said.

"How are Tara and FJ handling it?" Percy asked.

"Not well, FJ especially." Harold said. "I try to keep him busy helping around the house and his studies. But now he has a frown on his face constantly and he's not eating well."

"Yeah, like we've all lost our concentration. We start projects and they never seem to get finished." Missy added.

"This is taking one heck of a toll on your family, Missy. And this waiting is getting to us. The police say they have leads, but they haven't said much else," Jim said. "I still can't believe he got hold of one of Terry's tow trucks."

"Has FJ cried?" Percy asked, reaching over for one of Benita's fruit empanadas.

"No, he hold too much in. He blow soon." Benita remarked.

"Well, Val and Matt come tomorrow. That will cheer him some, and we have Staci and Irma here almost every day to help."

"Jim darling, you think it's taking a toll on the kids, but think of what this is doing mentally to Susan." Percy said.

Jim said, "No, my dearest I really feel this will harm us all for the rest of our lives, but it will be more horrible for Susan."

"Yes kiddo's, Jim is right; it's going to affect you children later in life more than now." Percy stated.

* * *

Susan awoke in the root cellar again. It was dark and musty, without the odor of a heavy chemical cleaner she smelled before. She lay for a long period, not moving or speaking. The door stayed absolutely firm. *How long will I be here this time without food, water or basic facilities? At least this time I'm not wrapped in a cocoon. God, I'm going on about such simple stuff, when I should think of a way to get out of here and back to my kids. I know by now they're more than panicked.* These and many more things went through her mind, but she remained where she was, without hope. She had tried getting out of this root cellar before without success. She could not cry.

She heard the key in the lock; the door flew open, letting in the little daylight left and the coolness of late afternoon. Without hesitating, Drew crossed the small distance of the cement floor. He looked down at Susan. His hand flew forward, whacking her so hard across her face that she was out before her head hit the wall.

* * *

Hours later Susan roused

"Man, you're lucky I came. You almost did it again. She can't take much more, you know."

Talking to whom? Did I hear right? Head hurts. Susan lost consciousness again.

This time when Susan awoke it was daylight. No lights were on; it was very quiet. Head still hurting she tried to move. *How long have I been out? Days? Hours? I can't be sure.* In her moving ... *well I'm in an anklet again and bathed, back in a nightgown ... well. Why doesn't he just kill me off? Then he can get a new person to abuse in every way possible.* Looking around the dismal room; *this antique furniture is morbid and ugly; downright depressing. At least I seem to still have my faculties ... I don't think anyone's here.* Feeling her head she realized she had stiches. *Don't recall any hospital visit.* Lying there, she worked her brain. Thinking seemed to even hurt and things were fuzzy. Lying still, she let some time pass before trying to think again ... Yes, he *hit me.* Staring at the ceiling, noticing the paint peeling ... *talking ... yes he was talking to someone. I didn't think Drew had friends. Sure, the kind that can get him dope, but not friend friends and this one sort of sounded that way, I could have sworn ... the voice ... sounded familiar. Feel tired, very tired...*

* * *

The front door opened. Abruptly Susan woke. Someone was moving around, but she could not quite decipher. The sounds seemed

95

different. She was not sure if it was Drew or the person he was talking with earlier. She lay on her side, face to the wall quietly listening and acting as if asleep. Obviously he had a key to get in. *Keep breathing evenly ... W*hoever was there was now in the doorway. "Susan, are you awake?" the voice asked.

Not moving, she stayed extremely still, she did not want him to know she was awake. She tried to look out from under her eyelashes ever so slightly. *That voice is familiar.* She could not see the face from her angle. The person moved into the room. "I'm here to help care for you. I want to mend you and love you. Remember I told you we would be together. Now that we are, I don't want to lose this time." He moved toward the bed, standing right next to it. *Together? He told me? Drew says things like that too. Who?* Time passed quickly between his standing over the bed talking like he was from another planet and Susan trying to figure out who this person was. She could not recall any other man saying something like this to her. She was not involved in relationships. *This has to be the one Drew spoke with the other night? Did Drew Ok this guy to have sex with me? Is this dude paying Drew? No, no, Drew likes owning his property. He does not share. Will he hurt me too? Speaks of taking care of me? Did he fix my head? Can he get me out of here? He has keys. He's contemplating coming into the bed. Stay away, I have to think. Get out of here! Please ... My God, no one is going to believe this!*

As if he heard her thoughts, he lifted his knee from the bed and left the room. Susan did not realize the last few seconds; she had held her breath so long and kept her body so rigid it felt like she had bruised her ribs, from holding her body so long in such an extreme manner. Letting the air escape from her lungs, she quickly took in oxygen, now feeling severe pain. However, this pain now seemed to feed her.

Susan did not dare move for fear he may be lurking right outside the room, sensing she was faking sleep. She was. *Is Drew trying to play some kind of sick joke? Teaching me a lesson? This can't be happening. Dear Lord, please let me be dreaming.* Having lost herself in her train of thought, she did not realize the person had entered the room again, observing her, admiring her until he could no longer take it. "Oh Susan you are so beautiful. I'm so glad you're awake. We have so much to discuss. You are safe now with me. I'm here to protect you."

As this person spoke, *I must have moved enough for him to see me awake. That voice ...* slowly

Susan turned to face this invading person, not paying any attention to what he was saying; she only wanted to get away. She feared what this person may do compared to Drew.

"Hello Susan, are you feeling better? I did such a super job stitching you up. Drew has a nasty hand. I would never hit you. I only want to cherish you. Give you everything you've ever wanted."

My God, how are he and Drew in relation? Is this for real? Well he is standing in front of me isn't he? Whatever is to come I best not panic. I know I must be showing some, but ... Dear Lord! He's repulsive, repels me. I told him that. Remember he's like Drew, don't panic. Think before you speak. Susan spoke softly, "Get me out of here please, Dr. Cohen."

"Susan, you must call me Ernest. We can now more than ever be on a first name basis, don't you think? I would enjoy taking you to my home, but I do not have the key to undo your ankle chain. So we must endure this horrible situation for now, but then we can enjoy each other too, until I can locate the ankle key. You'll see we'll be very happy."

"That's easy; Drew wears the key around his neck. Just take it from him and free me. That would really make me happy!" speaking with loud emotion, "Or better yet just contact the police. They'll make sure I get out of here. They'll get me out of the anklet."

"No dear, I can't do that! I was the one who stitched you up. I did not notify the police, so that is an infraction on my license. No we must endure this for now. It seemed the only way I could get to be with you and ultimately remove you from this place. But I never expected him to have chained you up like this either. You poor, poor dear, what you have endured. And even I would like it to be so different. I'm a doctor, I can control him, you'll see."

He's really schizoid! He may be worse than Drew, best be careful. "Tell you what, why don't you go get a pair of cutters to remove the anklet. Then we can go to your place." Susan was testing the waters for his reaction.

"Cutters? What are those? Besides, we can take advantage of the time right now to enjoy each other, I so want you." As he said the words he moved closer to the bed, lessening the space between them.

Susan stood her ground, "It would be better if I was free from this anklet. That way we could enjoy each other more perfectly. *This one has really been pampered.* If you get a paper and pencil I'll draw the cutters for you. You can take this to a hardware store and buy them. Then come back and cut the anklet. It would be much better with me free, don't you agree?"

At first he just stood there looking down at her, for the longest moments. Susan seemed to hold her breath, not sure what was to come next. Cohen moved quickly lying down next to her; he did not try to fondle her. Instead he placed his head on her left breast, his arm and leg across her body. "Isn't this magnificent?"

Cohen did not notice how hard Susan tried to keep the shock from her face. She had no inclination what to expect next. Slowly she took in air; *he's acting like a small boy needing motherly attention. Is this the kind of togetherness he's speaking of? Think! ...* Again long minutes stretched by; finally, without thinking, she reached up and started running her hand over his head, as if consoling him. Within minutes Ernest was sound asleep. Looking down she realized his left arm was no longer across her, but bent with his thumb in his mouth. *Damn this is the weirdest thing yet. Hearing the nurses and interns at the hospital, they talked like Cohen was a genius. Well this genius is not so grown up is he? He's really in need of psychiatric help. I felt like I was talking to my son. He seemed to respond to me better that way. Maybe that's what possessed him to seek this motherly attention. Or maybe he's playing games with me. At least that is the way I will play it until I know more. Let the games begin, asshole!* While he slept she checked his pockets for house and car keys, but to no avail. *He probably left them on the table. I must get him to help me. This may be the only chance I will ever have.*

THE WEEK

Cohen came every day to feed and care for Susan as if she were a sister or mother without making one sexual overture, and while sleeping next to her he was every bit the professional. But he couldn't let his thumb leave his mouth while sleeping next to her. *Did he do this when he was away from her?* Since he did not have the key to undo the ankle chain, he bathed her carrying linens, full water basin and clean gown to her, without showing any signs of arousal, except that his erection was evident.

This sure isn't the usual behavior, I've seen in any man. But then, I never had much experience with men or whackos. "You know he'll be back any day now." Ernest kept his hands moving over her body, taking thorough care to clean Susan. His only reaction showed in his jawline. "If you really care for me, you'll get me away from here."

Slowly losing his professional demeanor, "I ... I can't do that."

Looking into his eyes, *My God, you really fear Drew. I shouldn't be surprised, but I am. Is it because he's stronger? Probably that's it, or is it you don't have that insane quickness that he has. It seems to take much longer for you to get to that point. I must think of some way to get him to change his thinking and get me out of this dilemma.* "I appreciate all you've done for me. I want you to know that." Clothed in a new gown, she sat on the edge of the bed. "So, you're satisfied with the fact you will just keep patching me up, until I'm dead?"

"What do you mean?" Moving quickly away, he did not look her in the eye.

Damn brainiacs! They really have no common sense. No don't laugh, that's the worst thing you can do. Susan quickly looked down into her lap, "Drew will keep on hitting, choking, beating and raping me and I guess you will keep on fixing and repairing me for him, until one day he kills me. He has no intention of ever letting me go."

"Do you love him?" as he proceeded to cross the room.

Susan let out a vile laugh. "How can one love a beast?"

Turning he looked to her, "He says you love him and that you're

99

made for one another. You fell in love the night you met."

"And you believe him? That makes you as sick as he is!" Susan spit out a bit too harshly. *Oops, I shouldn't have said that. It just came out. Be careful, you're on scary ground here. There's very little time left before Drew returns. You don't know what things will set this psycho off either.* "The night we met, yes, he was the handsome artist who told me nothing but lies and I fell for it. I guess I was naive and felt I had finally met someone who would love me for me. Little did I realize it would be the worst thing to happen for me and my children?" Susan stood and started pacing alongside the bed, the anklet straining under the pressure of reaching its end and pulling her back. Little did she care if she drew blood! She was frustrated. "You really are as naive as I am when it comes to experience. What a sucker I was playing right into his sociopathic mind. Surely you see that." He made no reaction to her statement. *No, I don't think you do, maybe because you see yourself in the same ways. How am I going to get through to Cohen?* "Are you Drew's friend?"

For the longest time he stood directly staring into her eyes, but it was like he wasn't really seeing her. Eventually he did take his eyes from her. "I wouldn't say we are directly friendly, no. I know him through a nurse from work. He called on me because she is on sabbatical."

Should have known there would be a woman involved with Drew and not a man. "So you were to help patch me up, because she wasn't around; how convenient." Feeling deflated, no longer anxious to pace, she sat. He still stood before her, with one hand he tried reaching out to her. Susan pulled away. "Did you know it was me you were coming to stich up?"

"At first, no, but then I remembered about his nurse and how she spoke about Drew. Then I did put it together." He looked away from her, staring out the barred window, "I never expected to see you in such poor condition, nor being chained."

"So, what you're saying is you were willing to go along with this sort of arrangement?"

Having placed the soiled linens and basin aside, with hands by his side she could see he was clenching his fists, "I want to free you Susan. I really do."

"But not enough to save me, it's your own skin you're worried about." There was no reply. "Do me a favor, leave." With that Susan lay across the bed facing the wall. He stood quietly for another few minutes, and then left without saying good-bye.

* * *

"Darling, I'm home," came from the living room.

The bedroom was dark. *Must be sometime into the night.*

Drew clicked on the light over the bed, "Oh my red of fire, I truly missed you so. I thought of nothing else but you. I couldn't wait to get here. Let me look at you." He turned her to him. "You look marvelous." He examined her head. "You've healed wonderfully. Why did you do that to yourself?" *Expecting an answer? Anything to cover the fact it was you throwing me into the wall. Your simple mind just can't deal with it, eh?* Her mind so deep in thought, forgetting him, she found he was now lying unclothed on the bed beside her. *Something's way off he's being so gentle. Like when we first met. What happened to make him change? Did Cohen speak with him about me before he came back here? Something's awry...* Gently he fondled her breasts, removing her gown. He always made sure she had gowns he could undo from the front. Now he was sucking her breasts as if in a feeding frenzy. Susan almost felt arousal, as again his hands floated over her breasts bringing her nipples fully erect. Smiling, "Oh yes, this is what I've so missed." He suckled with such satisfaction; she could feel his manhood arise between them. As much as Susan tried to keep her mind free of him, he was actually getting to her; she could feel it in her lower abdomen. He placed his hand between her thighs, placing his finger into her wet vagina, smiling knowingly as he felt the luxury of her. He let out a sigh. "Oh yes, my fire, you are ready for me and I know you have missed me too. It emanates us." With that he climbed upon her, entering before she could catch her breath, wincing from the pain. "I'm going to your secret place and this time you will give me all."

* * *

I failed myself. You may have got me to come, but you will never

ever again have my heart. He's trying a new avenue to get to me. It won't make me ever want to stay and be with him. He's completely psychotic. If he truly loved me, he wouldn't beat me, chain me and he wouldn't keep me from my children. I've lost count of the days and or months I've been locked away. Have they given up looking for me? I've got to find a way to get out of here. There just has to be a way. He remembers to take the key off before lying in the bed. Wonder where he puts it? But he never forgets to keep the ankle chain on me. Only once he forgot. Plus there is nothing nearby I can reach to slug him over the head with. Susan fell asleep trying to figure different ways to get away and to find the key, while Drew snored lightly

RENOVATIONS

"The pool is almost completed. Soon we can start putting our efforts into the bungalow," Harold stated between his bites of apple.

"I wonder if Susan will ever get to see them." Staci mused, as if she was talking to the air. "I'm having a hard time getting excited about anything. The cops haven't given us any information in a long while. It's like they've forgotten all about her. I really don't believe they have any hint to go on."

"Sí, it seems so." Benita commented.

"Look ladies, we have to stay positive for Susan and the kids. We must keep a good face and attitude."

"Harold you're right." Staci said.

"It's hard enough dealing with the kids crying and getting depressed without you two doing the same. Now, let's discuss the things that we need to do to get this show on the road. Staci, we also need to set a date to go up to Val's to finish up the last details on her and Matt's home." Percy said firmly.

"You're right; I know Susan would get very angry with Benita and my pity party. But I needed to vent."

The phone rang; Harold went straight for it, as though he was expecting a call. "Hello? Yes? I'll be right there."

"Frank again?" Benita asked.

Harold shook his head, kissed Benita on the head, leaving without another word.

"What was that all about?" Percy asked.

"Mijo is being unruly in class all the time now. He no sleep bueno. Kids making nasty remarks about his mama; he fights."

"Wow, why didn't you say something? Staci was surprised.

"We hope it end, but no." Benita replied. "Happen ever since Missy goes back to college."

"Sounds like he's feeling abandoned," Percy offered. "Maybe we should home school him until this is over."

"That's a great idea. Irma is doing tutoring with Chelle, maybe she would be willing to help. Harold would also be marvelous with the kids, don't you think?" Staci asked.

"Sí, Tara and Missy are bueno at tutor. They may no want for you to interfere; very protective of Frank." Benita said.

"Well tell you what, Benita you talk with Harold, Staci you talk to Irma, and possibly I can be the mediator. If you need us to help we can." Percy said. "Oh my, look at the time; I must get to the schools. I sure can't wait for Susan to get back. How she keeps those schools from falling out of whack is beyond me. She's so terrific when it comes to keeping it all together." With that Percy stood, air kissed them all and walked out the door.

"Percy's tired. She can't run the schools anymore. She refuses to consider anyone else to take Susan's place. Wonder how long that will last before she is forced to do something?" Staci says.

"Sí, she look very worn out. She and James need to enjoy now; no work."

"Benita, you and Harold need to enjoy life now too, not take on three kids."

Benita reached across the patio table, placing her hand over Staci's. "We no feel it a job, love them like our own. Susan soon home, you see." Staci and Benita both had tears in their eyes. The workers were beginning to come into the back area, so they rose, took the breakfast plates and walked inside.

MAKING SUSAN RESPONSIVE

Drew lay in his hammock, observing Susan taking in the sun, as if she would never get enough again. He was having a hard time figuring out why she would want to see her kids so badly. These thoughts were dismaying. His mind could only see that she should be happy with him alone, for the great attention she received from him. Every other woman he had been with loved all his attention and craved more. *Why does she want to see her f'n kids? We shouldn't live with those brats. Those children do nothing but squabble with each other and whine to their mother.* To Drew the boy was the worst. "A pussy-whipped mama's boy," he whispered. He felt he had almost changed the boy to his way of thinking when he gave him that good beating. He still could not believe the cops put him in jail for child abuse. *I was only teaching him who was boss.* FJ's mother and sisters were always telling him how smart he was, but Drew felt the kid was dumber than a box of rocks. *Instead of tutoring the kid, they should have locked him away"* He could take the girls living with them, but not the boy brat. *The girls will be easy to manipulate, plus if needed I could dose their food or drink, just like I do their mother. Maybe I can drug his food too, but don't know what the repercussions will be with him being so loony. Maybe icing the boy is the answer. It sure wouldn't be hard. I could just tell him I'd let him come and see his mom. Take some real planning, but I could pull it off and no one would know.*

Hearing screaming brought Drew from his reverie. "My god, what is wrong with you?" now yelling loudly. No answer came, just loud screams. Coming off the lounge in one swift jump, hurrying alongside Susan, looking down she was screaming in her sleep. He couldn't believe what his eyes perceived. Sitting on the edge of her lounge he reached over gently to wake her, saying soothingly, "Oh, my poor darling, you've had a terrible nightmare. Now, now, you'll be fine." Taking her shoulders, he started to bring her into him.

"Get away from me, no, I will never surrender. The cops are coming. You almost killed him, I can never forgive you." Again Susan began screaming.

"Susan, wake up," he shook her so hard her teeth clattered; it didn't seem to do anything. He slapped her hard across the face.

Shock and puzzlement showed on her face. He didn't care that he had slapped her so hard, that blood now ran down the side of her face and one eye was swelling shut. Drew eyed the walls, to see if any neighbors were trying to look over. He was truly worried one of the neighbors had overheard. "What is wrong with you? I've never seen you like this."

"Hunh, what, what did I do?" now cowering away, not sure why he hit her. She tasted blood and her lip was swelling.

"You must have fallen asleep. I couldn't get you to wake up so I hit you." Making sure to say it loud enough, with the right tone of concern for the neighbors to hear; like his hitting her was quite out of the ordinary.

"Come, it's time to go in." Drew said, taking the key from around his neck to unlock the anklet. The sun felt so wonderful. It seemed to be helping Susan's ribs she knew were broken. She was so tired, just sitting there on the lounge she felt she could sleep forever. This seemed to be the only place he gave her any peace. *I wonder if he's afraid the neighbors will hear? Yes, that's probably it. If I yell, scream, or plea for help, he'll beat me even worse, but what the hell, he's going to kill me one way or the other. Why do I even try to hang on?* She knew the reasoning without answering herself. She did not cry out for help to the neighborhood.

As they entered the house, Drew carrying her draped over his shoulder, the front doorbell rang. Drew froze. "Damn." Lifting her head, using her tied hands to push off the back of his hip, Susan tried to look around Drew's back and arm to see out the window. She could not get a good angle. Drew did not move a muscle. The doorbell rang again. Finally he set her down off his shoulder to the floor, propping her against the sink counter. She felt the weakness in her muscles trying to stand. The counter helped somewhat, but no matter how hard she tried not to collapse she would begin to drop, pulling herself each time to stay up. She knew that muscle atrophy was taking over her body.

Drew walked to the window, looking out around the curtain. "Damn neighbor." Walking to the door he opened it slightly. *Should I cry out?*

Susan was so unsure of what to do. But this was an opportunity.

"Hello, I'm your neighbor Jake Haskell from next door. Is everything all right? We thought we heard a woman scream in your back yard."

"My wife fell asleep, she had a bad dream. Everything's fine."

"Oh? We're surprised. We didn't know Caroline rented the house before leaving on sabbatical. Usually she lets us know. If you need anything, just let us know. We're willing to help our neighbors. My wife is Jenni, here's our number if you need to call."

A loud crash came from within as if dishes had fallen and broke on the floor. "Gotta go; my wife's an invalid. She needs me." Drew slammed the door in Haskell's face. Jake still had the paper in hand with his number. He stood at the door a few seconds, and then pushed the paper into the door jam. Shaking his head, he left.

Rounding the corner to the kitchen, he found Susan sprawled on the floor, moaning. "My God, you fell? Oh dear, let me get you back to bed." He saw the large casserole dish he had placed to air dry smashed into pieces on the floor. "Susan, what were you doing?" he asked as he dumped her onto the bed.

Pain shot up through her ribs causing her to lose her breath, and almost cry out. *No, don't let him know you're in pain.* "I-I was trying to help. I wanted to put the dish away. I didn't realize how weak I am." For the longest he stood there looking down at her. *Will he believe me? Or hit me?*

Sitting on the side of the bed, he stroked her arm, "I guess I've not given you enough exercise. Would you like it if we worked out together as we used to, and you can start cooking again?"

Digesting what Drew said, *maybe he'll unchain me and I can get out of here. Hopefully that neighbor will get more curious and keep returning.* Inside herself she smiled. She could only hope this would help lead to her escape. Truly she was thanking the higher powers for being with her this day. It was the first day he had not beat her in some way, other than waking her from the nightmare. *Funny he never asked me what I was dreaming about. WHAT WAS I DREAMING ABOUT?*

FLAGSTAFF

"Auntie Val, we're here!" FJ threw open the door without knocking.

"You sure are sweetie," Val remarked, bending down to give him a hug. "How's my big guy doing? I'm so glad you came to see us. You beat them all in the door."

"I know, where's Uncle Matt?" as he kissed and hugged her.

"Well, he's out back with Oscar, and probably Blazer jumped out of the car with you and ran around back to join them." Without another word FJ kissed his aunt on the cheek again and was off out the back door.

Percy stood in the doorway watching the love shared between Val and FJ. "If I didn't know better, I think you like that kid." Percy said with a smile.

"Hi Percy, welcome; I kinda grew attached to those rug rats when we all shared a home. But not enough to change my mind about having kids." The rest of the group came loudly into the house, giving out hellos, kisses and hugs.

Staci and Percy enjoyed adding their finishing touches to Val and Matt's home. The rest stayed outside helping prepare the barbeque meal they were about to enjoy. "Harold, thank you for making me aware how desperately my Val needed these changes made to the house. She's a completely different person to live with. And I must say the house looks so alive now. I even feel better. The house doesn't feel so drab. I guess I was living in a dungeon and didn't realize it."

"Glad you liked everyone's suggestions. Putting those new doors in sure made a difference in your great room. The morning sun coming in is sensational. Noticed your animals like it too." Harold moved so his back was to the group, and facing Matt, dropping his voice. "I've noticed how happy FJ is. He's almost shut down at home. Here he's smiling and jumping around. He's a different kid right now."

Matt moved to the pit and added charcoal, "Well, with his Mom out of the picture, he's very frightened."

Harold automatically moved with Matt, handing him the lighter fluid, "Yes, we're thinking of home schooling him. He's been getting into fights at school. He's very angry. You and Val both seem to have a way with him."

Again, Matt moved and went to the cooler taking out two beers. He handed one to Harold, popping his, "He's a great kid. Maybe he would like to come and stay with us a couple weeks this summer. I can't speak for Val, but for myself I'd really enjoy taking him fishing and hiking."

"I was hoping you would say that. I think he needs to get some time where he isn't always thinking of his Mom and the situation she's in."

"Well, let me speak with Val. If she agrees we can ask FJ if he would like to come. I'm sure you and Benita could use the rest. How's the renovation coming at your place?" Even though the subject was changed, Matt looked over to FJ playing fetch with the dogs. His mind was on FJ and the damage that may have been done to him.

Later, Percy and Val were in the kitchen, "How do you like your place now, Val?"

Cutting the pies, "It's so fantastic with all the light. I never dreamed we could have such a wonderful place here amongst trees and cold weather. You and Staci have done wonders with it. I still think the both of you need to start your own business."

"Heavens no, I'm hardly surviving taking care of the schools until Susan's return. It's wearing me out."

"Oh Percy, is there anything we can help with? I just never thought you wouldn't be able to handle it anymore." Val looked up long enough to take in Percy's face, noticing how much she had aged.

"That's just it. I need to put in a new School Director; one who knows the cosmetology business. Those I've checked out don't have the ability Susan has. I even thought of calling Tracy to see if she would come back from Florida. Do you think Nick would come back?"

Val frowned at the mention of Tracy. "Well, none of us have heard from her since she left. When all this happened with Susan, I tried calling, but for some unknown reason she isn't answering any snail mail, text or email of my messages and or any of the others. What's more odd, is her not contacting Susan since she left. Something is very wrong there."

Looking to Val, she realized the concern Val was feeling for Tracy. Percy also noticed Val was now wearing western garb. This made her think the changes in their home had improved her outlook on living in Flagstaff. Maybe eventually Val's outlook on things in general would change. "But truly, there is no one who will be able to do as great a job as Susan has. I can never replace her. I just don't want the schools to die, after all these years. They definitely would lose their high ratings, if I hired someone less qualified. At my age I'm supposed to be enjoying travel with my hubby, golf or whatever else we decide. I feel like I'm robbing him right now. And down deep I know my dear Susan will return, but in what condition, only the good Lord knows." Percy piled the plates and forks together. "There's another pressing concern. FJ is having problems, fighting at school and declining scholastically. I noticed how well he takes to you and Matt. He's happy with you. Do you know that boy hasn't smiled or really spoken to anyone in a long while?"

Val stopped what she was doing and looked out the new window to where the family was sitting. FJ and Matt were talking and giving attention to the dogs smiling, "Ok, Percy, I hear you, let me talk with Matt. Benita and Harold could use some down time, also. Heck why not let all the kids come up here this summer."

"A woman out of my dreams; I salute you," Percy stated with a huge smile and tears glassing, quickly then taking a sip of wine before carrying the pies out to the family.

FJ

Drew sauntered around on the outside of the school yard fence, scanning for FJ among the other kids in rowdy play. FJ was not at his usual station. This unsettled Drew, because he had spent so much patient planning for this day these past three weeks. He paced the fence back and forth, checking to see if there was anyone who would notice him there, while he scanned for FJ. "Why isn't the kid here? Is he ill? This kid better not screw up my plans." He started to bite his nails. Slowly he scanned the yard again. "He's not here. Now what? Susan's nightmares are getting worse; all because I was teaching the kid a lesson. He's the problem; Susan won't give into wanting me completely until I take care of this situation. I'll check the house to see if he's there. It'll be easier to take him from there than it is here." Drew walked to his car, pondering a possible new destination.

* * *

The door opened waking Susan. Listening, she realized the footsteps were different. *It must be Cohen.* Cohen appeared in the doorway. "What the hell are you doing here, Drew's out?"

"I've been thinking of you so much Susan dear. Oh my…" He saw her swollen eye. *Susan dear? Walk lightly.* He slowly stepped into the room, taking in Susan's appearance lying on the bed. He wondered if she could tell he had an erection. "I'm sorry. Did I wake you?"

Making sure he could fully see her in light, she moved more to where he stood, "Doesn't matter I sleep a lot these days. Being chained, there isn't much else to do. Unless you came to get me out of here, there's no need for you to stay. He hasn't been beating me as much lately as you can see. Not sure why either."

Looking longingly at her, he wanted so to crawl into bed with her. "He called to ask some questions about nightmares. If he comes back, I can say that's why I'm here, to speak with you about them."

Smiling wryly, "He won't buy that. You didn't wait until he was here. He still lets you have a key? Odd, don't you think? Would you mind telling me how long I've been held here? I've really lost count." Susan said this without any emotion. *Why am I giving him advice? Maybe I should just let Drew beat him to see how it feels. Then maybe he would help. Shit he'd run away from the situation. I'd be the one screwed again without hope.*

Cohen took note of this. He knew immediately she was giving up. She had told him this on his last visit, but he thought she was using the situation to get unchained. Now he knew she wasn't. She was really giving up. He had to help her escape, but how? He couldn't call the police, he was too involved. He must try something. He had to make it look like she herself escaped.

Will he have the temerity to help me escape? What is wrong with this psycho? He can't even answer a question. Susan now moved to the side of the bed so she could sit up, dragging the chain with her to place her feet on the floor. She stood easily as Ernest reached out to help her stand. Susan laughed, "He has us working out together, so my muscles do not atrophy. Quite the joke don't you think?"

"What do you mean? Like he unchains you to work out with him?" He looked down at her.

He really has a puzzled look, "Yes, but then he puts a noose around my neck with a long lead, so I can move around the room, but he also makes sure to lock the door high above with bolts which I can't reach. He does not trust me, but then I wouldn't trust me either. One thing he's forgotten about is there are a lot of weights and dumbbells in that room. An accident could occur, you know. But to get out the window would be most difficult, since there are bars on the outside. Oh yes, and spaced close enough one cannot escape. Wonder if the weights and dumbbells could knock a whole big enough in the door? But then I would have to get a lot more muscular to carry all this speculation out."

Susan looked into the distance beyond Cohen as she spoke. "Oh, did you hear, we met one of our neighbors. Funny"... giving a small giggle ... "did you know Drew doesn't really own this place as he said? The neighbor usually takes care of the place for the real landlord. But then I'm probably giving you information you're already aware of."

"Ah, no, I wasn't aware of that but I never had reason to inquire. Susan, I really want to help you." Susan made sure not to look at him or say a word. *Does he really have a heart?* Cohen slowly walked the room checking out all the furniture and the amenities Drew had added for Susan to survive with essential needs. *Is he trying to figure a way to keep me captive at his place now?* "You see, I can't be found out. If I go to the police, they would find out I'm involved and I could lose my license to practice." Picking up her hair rake, he fingered it with compassion, almost getting lost in it, like he wanted to bring it to his nose to smell. Coming back to reality, "Two, Drew could beat me to a pulp or do away with me."

His safety first; it's a normal reaction. Susan purposely stared off into space as if she did not see him, letting the silence between them drag out. "You could make an anonymous call to the police giving them the location."

"I thought of that, but then they could trace the call. In this day and age that's very easy."

She noticed he had her lipstick up to his nose, smelling. *Disgusting ... he's as weird as Drew.* Susan looked away. "You could drive to an outside location of the city, saying you saw his picture on TV, followed him; give the location saying you don't want to get involved. They do still have roadside phones along the highway don't they? At least I think they do in small towns."

"I'm not so sure it will work. I'll think it over." Suddenly he was all over the room jumping like a madman, "It's so damn hard working everyday knowing you are a prisoner here. I've been doing some lousy surgery lately and people in the hospital are talking. I can't keep my mind where it should be. We've got to get you out of here." Not looking back, he swiftly walked from the room and straight out the front door.

She heard it slam. Shaking, as if from a cold chill, *I advised you how, now it's up to you. Please Dear Lord let him do this one thing to help me.*

FRUSTRATIONS

Drew sat in his car a good ways down the street from the house sipping coffee, trying to keep warm. He hated getting up when it was cold. He had arrived just before dawn. The only ones coming and going were construction workers. He considered making himself look like one of the workers, to get to the kid. Or he could do away with the alarm. Missy the so called brilliant one helped him more than she knew. She practically handed him the numbers.

At around 8 am, Tara with her backpack came bounding out of the house. This brought Drew out of his reverie. The girl took a few minutes looking up and down the street. She started to walk toward Drew's vehicle. Immediately he ducked down, even though he was positive she would not know the car. The window was cracked just enough to hear anyone who passed. Waiting ... he did not hear her pass. He waited a few minutes more. Still he did not hear her pass. Slowly he raised himself, looking down to where she had come from. She was not there; quickly he turned his head to see if she had passed and was well on her way. She was not that way either. Now he got up to have a better look. He did not see anyone as he viewed a complete circle. What happened to her? He knew he had not become hard of hearing. Maybe she forgot something and went back to the house. Yes that had to be it. As he was deciding this she came out, but not alone. That so-called adopted grandpa was with her. The garage door opened. A clue, he was going to take her to school. Where was the boy? Why wasn't he with them? Maybe the kid really was ill. He knew that would be the only reason he would not go to school. That kid loved school and Drew never figured out why from the way everyone treated him at his school. To him it was just another part of the kid being damn weird.

Drew ducked down once again knowing they would pass his vehicle going toward Tara's school. After the Cadillac passed he got up to look for the boy once again. There was no way he could go look in the back area of the house with workers around. He didn't have clothes with him to make like he was one of them. At least he didn't have to worry about the mutt anymore. He gave him enough poison in meat for six animals. As he was thinking of giving up for the day, Irma and Staci pulled into the drive, from the opposite direction. "What are they doing here so bright and early? Staci has never gotten out this early that I can remember."

Irma and Staci got out of the car, and he noticed Staci's two kids were with them. Something was a little off there. Those kids would normally be in school. Drew decided to sit and wait. He had to see what was coming about.

Forty-five minutes later the same group came out with one added child. Drew perked up, it was FJ. He was carrying his backpack and Irma was carrying a suitcase. Opening the trunk of her car, he realized there were more suitcases in the car. "Well this is wonderful; they're helping me get rid of the kid for a while. I'm sure not messing with Irma, I've done that enough. Enjoy your mini vacation, all of you. You're all out of my way." he waited until they pulled away. As he drove off he started humming to himself.

* * *

Tara started out of the house. Darn, Aunt Staci wasn't here yet. She tried her cell. "Where are you?" knowing her Aunt was giving another excuse, she started to walk.

"Sorry baby, we're running late, just now leaving the house."

"Aunt Staci, I'm already late for class."

"See if Harold can run you to class." Click went the phone.

Mumbling to herself, Tara turned around and re-entered the house. "Harold, can you take me to class, Aunt Staci is late as usual. I should have known better than to count on her being here on time and I have a test first period."

"Ok, meet you at the door," as he bounded down the hall for his keys. Leaving the house, Harold looked down the street. "Wonder whose vehicle that is, haven't seen it here before. Doubt if it's one of our workers, they usually come in the trucks. I'll ask the foreman when I get back. Meantime do me a favor and take down the license number when we pass. Do it nonchalant. We do have to be careful around here." Passing, Tara turned, being very conspicuous, like any teen would and started writing the numbers while looking at the vehicle.

* * *

Ten minutes later Staci, her two kids and Irma pulled into the driveway, jumping from the car. Staci got out her key, unlocking the door, "Hey FJ, are you ready to go see Aunt Val and Uncle Matt?"

"I've been ready since seven o'clock. Isn't that when you told me to be ready?"

"Yes, honey, but you know how your Aunt Staci is." Reaching down, she kissed him on the cheek, causing FJ to blush. "Morning Benita, are you staying or going?"

"I stay; don't trust workers without someone always here."

"You're right. What are you eating young'un?" Irma inquired.

"Benita made me a special breakfast burrito."

"More in freezer help yourself. Just wrap in paper towel micro for two minute."

Irma went straight to the freezer, taking out the burritos. "Thanks Benita, of course Staci got us all up so late there wasn't time for breakfast."

After breakfast and saying their good-bye's all walked out leaving Benita to a quiet empty house and the workers in the back. "I no used to this, no like."

ABRUPT CHANGES

"Oh Susan I've got the most wonderful news," Drew expounded, running into the room, waking her. Quickly he lay down beside her.

Opening her eyes, looking at him, *he's happy*. The light was dim, but she could tell it was, *something good?* All Susan could bring forth was "Mmm."

"We'll have the girls with us within the week. They'll live here with us. I know it'll make you happy. I'll move the workout equipment into the fruit cellar. We can all work out there. It will be good, you'll see. You won't be unhappy anymore and we can get on with living."

"Live with us here? And aren't you forgetting another child? My children will not be separated from each other and what gives you the right to bring them here without my consent?" She was definitely awake now, ready for battle.

Not looking her in the eyes, but up to the ceiling, "Oh, no Frank's gone, left this morning with Staci and Irma and her two kids. *He seems very excited about it.* I guess they're going on a trip. Anyway we can worry about him later." *He's lying.*

"What were you doing there in the first place? You aren't to be within twenty-five miles of my house."

Drew leaned back away from Susan, moving his head from one side of the pillow to the other, looking at her with disbelief. Like why shouldn't I be there, I have the right. "I…"

Suddenly the front door flew open, "Drew, I sure didn't expect you to be here! Where are you my baby, I could use a good kiss, hug and lov'in all in one package. I really missed you! I realize I made a horrible mistake running away. You know I was scared, scared of commitment. But I'm here now and hopefully you will forgive me and we can start again. Please give us another chance; I know I can help make it better for us this time. I just couldn't stand being away from you!" as this female voice was speaking, they could hear her dropping suitcases along the way as she searched through the house, trying to find that male person she missed so much. Before Drew could jump up from the bed, the overhead light switched on. "Just what the hell is going on in my house? And who the hell are you?"

Drew rose slowly from the bed, "Caroline! Ah, I, I can explain…"

This woman stood about five foot eight, with long blue-black hair. She looked to be a mixed race, of primarily Mexican decent. "Oh I think there's a lot of explaining to do! You've made quite a few changes to my home too! I could sure tell that on my way through. You had no right. You, sweetheart on the bed, can get your ass up and out of my house in your nightie, I don't give a damn. Just go, this concerns us." Everything was quiet for a few seconds while taking in this scene. Susan suddenly could not help herself, and she started laughing. Every time she tried to sit up the laughter took over, so all she could do was gesture to the chain around her ankle. "Oh God! Drew, what the hell have you done? You're the one they're looking for, aren't you? Why? What possessed you…"

Caroline never got to finish. Drew jumped her so quickly she never got a chance to protect herself. He took a swing, knocking her backward.

Susan got on her knees slowly, cautiously working her way to the end of the bed to watch. Even though Caroline staggered backward she did not fall; she seemed to brace her feet in the anticipation of another swing. *Did she anticipate he'd hit her? Is she used to this type of thing with him? Her actions make me believe she enjoys this type of life with him.* Caroline snarled, as she grew angrier.

This time Drew took another cross swing with an upward movement, his fist contacting her jaw, nose, and ear, knocking her off her feet. This caused her head to move hard to the side making a snapping sound in her neck, as a dried tree limb bends and then cracks. Caroline's eyes grew larger, while she tried to keep her balance in an almost musical dance. She faltered, while in midair, her head turning back, and then it seemed to drop abruptly backward. The tree limbs now hung opposite from front or side. Slowly her legs gave way as she sank to the floor. Silence filled the room, stretching out time. Mechanically Drew turned to look at Susan.

Susan was looking at Caroline on the floor; eyes wide, mouth agape, unmoving. Her head was tilted slightly backward yet seemed turned around. Trying to make sense of what she was seeing, she looked up to see where Drew was. Was he coming to kill her now? As if in slow motion she backed toward the headboard to get away. His eyes were open wide, but without anger, without fear, without satisfaction, just seemed unbelieving of the deed he'd just carried out.

Drew seemed to stop in mid motion and turned back to the lifeless body. Falling to his knees; he crawled to where Caroline lay, reaching out for her, "Caroline, please be all right. I didn't mean to hurt you; you know I don't like to hurt you." Still Caroline lay unmoving. On his belly, he picked up her dishrag-limp hand, crawling closer; he checked for her pulse and let out a painful whimper, then a sick wailing, loud cry came from deep inside.

* * *

Well into the night, Susan still sat against the headboard shaking, staring and chewing her hand. Drew did not bring in dinner, nor take her to the dining room. *He could still be lying on the floor talking to Caroline. But then I would hear him, I think. I've got to calm myself. He may have accidentally killed her, but the next time, if there is a next time could be intentional. At least from most things I've read; especially if someone has been able to get away with murder. I may be next or one of my children. I keep thinking of his reference to Frank, and worry about him. Could he be plotting something like this for my son? God, I wouldn't put it past him. He must not have realized Missy is away at college. I must find out what his plans are, but this may change everything. What made him think bringing my kids here would make me happy and want to stay with him? Sounds like he and this Caroline would have stayed together if she hadn't got cold feet. Then I wouldn't be here in this situation.*

She could now hear Drew mumbling. *Probably well soaked in alcohol by now; hopefully he'll pass out before long.* Still shaking, *I realize now I do want to live. I really thought I didn't, but with something like this, it's a great wake-up call. I must use this to my advantage, to keep myself and my family alive. He won't turn himself in, this I know. He'll dispose of the body. Most likely he already had her sign this house over to him, or he forged the papers. She most likely trusted him and just signed a paper thinking it was for something else.*

He talked as if he already owned it, but she didn't like the changes he made. I thought the house old and ugly. I'm so tired, but too scared to sleep. Not sure what he's going to do. I'll wait until he passes out before I even think of sleep.

TEENS

"Are you awake?"

Yawn. "I guess I am, I'm talking to you aren't I? Is it time to rise and shine? I sure don't feel like it is. Are you coming home this weekend?" Yawn … silence came from the cell phone. This made Tara come fully awake and sit up. "Are you ok?"

"I … I'm not quite sure."

Tara could hear Missy moving and fidgeting around in bed. She waited for her to say more, but there was nothing, "Are … are you doing that heebie jeebie stuff again?"

"I think so."

"When'd it start?"

Whispering, "Early this afternoon; ah, I'm not sure but every sign tells me it's Mom."

Flipping her strawberry-blonde long hair from her face, Tara then ran her hand over her face and into her hair, fingering to remove tangles. Sliding off the bed, she started pacing. "Do you think she's trying to contact you? Or maybe you're feeling something happened to her? You know like trying to get a message to us?"

Missy sat up in her bed, pulling her nightshirt down, in case her roomie's freaky boyfriend decided to wake up. Looking over to the other bed, seeing no one moving, whispering, "A little of all you just asked."

"So roomie is there with Mr. Disgusting and you can't talk. Is there anywhere you can go, so we can expand on this? Like you know Mom says, you have the best sensitivity of all three of us. FJ and I don't seem to work hard enough at it. But it seems you don't either and you know it just comes. She's trying to reach out to us, I feel that much."

"Nowhere to go at this hour and I'm not dressed for it. But that's just it, there's no message, it's just the sensitivity. Like you know, that time she went to the store, and he followed her. No words came through, but just the feeling. The problem is I never let her know I felt it, so how will she know if I do try to reach her in some way? I don't know, maybe she's not able to talk. Or maybe I'm just hearing some of her mind trying to figure a way out. I think it may be the latter. She's in a very bad position to even try to help herself, so it's super mental."

Tara walked and walked her room listening to Missy try to get her point across. A few minutes of silence passed between the sisters. Tara looked out her window realizing the sun was rising. "Missy, have you ever tried sending messages, you know like the heebie way? I've never heard you mention trying, other than getting those jeebies coming to you."

Lying back down in her bed, roomies forgotten, she yawned. "My Sis, you have a way with words. No I never tried. I've never really thought about it. We've always kept it just family, you know and we call Mom when she sends messages to us, but I don't think I've got the training or ah, skill I guess is a better word for the higher psychic stuff."

"Well how will you know unless you try?"

"Well…"

"No, no, don't do that. Don't doubt yourself. You always doubt yourself. What other avenue have we got? The cops are doing less and less advertising, and Percy finally hired a new director, so this may be the only avenue we've got. I may give you a hard time about the heebies, but that's only to get a rise out of you. I do believe you have a great gift." Silence came from the other end of the cell … "No, I really, really do! Now maybe you should put it to use and find our mother."

Missy smiled to herself. "Coming from you it's quite a compliment. Speaking of finding Mom, did you get anything on the license plate?"

"The car is registered to a Caroline, ah darn, can't remember the last name. She's a nurse. So far that's all we know. When you come home this weekend we can go off by ourselves and work on trying to reach her. Oh, and by the way, don't you dare tell anyone I gave you a kudo!"

Giggling, "You're so funny"… giggly still, "But that's another reason I called. I needed to tell you I wasn't making it this weekend."

Tara got quiet, looked to her cell then planted it back to her ear, "So I have to be FJ's tutor by myself? Or better yet maybe you finally got a date." There was silence on the other end. "Well holy crap, you did! That's fantastic! Ok, now you better give all, don't leave a thing out, you hear."

Missy smiled, "He's really nice, couple years older than me, dark hair, wears glasses, about 6 feet, not a great build, blue eyes and cute, not really, but what a mind. He's in one of my classes; he too is going for law. I really want to go out with him, but now with this sensitivity with Mom, I feel…"

"Oh no, you go on that date. You need to do this and Mom would be very mad at you if you didn't." Tara was telling her sister this with her fingers crossed. She really wanted Missy home to work on the heebie jeebies. But she also wanted her sister to finally have some good fortune.

"But Mom is more important than a guy. I would never forgive myself if we didn't try this."

"Sister dear, one never knows what the future will bring. This may be your guy and you are not going to miss this opportunity, ya hear? Is the date for Saturday right?"

"Yeah, there's a new club opening and he invited me to go with him. I really want to go."

"That's great, you go! Drive home Sunday morning; you can go back Monday night! I know you usually leave Monday for your studies, but it won't hurt you to miss one day. Knowing you, you'll find a way to study, whatever's necessary. So you see this is where you needed my common sense brain power," smiling once again with a triumphant 'gotcha'.

"Well …Ok, I'll do it. I can't wait for you to meet Jeff."

"Wow, you're moving fast with this one. He must really be special. But be careful, he might not be the guy you think he is."

"He was in three of my classes last semester and we sort of got to know each other. We sit together in class every week and then lunch in the cafeteria. So I do kinda know him. He's geeky like me."

"I figured he would be for you to like him. Don't know if we can handle another geek hanging around." She said this smiling, enjoying giving the jab to Missy. "FJ is going to be disappointed you aren't coming Friday, but at least you're coming. You know what I mean."

"Yeah, sorry to load FJ on ya all alone; he can be a handful."

"Boy, what Mom has endured with us is something. FJ is so much to deal with and us two, can you imagine Mom not getting any help in the beginning. It makes me miss her so much and appreciate every little detail of what she has done for us. When she gets home I want to let her know just how much I appreciate her."

"Now you see why I don't want kids. I'll be happy just to be an aunt."

"Right, mark my word, you'll have kids. You'll change your way of thinking."

"I don't think so." Missy could hear Tara's alarm going off. "Time to run, text me if you know if you find out more about the license plate. OK?"

"Ok, give me a text during your date. Love ya."

"Kiss, kiss, love ya back."

* * *

FJ rose early on Sunday morning. He dressed quickly, without checking himself in a mirror; he scurried quietly down the hall and sat in a chair facing the front door. Every few minutes he looked at his watch checking time, as he chewed his lower lip. He got up and walked to the kitchen, coming back with a glass of water, petting Blazer. "Go get your own water."

The front door then opened, setting the alarm chiming. Missy set her stuff down and punched in the numbers to stop the chimes then re-set the alarm.

"Missy, you're home, a whisper came from the living room. "I was thinking you weren't coming, I was worried."

"Frank, it's way too early for you to be up." Instead of picking up her bags, she met him half way crossing the room. He banged into her with full speed with arms spread, wrapping them harshly around her, almost knocking her over. *He's getting so big. He's almost as tall as me.* "Wow, you really grew this summer. What made you get up so early?"

Blazer finally made it over to where his pat would come from, with his greeting for her as well. Missy noticed how slow Blazer was moving, causing her to frown.

"I wanted so bad to give you a hug and kiss. I was afraid you weren't coming," tears showing.

"Hey my man, you shouldn't be afraid of such a thing. Besides you have so many people who love and help take care of you, what makes you so afraid?"

"Mommy isn't ...."

"Oh no, Mom's coming back. Don't you go there; maybe not now, but she will come." Pulling him from her grasp, she stepped back looking slightly down at him. "Don't you ever consider she's not coming home, cause she will, I feel it!" Blazer again nuzzled in for attention.

"I feel it too." came from the hall entry. Tara stood before them in her nightshirt leaning up against the wall.

"I guess the alarm woke you." Missy said.

Just then Benita's door opened, and at the other end of the hall Harold opened their mother's bedroom door.

"Well I guess I woke up the entire house this morning. Hello everyone, I'm home." Missy called to all.

All three in robes and pj's came to greet Missy and FJ, smiling and sharing their good mornings with hugs and kisses.

Benita immediately headed to the kitchen to make coffee and Tara was already at the refrigerator, bringing out fruit. "Mijo, why you up so early?" Benita asked.

"I wanted to welcome Missy home first," looking to Missy and Tara as if to say 'don't say another word'.

Harold said, "Here, let me help with your bags, Missy."

"How was the date with Jeff?" Tara asked.

"Oh, my gosh," Missy ran for the door. "I forgot Jeff."

"He's here? Now?" Tara inquired, while the others looked on with curious surprise.

Smiling very cunningly, "He's waiting in the car." Fidgeting with her sweater," I hope y'all don't mind." Quickly turning she hammered out the numbers to disarm the alarm. Everyone who wasn't dressed scrambled for their rooms.

FJ followed Missy to the door, watching as Missy and Jeff arrived at the doorway. "Are you my sister's boyfriend?"

"Well you must be Frank." Holding out his hand to shake FJ's, "Yes, Frank, I guess I could kinda say I am Missy's boyfriend, if she'll have me. Do you think she might approve?"

FJ finally shook hands, "Well, I don't know. If you're staying overnight; you can either sleep with me or on the couch or on the floor. Missy and Tara have to give me lessons you know, then maybe we could go to the park and play some ball. My sisters always need girl time alone, you know. Before you leave I will let you know how I feel about you, but it is up to Missy to decide if she wants you for a boyfriend."

Jeff couldn't help but laugh. "Boy, Frank, I was told you are a special man, and I believe the person who said it is very right. May we come in?"

"Oh, sorry," Moving aside FJ let them both into the house.

Slowly the rest of the family made their way back into the living area. Missy introduced Jeff as each returned. Once all were back, "I apologize for not giving Missy time to prepare you for my surprise arrival. It's my fault I'm here, not hers. You see I kept her up most of the night talking before we realized the time. Hearing she was still going to drive home this morning, I did try to talk her out of it. She wouldn't listen. So, well, I came along hopefully so she wouldn't fall asleep at the wheel."

"I thank you for looking after our granddaughter, Jeff. That was very thoughtful of you." Harold looked to Missy, staring out to the patio, smiling with a blushed glow.

"I'm hungry, Benita," FJ chimed in.

"Mijo, you have hole in your leg; you always hungry," smiling, "Before you eat, you go back brush teeth and comb hair please."

"Yes ma'am," answering as he ran down the hall.

* * *

The weekend became a whirlwind with Jeff in the mix; nothing ran per usual. He seemed to be right beside Missy every available minute, not leaving space or time with Missy for anyone else. However, FJ did receive his lessons amongst the chaos, and next assignment outlines were handed out for all in the household. Jeff and FJ did go to the park for ball, so Missy and Tara tagged along.

After the house quieted to a slow purr, Tara sat in her usual living area chair, feet thrown over the back of the chair, with head toward the floor.

"Mija, pouting?"

"Do you like Jeff? Doesn't he seem to cling? I never got time alone with Missy and we had a project to work on this weekend."

"Well maybe next weekend?"

"No, Benita, if she brings Jeff again, I doubt he will let her be without him around."

"He seems muy bonito for her. Cute together, no?"

"Yeah, but will she put up with his clutching? That's not my sister."

"Give time; that will change; relationship new."

"I sure hope you're right, 'cause it will make Missy pull away if not." Just then the door opened, chimes going off and Missy punching in the numbers. "What brought you back, did you forget something?" Tara now turned upright to get a clearer view, "Where's dream boy?"

"I left Jeff at the bus depot. We have a project to work on don't we? We best get started so I can get a nap, before I drive back to Tucson. Oh, Benita, is it ok if we use the new house for the project? We won't destroy anything."

"Of course, just go into bedroom suite and no one will bother you. I told the workmen to stay out of the area for a couple hours." Benita said everything with a knowing smile.

Looking from Missy back to Benita, Tara placed her hands on her hips. "Benita you knew all about this didn't you? You let me go on like a screwball."

"Of course she did, she knew I wouldn't possibly let Jeff interfere with any efforts to get Mother back. It's way too important. Benita also agrees, we should try, oh and Benita I think you should come and help in the circle. Matter of fact maybe we should have the whole family involved. This way she may be able to reach one of us better."

"That mean we don't have to go to back home, we do here."

"Well, Benita, you'd better call me absent for the day." Tara remarked. "We have plenty of work to do."

BURIAL

Three days later

"Wake up; it's time for you to be bathed. It smells like a pigsty in here!" Drew yelled at the top of his lungs. Susan jolted from the bed like a rocket, pulling the chain so hard it jerked her leg and she toppled back onto the bed. He grabbed her foot and undid the chain from her ankle.

"OW!" Susan almost started to cry. She gritted her teeth.

He never mentioned the blood oozing from where the chain cut through her skin. The look on his face was stern, hard, and pale. She could not see his eyes; he kept them turned from her. This was the first she had seen him since that terrible day. She had heard him moving around in the house, but could not know what was occurring. Her thoughts were many; *what did he do with the body? I do believe he buried her in the root cellar. The neighbors are now nosy and are watching so he couldn't have buried her elsewhere. I'm so thirsty and hungry. Doesn't he realize it's been three days? I don't know whether to ask for anything, I don't know his state of mind.* He took her arm to help her stand, she found she was shaking. "You're weak; I'll feed you after I bathe you." Nothing more was said. *Odd he doesn't seem drunk or high.*

* * *

One hour later

Sitting at the dining room table, *He was manic the entire time he bathed me. I couldn't see any emotion in his eyes or body language. Now what? I must rethink this program over entirely. Just when I realized I didn't want to give up, this happened. Where do I start? He mentioned bringing the girls here, but not Frankie. Do I dare ask?*

Drew appeared in the dining room doorway, leaned up against it,

128

and looked at her like she was a stranger. "Because of you, Caroline's dead."

Susan stopped eating the ham sandwich. Slowly placing the sandwich on the plate, *do I dare say what I'm thinking? I don't know his psycho state.* Looking up to Drew, taking in his posture she felt only pity for him. *He's truly insane. He doesn't know how to take blame for his own actions.* "I'm not to blame. You brought me here, chained me, and for the second time you're holding me against my will. You led me to believe this was your home, your car and then this Caroline comes in spouting love for you. I think you used her as you do all the women you've been with including me. No, sooner or later you must accept what you've done to so many. How long are you going to keep blaming others?" *Well I may die right here and now, but someone has to confront him. Don't take your eyes off him. That's the worst thing you can do.*

Still standing in the doorway, Drew silently swayed, it seemed ever so long but it was only seconds. She felt any moment he would fly across the table and hit her, beat her or maybe even kill her. Purposely he moved but ever so slowly rounding the table. Standing stiff and straight; as a wooden soldier right next to her, looking down. She did not look up. *Is he going to hit me, beat me, I'm sure he will, but it had to be said. Why I haven't died from all this I'll never know ...* slowly he raised his arm and placed his hand on her head. He held it there without moving for a good three minutes. It was absolutely unnerving. Susan dared not look up. *He could break my neck right now. It would be over in seconds.* His hand moved slowly down the back of her hair. He grabbed a handful. "Your hair is finally growing out nice and long. I like it so much better long. It's better than those freaky hairstyles you insist on wearing to help your business. Men like long hair on women, not short. Caroline had long hair, but it wasn't as beautiful as your shiny auburn hair." Slowly he bent to smell her fresh wet hair. Releasing her hair, he turned away leaving her to finish her sandwich.

With a sigh, letting out the breath she had not realized she was holding, *what was that all about? Please dear God, make him let me go free!* Susan swallowed bile, sandwich forgotten.

PHONE CALL

"Pierce, have you got any new information for me?" Percy implored more than asked.

"No, 'fraid I'm completely empty-handed." Saying this he happily put aside the paperwork on his desk, relaxing well into the back of his chair, smiling while picturing Percy on the other end of the line. He still loved her after all these years, although he knew it would not get him anywhere. But just hearing her voice every chance he could made his day brighter. "You know, I do wish I could give you a yes on that question. It's just grand to get your call, my dear friend." Pierce knew he wasn't telling her the whole truth and it bothered him so much he got out of his seat to pace.

"Flattery will get you a smile, Pierce."

Turning Pierce now did a good pace back and forth in front of his desk, "You can't say I don't try, eh? There is absolutely no trace of this guy. It's like he dropped off the face of the earth."

"I grant you, he's very good. After all he is a sociopath."

Pierce came to a complete halt, "Percy?" looking to his phone as if he could see her face, "How would you know information such as this about this guy?" He did not want to let her know, he never saw anything in the paper work he received about this Drew character. "Was he ever diagnosed?"

"No, Drew's never let anyone get close enough to do a full diagnosis, but hearing about his past from Susan, he's a definite, I've no doubt. I was really hoping to give the kids something to help raise their spirits. It has been a very long six months for all of us. And another thing that still bothers me; why checking out this nurse from the hospital never really led the law anywhere. She takes a leave of absence and no one has heard from her since? Seems she up and left the country. Sabbatical I guess; she does it a lot, the news media said. You checked out her house and I can't figure why that was a dead end. You know like did any of your people talk to anyone in the neighborhood? One of those neighbors might have a key to her place. Or maybe she has a service keeping an eye on her home while she's away, if she's really on a sabbatical. Did your guys show Drew's picture to any of the hospital staff? Like did they think maybe a nurse would get close with him?

Now he was leaning on the front of his desk, he smiled; she would have made him a good wife. She thought like a cop. "Well that too led us into a dead end. Most of the neighbors, average of two at least work in each household, so they're never there other than at night. So they really have no concept of what's going on. Hospital staff didn't remember him. So many say they see too many people in ER, they all start to blend in and they really never individualize them. But a few said he looked familiar, nothing substantial."

"Pierce darling, I don't buy that. Besides you don't either from the way you're speaking about all of it. I bet if you sent one of your own detectives out there, you'd have got tons of information from the neighborhood than you're letting on. Do you even know if she was entangled with Drew?"

He was still smiling broadly, he loved she truly pricked him, "No, we never got anything that would lead us to think they were an item. Funny you should mention this, because I've been thinking of a new angle to get them back out there," he lied, partially. He just could not tell her he was forced to close the investigation.

"I'm telling you if she's single, Drew would play her. That's part of that man's MO. If he can get something he will. He's fabulous at swooning women."

"Well you've just given me an angle to play with to get the department to allow a detective back on the case. Thanks."

"Glad I can be some help." *So they did close the case, she thought.*

"I'm going to cut this short my girl, but I will keep you posted."

"Thanks Pierce, talk with you soon, kisses."

ANGLES

"Mr. Haskell?" Detective Harrison queried. Haskell had shorts on. Harrison wished he was in shorts, instead of his required monkey suit.

"Yes?" as he turned, he carefully watched the person approach his driveway. Wary, he made sure the hose nozzle pointed directly toward the approaching man, who was lean and tall. Right away he knew it was probably a cop, because he had a suit on in this sunny ninety degree weather.

"I'm Detective Harrison, from the Maricopa County Sheriff's Department. Could you give me a few minutes? Asking as he flashed his badge so it could be seen.

"Has something happened I should know about?"

"No Sir, nothing like that. I was just wondering if you know the neighbor who lives next door to your right."

Body language and the shocked look on Haskell's face made Harrison give him full attention. "Are you speaking about the owner, Caroline, or the renter?"

"Oh, she's renting the place?" Harrison couldn't believe his success with the first person he encountered. And on such a hot day no less; maybe his work could end out here before it went into the triple digits. He wondered how the regulars had missed this guy.

"Yeah, and the new guy isn't friendly. I usually keep an eye on the place for her. My wife and I are good friends with Caroline. She rents it out when she goes on long trips."

"Does Caroline often go on long trips?"

"She'll work until she gets enough saved for a special trip to another part of the world, take an LOA, come back when the money runs out and starts all over again. She's been to many places. She's single, so she hasn't much to worry about. Caroline would be quite the catch, are you single?"

"'Fraid not. She sounds like a real catch. Did she take an LOA recently?"

Mr. Haskell's body language again gave much away. He started looking toward his feet, moving side to side, then put down the hose, and crossed his arms across his chest in an effort not to say more. Harrison knew he had to take it more slowly, but he knew this man had most of the information he needed on this nurse to possibly help with the case.

* * *

Two hours later

"Boss, you told me to call you at home, right?"

"Yes, do you have something for me?" Pierce asked.

"I think we have our man; got a pretty good description of him. The neighbors next door knew plenty and have the same house layout, so it would be easy for me to draw it if we needed to have the heavies go in. They also have a key to get into the place. Seems they're the ones who usually care for the place when this gal brings in renters. However, they knew nothing about the new renter. When Haskell, that's the neighbor, went over there to check it out, the dude slammed the door in his face when he started asking questions."

"Harrison, can you get the report written up and on my desk within a few hours?"

"Way ahead, boss man. Already dictated to that cute newbie you gave me and she's typing away. I can't figure how the regulars missed this information."

"Me either, I'll meet you at the office, say after lunch, so we can talk more."

"See you then."

VISIT

"Where is everyone?"

"The girls are taking naps. Supposedly FJ's doing homework, and Benita and I were having some quality free time, until you so kindly interrupted."

"Gee Harold; you really know how to make a best friend feel wanted." Kissing him on the cheek, Percy walked right past into the living area. "Hi Benita, I guess I'm interrupting private time, but guess what, I don't care. I need to be here, can't stand being at the school right now. Jim's on his way over too. I thought we might be able to do something together. We need family right now." Percy unloaded in a matter of seconds, kissing Benita on the cheek and plopping down in the chair next to her.

"So you hear no bueno from Chief?"

"No, no new leads. Everything has gone cold. I did ask him to send out one of his detectives to re-investigate that nurse's neighborhood."

"And the Chief took your advice?" Harold asked, with a smirk on his face.

"He didn't say yes or no on the subject. I was just hoping to make him think a little. They never really combed the neighborhood for information."

"Now, how do you know that?" Harold inquired. "Don't you think you're just assuming?"

"Not really, he alluded to it when we were talking. I do have my ways."

"Really? That doesn't sound like Pierce, but he's probably just trying to throw you off track for constantly nagging him."

"Harold sometimes, you ca—"

The doorbell rang, interrupting the conversation.

ABSENCE

How many days has it been this time? Think it's a week. I'm so-o-o hungry and thirsty; never left food, just water. I smell foul. There was no way she could get away from laying in her feces, the foulness sometimes making vomit and sometimes not.

The door slammed shut. Jumping, she woke from her thoughtful fog. The light flipped on overhead with a nightmarish glare, causing her to lift her arm over her eyes to block it. "God, you look like hell. This room reeks, what've you been doing? I thought I told you to make sure you put cosmetics on every day. I can't stand the sight of you without it. Don't you listen to an f'n thing I tell you? What don't you understand?" He was suddenly there by the bed looking down at her. Without warning, he hit her so hard in her ribs she flew across the bed into the wall. Groaning loudly, she knew she could not move. *The pain is excruciating! He broke ribs, again or more. This must be it; my day to die. Well I'm not going down without a fight! I never got to see my kids one last time.* Drew now stepped onto the bed. Susan realized he was getting ready to kick her; unconsciously reacting she pulled hard on the sheet. It was enough for him to lose his balance. Instead of falling off the bed, he fell into the headboard, sideways. Using his arm to straddle with the aid of the headboard he struggled to get up on his knees for leverage. She pulled the sheet again, and this time his foot slipped in her feces. Drew slid from the bed to the floor. "God damn you, you couldn't even go to the bathroom in the portable john?"

Susan smiled slyly and then glared at Drew with complete hatred. *If I'm going to die here and now, I'll let him know why.* Snarling, hurting with every breath of air taken, "You neglected to leave me the portable john or food, you asshole!" His eyes opened wide enough to show the brilliant red of the whites. *He's on drugs, irises and un-whites tell the story. He won't remember this when he comes down, but I won't be here to see it either.* Blood showed through her gown. *I think a rib broke skin. How'd I manage to pull the sheets, or find air to speak?*

He stood up from the floor, rubbing his hands on the sheets that were full of feces. This soiled his hands more, which made him angrier. "How dare you speak to me this way! I'm your husband; you're never to speak this way to me again. Do you understand me? I do everything for you. You complain day and night. You should have died, not Caroline."

"Well now you sound like the old Drew. I was wondering when I would hear the true Drew come to the surface. You are the one who swears with every other word, and always finishing with, 'do you understand.' Only most of the time, it is with a slur and or with some sort of hitting. Guess what, I don't respect you. You were the one who kidnapped me remember? I sure as hell didn't want to come here or be with you. Why would anyone want to live under these conditions?" She hurt badly, breathing was getting more difficult. *Did he damage more than ribs?* "Wake up, get with the real world. You live in a world of make believe. You can't force someone to love you. Complain? How can I complain, when I try to not talk, for fear I'll get hit opening my mouth. This is the first I've said this much in all the months you've chained me. But then you don't chain me do you, or beat me, do you? In your mind I'm in love with you, but believe me, I'M NOT! Whatever I saw in you left years ago! All I want is to be home with my kids, please let me go!" Susan's voice rose higher the more she talked. Now she was crying uncontrollably, while struggling to stay upright, shaking from nerves, pain, exhaustion, and the ankle chain now coated with fresh and dried blood. With blood and feces on her gown, ribs broken, choking and trying not to cough, "Just please, go ahead and kill me, I'm too tired to care what happens."

Five minutes after this speech, Drew remained in the same spot, quiet, unmoving. *Now he's become a statue? Catatonic? Maybe he'll fall over onto the bed, pass out and I can get the key from around his neck. That would be grand. But can I walk? Dear Lord do something, I can't take much more of this.* Still sitting against the wall, *should I move? I need to lie down, not sure I can ... afraid to move for fear he'll jump me. But then, he will either way.* Watching him closely, she slowly tried to lie down on the half torn sheets. Struggling to achieve this, she never realized that Drew had turned and quietly left the room. Susan passed out.

PEST

"Good morning, Pierce."

He did not want to speak with the voice he most loved to hear. He could not begin to explain what his detective had uncovered and what he was about to do, and now he truly feared she would worm it out of him. "Percy? What, two calls in one week? That's surely not you. You're a busy woman." He tried very hard to rustle paperwork to sound as though he were extra busy and did not have time for her, even though he wanted the conversation to keep going deep inside.

"Not busy enough to check and see if your investigator found out anything. It's been preying on my mind ever since we talked."

"You know I can't divulge anything about that. Oh, and he's a detective working for my department, not privately."

"Well then, I guess I won't keep you. That's telling me you didn't find out a damn thing." Percy too was rustling papers in front of her. "Oh, ah this may sound weird, but ah, my niece Missy, woke up yesterday morning telling Benita she dreamed her Mother was in a very dark and dingy, damp cold place. You know it could be a cellar or maybe a cell. Around here we don't have many of those. It could lead you to something."

Chief Pierce stilled the papers. "You say Missy dreamed this?"

"I know it sounds strange, but she's somewhat like her mother when it comes to being very sensitive. You see, sometimes Susan sends brainwaves to her kids and they ah, well ah, hear her without knowing and they'll call from wherever they are." Percy closed her eyes knowing how idiotic she sounded. She waited for some kind of response to come from her longtime friend; she counted on his trust in her. She did not want to go heavily into the details of other things Susan was able to do without sounding whacked out.

"Then why the heck wasn't she able to foresee this character who was kidnapping her and also the first time charming her into marriage?" he smartly retorted. Pierce could not believe what Percy was telling him. He moved some papers, and re-read what the report had said from the investigation with the neighbors. This was downright spooky. "Do you expect me to…"

I knew he would think me whacko. "No, no, I was just thinking about what she said and I don't know, I … well I just thought it might be of help. From what I understand, very few sensitives can see their own destinies, only see that of others. Sorry to have bothered you." The call abruptly ended.

The Chief held the phone, while re-reading the report again. Then laying it down, he pushed the intercom. "Jill, locate Harrison for me."

"Yes, sir."

Harrison entered while knocking on the door. "Hey, you wanted me? I was in the midst of making the call to the Judge for the court order, to get into the house."

"We'll let Jill do that, there's something else we should talk about." He pressed his intercom and relayed to Jill what he needed. As he did he motioned for Harrison to sit. "Ah, what we are going to speak of will not leave this office. It will remain between us. Percy helped me more than she knew. This may sound crazy, but I just had a very weird call and … His intercom beeped. "Yes, Jill?"

"I think one of you better pick up line one. I've already made contact to have a tracer put on the call."

Immediately he pressed a button to put it on the speaker. "This is Chief Pierce Daniels, to whom am I speaking?"

"It doesn't matter who I am. About an hour ago driving, I think I saw the man you've had a hunt on for a kidnapping. I don't remember the name, but he was in a neighborhood I got lost in. He came out of a house. Anyway I already gave the address to your secretary."

"Can we have you stop by the station to fill out a report?"

"Afraid not, I'm already on the highway leaving this state for another. Have important business and don't have time to get involved. Hope it helps." The line went dead.

"They didn't have enough time for a trace, I bet." Harrison commented.

"You're probably right." the Chief pressed the intercom, "Jill, what was the address?"

"2695 E. Spring Street. They didn't get a trace, but the Judge says come on by for your warrant."

"Same address, let's go."

* * *

Why am I still alive? I should be dead. I no longer feel hungry. He really wants me to suffer... smiling ... but I'm no longer suffering. I no longer feel pain. I'm numb; joke's on you Drew. Now it's agony for you to live. I want my brain to shut off. You took advantage of my naiveté. At that time in my life I was so vulnerable. I'm sure you've hurt many more than me. I forgive you for what you did to me, but not what you've done to my family. Now you've accidentally taken a life and you can't live with the thought. You're probably placing the blame elsewhere. It will come back to get you in a huge way. I should have never married Frank, either. I truly didn't love him. We just both wanted the same thing in life: power. Once Frank achieved his power he used it in the wrong way. Lying here week after week I've re-lived every part of my life over from beginning to end. Made some horrible judgments in my life; hope I'm forgiven. Dear Lord, please take good care of my kids and family. When I get there I'll help oversee them too. That is if you'll have me in heaven. Benita, Howard, Percy, James, Staci, and Irma, all will help raise you kids right. I'll sure send messages to help them raise you the very best way. Also Val and Matt will pitch in whenever needed. I do hope they have some young'uns; it'll complete them. They just don't realize it yet. Tracy, why did you fall off the face of the earth? You need to be here with my kids. They counted on you always when I wasn't there. You just don't walk out on people you love. I know its Nick keeping you from us. Just surprised you'd put up with it. But then we all have our breaking point.

Susan tried to move but she could not. There was no strength left in her. Her mind did feel like it was slowing; it was. Suddenly her body began to shake. She did not know from what or why. Instinct told her it would not be long now. There was so much blood, vomit and excrement; she knew she had to have contracted infection through her skin. *I won't see my children graduate, marry, or become professional assets to this world. No ... not true, I'll watch from above. I plan on it. I won't let them out of my sight, but looking down on them, not able to give council; physical love ...* Susan closed her eyes. *I'm ready ...*

Susan slept. The setting of this dark and dreary room seemed perfect for her to die. The added feature was this hideous and dreary antique furniture she so hated. *I'll see the glow better to take my soul...*

* * *

Late afternoon

An undercover car sat down the street from 2695. There was one person in the car reading a newspaper and drinking a cup of java. He was watching a particular house, but made it appear as though he was waiting for someone in the house where he was parked.

"Chief, there is no car in the garage and no one in the back yard. All are in place back here. All's quiet." The voice spoke into his ear piece.

"Bring in the landscapers." Soon a small pick-up truck with trailer and gardening tools turned onto Spring Street. There were four gardeners crammed into the vehicle. They stopped in front of 2695. Getting out of the truck, they slowly took their time peripherally surveying the yard within the surrounding area, as they grabbed tools. Slowly they moved one by one, going into the Haskell yard next door as pre-arranged. Other police were scattered throughout, but unseen. "Give it about eight minutes and then bring in the four cars. Everyone, check your ear pieces," The Chief stated. Those eight minutes seemed to drag on forever. Pierce couldn't help think how the waiting was always the hardest part to endure.

Four police cars entered the street, each from opposite ends, pulling their cars in at an angle just before 2695. One officer each popped from the cars, leaving the doors open and standing behind the cover of the doors.

Four other officers removed themselves from the cars, doing the same. Four more stepped out while unclipping their holsters. Two walked on the sidewalk toward the front door while the other two moved into position on the gravel walks along each side of the house. The drivers remained in their cars. The landscapers stopped to watch, talking amongst themselves.

One officer stepped to the porch with paper in hand, knocking on the door, while the other turned trying to see in the window, keeping his back to the house wall; it was too dark. He shook his head in communication. Now he removed his weapon holding it up and to the right of him. In the meantime the officer holding the paper rang the bell and knocked loudly on the door, "Miss Caroline Cinch, we have a warrant to inspect this home, please open up." Everything remained quiet. Again the Officer repeated his sentence; still nothing.

"No sign of anyone trying to come out the back?" Pierce asked.

"No Chief."

"Ok, Princeton, you guys try knocking on the back door to see if anyone comes." The Chief said. "Oh, Princeton, can you see the door to the fruit cellar?"

"Sir, yeah, there are four steps down to the door. It's right next to the kitchen window. No one is in this area of the kitchen."

"Miss Caroline Cinch, we have a warrant to inspect this home, please open up," the Officer banged louder on the door; again nothing, "Seems to be no one's home. How do you want to do this, sir?"

"Well, since all the windows were pre-checked, guess we're going to try the key the Haskell's gave us. Best try the front door first.

After a few seconds, "Sir, the lock's been changed," the officer announced.

"Princeton, try your key." Pierce Daniels said.

"Same here Sir." Princeton said.

"They never want to make it easy for us do they? Well Princeton, we best not let the neighbors know what we do to their homes. So we'll do the busting of the door from the back of the house. Are they the usual prefab wood doors or heavier?"

"Pre-fab," was the unison from the officers at the doors.

"This front door has five dead locks, sir."

"Mine also, Sir. The fruit cellar door is metal."

"Well, guess these folks just don't want company; too bad. Bring the ax out."

One of the gardeners went to the trailer, got an ax and carried it in a manner to conceal it as he went toward the back of the house. Hitting the door with the ax, he soon realized there were also three chain bolts at the top of the door. It made him think they should have broken down the front door instead of the back. But they could have also been on the front too. He knew whoever was inside did not want company. It also made him wonder if the garage was concealing something other than a car.

The Chief listened to what was going on, with thoughts of Susan in there and what they could find. Possibly they could find her dead. How would she be psychologically, if alive? He would have to explain all this to Percy and her loved ones. Percy! He still loved her more than life. He'd been married to Jan forever, but still his love was for Percy. All through school, until she met James in college and he lost her to him. Life sure had weird outcomes. He should have moved away, it would have been easier. His sitting here in the realm of things to get her kidnapper was all for Percy and Susan. Susan was like a daughter to Percy. This he knew full well. He felt mundane about being here. No longer did he get a high from going in on an assault to grab a kidnapper, if he was one. His men knew the job now better than he. But it was protocol, so here he was. He wondered if it was time to let go and retire.

"Another whack and we're in. Get ready Ozark."

"Roger that." A sign from Ozark, four of his team followed, in single file, guns drawn, checking the scene and each other's backs as they entered the kitchen. "Kitchen clear," Ozark announced.

The officer behind Ozark entered the dining room, while one officer headed for the hallway, where he immediately saw a doorway to the living room on his left, and across the way the bathroom, down the hall the bedrooms. He motioned for the back-ups to follow, and then they all proceeded single file to enter the hall moving toward the bedrooms.

One man moved to the door of the first bedroom, one hand gingerly turning the knob while the other held his gun upright but ready. Another officer was covering from a crouched position, in case of gunfire or another form of attack. As the door opened in, one could see gym equipment filling the room. Sweat poured off every brow now in anticipation. There was no one behind the door. The closet was wide open and clear. This gave them a few minutes before moving on to calm their nerves and breathe more freely.

Proceeding down the hall the stench hit their noses, causing them to gag, the rawest officer feeling bile coming into his throat. Immediately he stepped back out of the way to get himself together. The experienced officers looked on, with smiles remembering their own early trials.

Again with apprehension, the door to the last room was open with only darkness seen. The smell was so foul they all brought out bandanas, wrapping them around their noses and mouths. One officer knelt down on the floor, looking around the door frame to try to see inside. He thought it extremely odd the room would be so dark in the middle of the day, causing him to take immediate precaution. He did not have a light nor did the other three. He motioned that he would run his hand up the wall to the light switch, and also motioned for someone to check behind the door. There was no sound coming from the room. Moving up the wall he found the switch. Turning on the bright ceiling light, he quickly ducked down in case someone fired and or jumped into the doorway while the others took over for this action. It was quiet … no doorway jumper… no gunfire … spying into the space behind the door they knew there was no one hiding. Entering the room they were not quite prepared for the scene before them. They saw a bed with sheets and blankets in chaos, stained with dried blood. At first sight it looked unoccupied.

Cautiously the officer in front leaned forward to look more closely. He raised his arm pointing to the bed. The figure of a woman, in a bed gown covered in fresh and dried blood and smeared with excrement from head to toe. The sheets were covered in the same fecal matter. The walls and headboard were splattered with dried blood and smears.

One man gasped, covering his mouth as he moved out heading for the bathroom. Not making it, he realized he had not done that since he was a rookie.

As the other three entered, one man went straight ahead with his gun pointed to the back of the sunroom making sure it too was clear. He opened all the blinds, letting in the light. One of the men moved to the bed checking to see if the woman was alive. He nodded his head yes, but see-sawed his hand to indicate 'barely', advising the officer in charge.

"Sir, all's clear, bring in the EMT's. They're badly needed." He said this as he headed to unlock the front door. "You may want to have very few come inside."

Pierce notified the paramedics to move in, as he walked up the steps of 2695. He knew it was Susan in there, but unsure of what else he would find. His stomach was cramping as he entered.

THE LONGEST DRIVE

She knew she was blessed, looking over at Jeff handling the wheel. Missy now knew that this was quite a man offering to drive her home. He never winced, he just took over. When they came to get her out of class, she went into a fog, not sure what to do or where to turn. For them to take her out of class she knew it had to be bad; especially when they told her to meet her family at Good Samaritan Hospital. It was her mother and it was bad. Susan was in surgery as they were driving. She looked; he was doing eighty-five in a seventy-five mile zone. They were on I-10 north going toward Phoenix. Right now this seemed to be the slowest speed in the world. Maybe her mother was now out of surgery and in recovery. But she also knew they would call or text her giving a progress update if so. Would she have to quit college to care for her mother and siblings? She didn't care; she knew she would if necessary. This was not a question, just speculation. Without realizing she spoke aloud, "Don't die on us Mom, I promised FJ you were coming home to us."

Jeff looked peripherally at Missy. He would not interrupt her thoughts. He loved her too much for that. But he could not help but wonder if he could compete with this mother who seemed to have such a heavy impact on her children. He had never realized how much hold a mother could have on her children until he became involved with Missy. But then, his parents never divorced. This probably explained the strong hold. She was both mother and father, even though their father was still in the picture; seemingly somewhat uncaring for them. His frats had warned him about Missy. Smiling wryly, remembering, they had said she was weird. They advised him not to get entangled with her. But he and Missy always seemed to connect in so many ways. He had never had a relationship quite like this before and he really wanted to keep it. Was he strong enough? Time would tell. Reaching across to her, he grabbed her hand. "We're almost there honey, just try and hang in there."

Looking over to him, "I know ... thank you for driving me. I don't

144

think I could have made it without you." Missy said, and meant it.

Squeezing her hand, "Missy, I want you to know I'm there for you no matter what." He wondered if he should say more. He really wanted to tell her he'd be there forever if she would have him. However they had not been dating long enough. He felt it best to wait.

Is he trying to say forever? I'm so not ready for this. Will I ever be?

* * *

The scene

"So what do we have?" Pierce Daniels asked.

"Chief, it's Ms. Susan, Sir. She's in a bad way. Figured you'd want to keep most of the guys out since most of us go to the schools for our haircuts. You know, like things would get into vendetta mode." Ozark reported.

"Good thinking." Pierce meant it. Reaching out, he moved himself and Ozark out of the way of the EMT's.

"I best get in there Sir. Oh, and there's so much for our lab folks, they'll be here a good week or more. You won't believe the mess." With that they followed behind the EMT'S into the room of tragedy.

Immediately the first EMT took Susan's vitals, and then lifted his pack phone calling into the nearest hospital for an available air-evac. As they were making ready to move Susan from the room, the Chief looked around. He did not want to fully look at Susan. All he could think of was what he had to tell Percy and her family. Slightly removing his handkerchief to speak, "God, it's a wonder she's still alive." The room was silent except for the sounds of the EMT hooking up more tubes and equipment to Susan. "Did I just hear her moan?"

No one answered; they all just wanted to hear her moan or something to that effect.

HOSPITAL

Two months now. I didn't come out too badly so they say. Drew did want me dead, that last day we had it out. He blamed me for Caroline's death. In his own way he did love her. And I believe she loved him. I truly believe she enjoyed the life they had with the arguing and physical fighting. Looking in the mirror; *Drew, you did pulverize my face. They say after facial surgery no one will ever know how horrible you made me look. I forget how many concussions they think you gave me.*

It seems I'm not needed by my kids anymore. They grew up while I was gone. They've gotten so used to the others caring for them now. Not one of them has asked for advice from me. I think this has been the hardest thing to take. You expect things to remain the same, but it never is.

Therapy every day, the boredom here is beyond normal scope. But then I seem to not care about doing much of anything anyway. God, the bills I'm racking up. Doubt if I'll ever repay all this before I die. I will walk with a limp the rest of my life, but only two more surgeries to go; two under my belt now. My internal organs are for shit now. I'll probably have plenty of problems, like I have now with going to the bathroom. Wonder if I'll be able to work again? No one wants to speak of it. They talk around me, but not to me. Act like I can't hear a damn thing, so I just go along with the program. Maybe they think I'm catatonic, because I just stare out into space. They don't know how damn scared I am. He could walk in the door any minute and whisk me away again, only to kill me for sure this time; especially after I faced him with the true facts. But I do know I must get myself together. I must work. There's no one else to care for our needs.

Drew you've screwed me and my entire family up. How many other lives are you screwing up out there? Well I no longer have to put up with Cohen. He's long gone, buried and practicing somewhere in California. Frankly I don't give a damn as long as he's out of my life. Sure hope he doesn't go for another woman in his lifetime.

My girls were smart to think of the jewelry. They're pretty good. I know they'll be fine. This guy after Missy seems very nice. He does love

146

her, it shows. She's very afraid of that, but she must try. No, he won't go away easily if she tries to push that button; must talk with her about this.

The pictures of the renovation are fantastic. Harold made a great deal of money on the sale of his old home. He and Benita are so happy together. I doubt I'll find a man that is wonderful like that. Besides men are the farthest thing from my wants and needs. Plus I'm a complete wreck, and no more children can be had. You made sure of that Drew.

I want to go home so badly. Recovery time is going to be long. It'll be awhile before they will do surgery again, so they should let me go home.

Three days later Susan did go home to recover before her next surgeries. Her therapist felt it would be better for her. But was it really?

* * *

Six months later

The door opened abruptly after the bell chimes went off for the third time. "What?" Tracy spouted venomously, shock on her face, "Oh ... ah ... Percy, what are you doing here? Oh my God, what's happened to Susan and the kids? I know that's the only reason you'd be here."

Percy could not believe this was the same up-to-date fashion statement that had helped keep her schools prosperous. "Well honey, if you let me in, we can talk and not let all the neighbors know. Yes I have a lot to say to you. First off you look like shit! Now let me in."

Tracy obediently stepped aside. "Where's the man of your dreams?" Percy looked around.

"He's out. I thought maybe that you were Nick. We don't get many visitors. I, ah, I was in the bathroom when you came to the door."

Percy knew Tracy wasn't telling the truth, but left it alone and followed her into the living room. She noticed Tracy was walking slowly and holding the wall. "Have a seat wherever you like."

The atmosphere was very uncomfortable, so Percy decided to get things out right off, "Tracy, why haven't any of us heard from you?"

The inner garage door opened. "Tracy," Nick said, "There's a car parked in front of our house. Call them damn neighbors next door and tell them to remove it immediately."

The person Percy saw was Nick, using a white-tipped cane, moving into the hallway. She was unable to hide her surprise. Bouncing back more rapidly than most would, she said "Nick, it's my rental, I came to visit, but I guess you don't like visitors anymore."

"Who's that?" Nick asked. He did not seem to mind someone being crass. "Ah, excuse me, but who are you?"

"You forgot my voice that quickly, Nick? It's me, Percy." She moved ever so slightly toward him.

"Well, what brings you to Florida? We don't get many visitors around here. Did Tracy call you and ask you to come? Maybe help out?"

Tracy was about to answer, but Percy motioned her not to speak. She moved alongside Nick, and spoke into his ear. "Now I know why Tracy hasn't been in touch with anyone. You are taking your problems out on her and everyone around you. Why would she want to have anyone come here to visit? I'll remove myself and the rental from your premises right now." Percy moved to the front door, opened it, and turned, "Tracy, I'm sorry I was going to bother you. Obviously things are very different in your life now."

A SURPRISE

"I still can't believe you're sitting here." Percy said, taking in this shocking change. "What happened? I'm sorry I ever came to see you like that. But we never knew and I was desperate to get help for Susan, and you were my last resort."

"I can't believe I'm here either. So many times I wanted..." Tracy stared off into space as if Percy and the others weren't there, and then shook her head. "Things were wonderful in the beginning, but slowly went downhill with his blindness and his jealousies, and then..." again she stared off into space. "But that's not why I'm here. How long has Susan been this way?"

"Since the day they brought her out of that house. At first, everyone assumed she was in shock when she was in the hospital. With surgery again and again and the long months of recovery in between each one, Susan gave up speaking other than when spoken to. She's here but not here. After the first kidnapping, she bounced right back, but this time is different. She stays in her bed clothes, sits outside most of the day staring off into space, then comes in for a meal and goes to bed.

"Yes, Percy's right, she does talk with us, but it's only when needed. We all know it's not my sister." This time no one laughed at Staci's words. "We've had her to another shrink, but she wastes money by sitting there. I think after the first shrink encounter she's scared to speak out.

"The kids can't even get her to come out of it." Val said.

"I tried bringing paperwork over for her, it just lies around," Percy said. Everyone sat quietly for a while, contemplating what else to say. "Tracy you're so pale and thin. Are you ill?"

Tracy ignored Percy's question. Looking out toward the patio, "I guess I'll go out and see how she responds."

After hearing so many good things about this Tracy woman now in her presence, Benita could not believe this was the right person to help bring Susan back to her senses. Immediately she responded protectively, "Must prepare for her to see you."

"No, it's the worst thing you could do. She may clam up more than she already has. She's one stubborn cuss, you know. I think a surprise attack is best." Tracy answered a bit too aggressively for Benita's liking, plus she did not look at Benita when responding.

"She not strong now, fragile, been muy hard for her…"

Tracy lifted her head, looking fully into Benita's eyes. "Benita, I do realize how fragile she is, believe me. I would never intentionally hurt this woman. She's my best friend, and I know you feel the same way. Believe me I do love her as you do. I may not have been here all these months, but I am now. We can get to know each other better after we check this out. Maybe with all of us together, we can get somewhere with her. Before you and Susan lived together, we all as a group did just this type of communicating years ago. So no matter how long I've been gone, it doesn't mean I haven't been here. It's hard to explain, ya know?" With that Tracy rose, turned and walked out through the patio door.

My word, Tracy has no life in her. Can't see how she's going to be any help. I guess I made a mistake going down to get her to come for Susan, Percy mused.

* * *

Tracy pulled a lawn chair alongside Susan. Sitting, she too stared out at the pool of water before her. Peripherally she took in Susan. *She looks like hell, but so do I.* Five minutes passed; "You look like hell."

Susan sat like a statue; acting as if she was unaware Tracy was beside her. *I can't believe she's sitting here next to me. How or why is she here? Who called her? We all called and she wouldn't answer her phone, now why? We also wrote, but no reply via email, or snail mail, or texting.* "Speak for yourself. Did your phone bill not get paid, or no internet?"

Tracy got a huge smile on her face. Turning, she looked at Susan. "Why you little shit of a devil. No, I just couldn't see talking small talk without much to say. You know Florida sucks. It's hot, humid, too many white hairs running around and they f'n roll up the sidewalks at seven o'clock in the evenings weekdays and nine on weekends. And finally it's wall to wall people, allowing no space to breathe. If you have your window open, you can hear the damn neighbors talking in their living rooms, the houses are so damn close. And get this, if say there's a fight between you, one can hear with the damn windows shut. And I'm not exaggerating. So … do I like it there? Hell no. What's even worse in our profession, they really don't teach but one hair shaping in the schools, so everyone has the same haircut, which is usually a chopped up mess. It makes a person want to set up a chair in the grocery store, just to help these people out." Tracy smiled again; she noticed Susan smiling also. "Man I feel so much better getting that all out. I hate not having anyone to talk with."

"You sure haven't given up swearing. I presume I'm right about Nick wanting you to break all ties here? Is he that jealous?"

"Yep, he just wants me solely to himself. It didn't work, so, here I am!" Silence fell between them; Tracy re-adjusted herself in her chair. "From just these few words we've exchanged, this group has been way too easy on you. They think you're too fragile to accept your own responsibilities. So, what do you say, isn't it time you get over your pity party and get back to your senses? You sure don't sound f'd up to me. Your kids and family need you, ya know?"

"From where I sit they get along fine without me, so I'm not needed. So I just keep my mouth shut."

Tracy turned her chair more towards Susan, as she snickered at the comment. "Evidently you've not looked beyond your f'n nose," talking in her usual dramatic way as her arms began to rise up and down. "Right this minute our girl crew is inside, awaiting Dr. Tracy's assessment on how we're going to get you back to the real Susan. And don't try to look so surprised. You can't tell me you didn't hear the alarm buzzing people in this morning. I sat and watched. Oh, and I spoke with your kids last night; they're all struggling with school, friends, and the pain of their mother not being there for them. Another thing; all the paperwork Percy's been bringing by for you to look at is still waiting for you. She asked me to look things over. I did. Guess what, the schools are going under! The new director just doesn't have what it takes to run our schools and Percy is too old and wants to enjoy retirement with her man. Also there are now a couple of law suits up on the schools. I don't know much about them yet, but it seems to me it's time for your damn pity party to be over with! I could go on, but from your look of surprise, you assumed all was going along just fine. Wrong, eh? For the life of me I can't see how you've assumed no one needs to have you around. You're letting everything fall apart around you, even worse than before you got back here. How about your house? It may soon not be yours! It can be taken away from you, you know if you keep up this act! You know all this shit, and you've just sat and ignored it, but I guess you needed someone to explain it to you out loud!"

My God, have I really been that far away from it all? Evidently or she wouldn't be putting it out there. She knows I like everything straight and frank. Susan and Tracy sat quietly a good five minutes. Tracy noticed Susan begin to shake, "I-I doubt the same Susan came back. I'm ... I'm afraid to move for fear he will come here again, taking me away forever. I fear for my kids and family. It seems easy for him to get away from the police; like he ... maybe he is taking on new identities. They think he went over the border into Mexico. But I don't for one minute believe that. Yuri will protect him because he does such a wonderful job getting drugs for his market; like they're both protected from being arrested." Again the silence between them hung in the air. "I was so sure he would not come for me again, after the first time. That was such a mistake. They've offered us protective services, you know with new identities, but that's never a sure thing either. Also I have to make that decision soon, but they don't know I know all this. I do listen. I just don't really know where or how to begin. Do you?"

"Well, when Percy showed up at my door a few months ago, no I didn't."

So that's how and why you came.

"But I do now. I guess I have to give you a road map. Or you're just enjoying the play. I do think it's the latter. You haven't had anyone challenge your brain for a long while. First get out of that damn bed wear, maybe enjoy a good swim in your new pool, which I bet you haven't even tried and let me give you a sparkling new hair shaping. My fingers are dying to get at that red mess." Susan smiled and shook her head indicating she hadn't. "That would be a good start. Next see and talk with your kids. Give them time. Then the rest will come. You'll know where to go from there."

Sitting and looking at each other for a good time, Susan finally broke the silence. "Ok, now will you tell me why you look like shit? I guess I'll get my shears into your hair too. Why, aren't you wearing cosmetics? Not the usual outfits I'm used to seeing on you, Ms. Fashion plate." *Something is very wrong with her.*

Tracy quickly lost her smile, almost to the point of tears, but instead turned to stare off into space; the need to avoid looking at Susan. Staring at the clouds helped keep her from collapsing inside; they looked so gorgeous and fluffy. Pulling herself together, "Well, the 'big C' returned."

Dear God, me and my big mouth. *I should have known.* Choking, Susan almost let the bile rise high enough to spew out, but she gulped it back down.

"When Percy stood at my front door, I knew I had to come home. Like you, all I was doing is sitting there day after day feeling self-pity. You know, like why me? She wouldn't have come unless something was seriously going wrong. It made me get enough nerve to let Nick know how I felt, about Florida, him and what all was going on. So I advised him I was coming home to be with my family for the little time left."

Little time? Susan's hand reflexively reached out for Tracy's, but she thought better of it.

"If he wants me he can come here and be with me. It's been two weeks and he hasn't called or come. It's not that he doesn't want to, but he's afraid to come by himself with the blindness. He wouldn't go to therapy they offered him. He too is wallowing in self-pity. And the treatments don't seem to be helping. I … I believe I have about six months."

Susan reached out her hand, this time grabbing Tracy's tightly and holding it to her chest. "Guess we both have heavy issues to deal with." *Six months? No, I won't accept that. I've nothing to pity myself over. My problems aren't anything compared to hers. I've now got to be there for her. Still holding Tracy's hand,* "I'm so sorry, Tracy. I am here for you; we're here for you. Now we have to get you with a good doctor, and get the best treatment possible." Tears welled in both women's eyes, but they still did not look at each other.

"Now you sound like someone I know. Guess maybe the pity party's over for both of us?" Tears streamed down Tracy's face. "Please help me get through this Susan, I really need you."

Susan laughed through her tears. Reaching over she pulled Tracy into her and hugged her, both laughing and crying. "Oh Tracy, I thank you. I really thought you were out of my life for good. I've been so worried about you. Now I understand, but I really never left mentally, just some asshole took me away making things impossible for me to come to your aid. Seems we both have a lot of work ahead of us. Give us time, we'll make it together."

"Percy, Tracy looks really bad. Did you ask her about herself?" Staci said.

"I didn't feel it was my place. My intentions were only to get her help with Susan. But I agree with you, I think Tracy is ill again, like you know possibly the return of the 'big C'?"

"She muy ill." Benita stated.

"Did she tell you what's wrong?" Val asked.

"No need, it show." Benita commented. "But she should tell." Everyone in the room knew Benita would not say any more.

"This sitting here waiting for something to happen isn't my idea of projecting. Val turned to look out to the patio. "They're conversing, and hugging, right now, so I think she's getting through to her."

"I pray so. Don't like this stand-still life." Benita slid out of her chair and stood. "Think I start food, kids' home soon and all need fed."

"I'll help, Benita." It was not an offer but a statement as Percy rose. "Where's Harold?"

"Our house; wanted to give us time. Oh, you phone James, he come eat too."

"OK, that sounds good." Percy took out her cell and texted Jim. "Harold is quite the guy! But don't tell my BF I said that." Percy said with a huge smile.

"Oh look, they're hugging and crying." Staci called out, as she jumped up and opened the door to the patio. "What a great sight to see! Move over you two, we're coming in for a group hug," as the others moved to the patio.

The hugging and kissing went on for a good spell. Benita and Percy chose to stay in the kitchen. Both women quietly enjoyed watching from a distance.

"Well, it's about time I saw all you women together again," Harold said, coming from his new home. "Are Matt and FJ, back from the store?"

"Not yet," Val said, giggling. "They sure wouldn't be quiet if they were."

"Well I'm really hungry, sure wish they would hurry." Harold stated as he entered the house. "Hey there's two gorgeous Señoras in the kitchen preparing food, and a slow moving Aussie trying to get food droppings or handouts from the floor."

Hearing the alarm chime, "Hey, Aunt Tracy's here too. Wow, all our aunts are here," FJ commented, starting to make his way around to pass out hugs.

Tracy noticed how quiet Tara was upon entering; totally out of the norm for Tara. She looked to Susan to see if she was also aware. She was happy to see Susan sizing up things since they spoke. This brought a smile to her face as she went to hug her niece Tara.

* * *

A few hours later still at the table enjoying their time together, Staci went back to prying into Tracy's un-well look. "Ok, Tracy, it's time for you to give." Standing back, looking to Tracy, Staci asked, "So Tracy, you have a lot of explaining to do. From the looks of you, you need us around. So what gives?"

"Staci, can't you wait for Tracy to tell things in her own time? You always go for the meat of things." Irma commented, with more irritation than usual. "Besides, your sister is in need also and we need to investigate that too."

"That's one of the reasons you fell in love with me, dear." Staci reached over and kissed her cheek. Irma blushed, smiling, but also showed an edge underneath.

Fidgeting in her chair and looking to FJ and Tara, "I don't think this is the right time. We'll discuss it later," Tracy warned.

"But…"

Irma put her hand over Staci's mouth, "Not now, Staci."

"Yeah, Aunt Staci, we aren't supposed to hear." FJ blurted. Everyone broke out laughing.

"I've got a better discussion to put before us. Do you think we can get this wedding over with? I can't wait forever for you all to get things ready and happening." Harold blurted.

"You waited?" Susan asked, completely surprised, looking around the table and then back to Harold and Benita. *Oh dear, this is my fault too, it's written on all their faces. What else have I caused?*

"Well where have you been? Harold is sleeping in the new house and Benita's still is in this house. Like that wouldn't be happening if they were married now would it? And do you see any rings on their fingers we helped pick out? Wow, you have really been out of it." Staci said.

Embarrassment showed on Susan's face. "I was away for such a long time, I … I just assumed it was because you all felt I needed the care, right now." *I've been really ignoring everything around me. Tracy is right; I've been really playing the pity person. I've got to change this, and immediately.*

Harold laughed, "No way, Benita won't marry me until you're well and can stand for her. So you best hurry, I'm getting impatient." Gently he pulled Benita into him to kiss her blazing cheek.

"I'm truly sorry, I … I've been in a fog for a good long while. Yes, dear Harold, I'm very sorry about all this and the burdens you've all been carrying. This will start changing as of now. Tracy also says, you've been treating me with kid gloves and I've just been sitting like a sap not doing a thing about it." *Not so sure I'm ready, but I must do this. Not one of you knows the daily fear I'm living with. I've been too long letting others do for me and my children. Why have I let this happen? Do I distrust myself? Am I capable of it? Well here goes...* "So do you guys want to get married next week?"

"So fast?" Percy asked. "Jim dear, do you think we can have the back yard ready by then?"

"We can have the wedding right here, our landscaping is done. What do you think, Benita?" Harold asked, with begging eyes.

"Dress ready, been ready. Foods in freezer, only dress need work is Susan's. Jes we can do next week; must bring Missy home."

"Ah that's not quite right Benita," Val stated smiling, "I've kinda gained some weight and I think we will have to alter mine too." Val looked at Matt; he pulled her in and kissed her forehead.

"Jes thought you pregnant."

"What?" "No?" "Really?" "Fantastic!" happy excitable words came from all areas of the table.

"Is this the woman who was never going to have kids?" Staci couldn't help herself, jumping up, to give them both a great hug, smiling, "And I told you you'd change your mind! When are you due?"

"This is going to be a Christmas baby," said Val, smiling. "We don't want to know the sex, but I have my suspicions."

"Wow, we're going to be grandparents again." Harold said.

"We sure have a lot of things happening all at one time." Percy piped in. "Beginning to think this is our normal; never a dull moment around this family."

"So Aunt Val, will I be an uncle and my sisters' aunts?

"Yes, Frank. And we have built in babysitters."

Everyone was so happy and loud, they did not hear the low growl that came from Blazer on the other side of the couch.

Tara spoke for the first time that day, but almost in a whisper, "Oh dear God...."

Slowly all realized Tara had spoken, and the low growls could be heard from Blazer. The talking idled slowly, stopped, and they all followed Tara's eyes to the patio door, where Drew stood, slightly weaving. "Iv'f bout had 'nough of this shit. Y'oure dissgust'ng." Staggering into the room, "Ar' yus alw's this disgust'ngly nice to one 'nother? Val you brr..ng bastard into thisss world? You sh..ldn't enough al...rdy."

Susan automatically was giving Blazer hand signals under the table. *Blazer isn't well enough yet, but that won't stop him from defending us to the very end.*

The shock of Drew standing in their presence was more than anyone could take in, except for Susan. There was no shock there. She knew he was not far, and she had shared this with Tracy. *I guess this is the reason for not sharing in the communal euphoria. But now that I have, he shows up. Dear God, I can't believe it. He's so sure I'll go with him, after all that's occurred.*

Drew hung onto the patio door for support. "Sus'n, les go home."

Not one person moved.

"I don't think you're in a position to drive, Sir, may I ask who you are?" James asked, to everyone's surprise. All were quickly aware that by the way his composure changed to try and buy time for someone to send a message, somehow, to the police. "If you tell us who you are, maybe we can help you in some way."

Percy slowly dipped her hand into her pocket, and hit an auto-dial number, praying no one would hear it dial and or answer. Little did she know FJ would come to the rescue? But of course the child was not aware he was helping at the moment.

"You can't have my Mother! I won't let you take her!" FJ screamed at the top of his lungs, as he pushed his chair back and stood hands fisted by his sides.

Drew's eyebrows raised high in expression of misbelief, as he looked at James, now taking on a new expression of a cat ready to pounce. ... Laughing, with sheer pleasure ... spying FJ standing almost in front of him; just as suddenly he stopped laughing, replacing it with a scowl across his brow, then taking a few staggering steps, he started laughing again, but harder with a slight snarl added. Unable to balance well he grabbed a chair to steady himself while he reached out across to pull on little Frank's shirt.

A hundred-fifty pounds of fur growled only once in mid-air slamming into Drew. Blazer and Drew flew into the patio window, busting it out causing both to hit the cement abruptly. This caused them to fall slightly apart. Drew showed astonishment seeing the dog was still alive. He seemed able to regain himself but Blazer did not. Everyone wondered if Blazer was hurt. At first it was difficult to tell. Slowly the dog moved, in a flat crawl using hind legs, ready to defend and protect his family again.

While all this occurred, Matt had gone straight to his truck, entering again with a shotgun, moving toward where Blazer and Drew lay.

Harold was also moving toward the scene outside on the patio, first quickly checking with an eye exam of FJ, and then sitting him next to Susan.

Matt raised his gun trying to get a sight on Drew, but was having difficulty due to Blazer's resurgence, biting on Drew's wrist, as well as pulling and ripping his clothes. Drew was screaming at the top of his lungs.

"Susan, call off your dog!" Irma cried out. "You don't want him to kill Drew. They'll down him if he does."

It seemed Susan did not hear Irma; she was smiling as she watched the scene. *Drew is finally getting some of the medicine he's always dished out to others.* After a few minutes passed, Benita reached out to Susan, shaking her shoulder. Without looking back Susan limped forward, getting a grip on Blazer's fur signaling him to stand aside, but having him stand masterfully ready in case she needed him again. He stood down next to his mistress, in front of FJ, the fur around his mouth showed blood. He never took his eyes from Drew.

Matt pointed his gun at Drew. "Best not move, man; I'm excellent with a shotgun."

Harold moved in on the other side of Susan and Blazer.

"The police are on their way," James stated as he moved toward the front door to be right there to let them in. Drew kept on screaming as if the dog was still on top of him. Out of the blue Frank Jr. came alongside and kicked him in the ribs. This made Drew abruptly stop screaming, as he reached out clasping FJ's ankle.

Harold and Susan both reached out for FJ ... but Blazer and Matt were faster ... Blazer had him by the throat now and Matt smoothly placed the shotgun to Drew's head. Oddly he did not raise his voice. "I don't think that's a wise move, Drew. Unhand Frank. It won't take much for me to pull this trigger. But first, I'd let the dog have some fun. I sure didn't like the way you came in to mess things up. And you spoke quite vilely to my wife. I've half a notion to mess you up myself. I guess you think you're some kind of God. Funny you don't have that look now."

The tension was thick in the group. Drew found himself looking to every face staring down at him. He was cornered, and knew if he tried anything he would truly die. Especially with that horrible mutt showing his canines ready to jump again; most likely the dog would get him before the dude could get a shot off. And now, he could hear sirens coming up the street. Knowing he was had, he immediately let go of FJ's ankle, raising his hands slightly in the air, "I jus' came to ge' my wif'man. We're in luvf. I must take her home."

"You'll never have my mother, I'll kill you first!" again Frank yelled.

"Not if I kill you first, but then in my mind you're already dead!" Drew screamed, smiling evilly, not slurring one word.

Oh my god, how could he say such a horrible thing. But then did I really hear such a thing come out of Frank? Somehow Susan found herself speaking, "No, Drew your mind is a very sick one. You need severe help. My family is the most important thing to me. I don't expect you to understand. We all love each other so much we would all do something terrible to you if you ever in anyway tried to harm Frank. Frank is just very upset over how you took me away from the family and hurt me. He would otherwise never do something so rash." *Would he?*

Drew looked at her as if at an insane person, and laughed as if she had said a joke, "Of course he'd kill me. We're all capable of it, you know." He looked at her silently, knowing they were both reliving seeing him kill Caroline.

God how I want to say something back, but I know it will make him think he's getting to all of us. It's a waste of time for me to think he'd understand.

Suddenly police swarmed through the front door and around the back of the house to the patio. An officer immediately held all of them at gunpoint to make sure he had everyone's attention, while another said, "Sir, please move your gun away and drop it to the ground over here next to me. Place your hands in the air and drop to your knees. We will take over from here." Matt did as requested. Just as he did, Drew reached out for Susan's ankle, but found teeth clamping down on his wrist. He screamed at the top of his lungs.

Again Susan smiled to herself. "You really did forget about my dog being a guard dog didn't you? Funny he's still very alive isn't it?"

"Ma'am, please call off your dog or I will have to shoot," the officer stated, in a matter-of-fact way. Susan reached into Blazer's fur, giving the sign needed for him to stand down.

"Help me, help me; they're trying to kill me! Look what that vicious dog did to me!" holding out his wrist to show the blood dripping. Drew was playing his role to the hilt for sympathy.

Funny he didn't have a drunken slur when he spoke those words. Seems odd he's turning it off and on so easily. Wonder if he was just playing that he was or is drunk.

"Everyone step back, so we can do our job. No one can leave until we speak to each and every one of you. Those of you without your hands in the air please step into the house and someone will question you. Ma'am, you with the dog had better stay here."

"Susan, you know how much I love you! Tell the'm I'hm here to take you ho'm. We b'long to'gth'r."

"No, Drew, this is my home. You invaded my family and home too many times. I will never forgive you for that. Maybe in time I can forgive what you did to me, but I'm not sure I can. You need help and you must pay for the horrible things you've done to others." Susan took Frank's hand, and then turned to the officer holding the gun, "Sir let me take my son inside and I'll return here to the patio. The dog will come with me."

"Go ahead."

Slowly the others followed.

* * *

Hours later

"Más coffee?" Benita queried.

"Heck no, I need something stronger, I'm still feeling jaggy from that insane person who keeps invading our lives." Percy remarked, moving toward the liquor cabinet. "I still can't believe he had the nerve to come here. And I can't believe you're all so calm after this episode. Maybe you're all just getting used to it, but I'm not! God, Drew is such a stupid determined man."

FJ and Susan were sitting on the couch, while the others were scattered on bar stools, chairs and on the floor, looking much worn, but not speaking.

"Percy, It's a good thing you're friends with the Chief. Otherwise who knows what would have happened." Matt commented.

"Mom, will they put him in jail?" Tara finally spoke, looking to the ceiling as she sprawled herself on the floor with Blazer lying next to her.

"They should, since he did kill Caroline, even if it was an accident. Maybe he can finally get the help he needs." *I wish they would throw the key away when they lock his ass up! He's done more than enough to us; I can hear it in Tara's voice. The fear is there!*

"Yes!" Tara raised her head from the floor, causing Blazer to jump up wagging his tail ready for fun, thinking it was he who was going to get the attention. "You finally sound like my Mother! I've been afraid you wouldn't sound like her ever again." Tears began to flow. Automatically Benita got up to get Kleenex; bringing the box she dropped it down to Tara.

Susan moved to the edge of the couch so she could reach her hand out to touch her daughter. "Tara honey, I ... I don't know why I've been living in this fog for so long, or why with Tracy coming today that I'm able to see things more clearly. Sometimes the Higher Powers make us do quirky things, before we can see straight. I'm so sorry if I've hurt you, my children and all of you," looking at all those present. "I really do plan to make things right again, please forgive me."

"No' ting to forgive. You been through lot. Time to get on with life." Quickly Benita changed the subject, "Tracy, thank you for coming. You stay for wedding?"

"Well, as I was telling Susan, I've come back home to stay. I need to be with my family. I must say you and Harold are a mighty addition to this changeable, weird family," saying this with a cat-like smile, "But I must find a place to live and get back to work. I can't afford to stay off work long; thankfully Percy has asked me to come back into her schools again."

"Where you stay now?"

"Right now I'm at a hotel, not far from here."

Benita and Susan looked at each other. Neither needed any words, it was understood immediately. "Señor Harold, you take Tracy to hotel, get t'ings and bring her back here. We have room for her here until she finds house."

Shocked into surprise Tracy, fumbled for words, "I don't..."

"You bet, Benita darling," Harold jumped up all smiles. "Now, Tracy girl, go get your purse. Soon I can have my woman with me in our house." Harold was at the door before Tracy could respond. Everyone started to laugh, as she was uncrossing her legs to remove herself from the floor. As Tracy walked out the door she was still laughing, but tears filled her eyes too.

FJ leaned into his mother and whispered into her ear.

"Tracy really needs us doesn't she?" Val directed the question to

Susan.

"Ah, yes, things aren't good for her, but we'll get her back with her doctors again. Florida was not a good place for her mentally or physically." This answered the silent questions they all had about her ill appearance. And now they also knew her marriage was on the rocks.

The rest of the evening went well, but soon all made their way to the door. Tara and Benita went into Benita's room.

"Mom? You didn't answer my question." FJ stated.

"Let me discuss it with Benita privately first. OK?" FJ nodded his head in understanding.

Benita stopped at the doorway to her room, looking questioningly at Susan and FJ. Susan moved to where Benita stood. "We've got a small problem. Frank realizes the two of you aren't married, so you aren't supposed to sleep in the same bed yet." This made both women giggle.

"Harold be upset," she whispered. "But we did raise child to be aware, so … Harold can share with FJ in cottage." Benita said to FJ with a smile, "Mija, muy right. You and Harold share cottage this week and give Tracy your bed."

"I can sleep on the couch until then. Then when you marry Harold things will be right."

Just then the door flew open with Val, Matt, Howard and Tracy all coming in at once.

Benita smiled her warm smile moving close quickly to Harold, pulling him off to the side. Harold turned four shades of red as she whispered to him. Then Harold shook his head, knowing the circumstances. "Frank, I want to thank you, for reminding Benita and I about sleeping in the same house before marriage. I guess I am in a hurry to have this wedding done." Disappointment was written in his expression. "Matt and Val, you take the cottage tonight. Frank and I will take the couches and the rest all have beds. Tracy, you can sleep in Frank's room. That is if it's ok with you, partner?"

A huge smile lit up FJ's face. "Yes, we will watch over things; right partner? I'll go get into my pj's, Aunt Tracy."

"What is going on?" Tracy asked when FJ left the room.

"My brother is being my brother. You know, like they can't sleep in the same house because they're not married yet." Tara stated, giggling.

"He really got ya, Harold." Tara walked down the hall as FJ was coming from his room. "Come on FJ; help me change your sheets for Aunt Tracy. Then we can go change the sheets in the cottage for Val and Matt." Tara said as she went to the linen closet.

Everyone was enjoying solving the monumental problem except for Benita and Harold.

WEDDING DAY EVE

"We did the right thing by sending them to the El Conquistador for a week. This will give them time together without any of us interfering; also a good rest for Benita to not cook. Can't keep her out of the kitchen," Percy commented, rubbing her sore feet.

"It was a wonderful wedding. Harold looked so dreamy and Benita looked sooo beautiful. I didn't know she could sew so beautifully. Maybe she'll make my prom dress." Tara mused. "I'm going to have a wedding just like that and Benita can cook all the food, just like she did for her wedding."

"Maybe you should learn to cook, Tara." Missy sassed.

"I will, but I'm just too young yet." Everyone just looked at her, 'like really'?

"Wrong, you used to cook most of the time with your sister. Now all of you take advantage of Benita." Susan made sure to stress 'all'. "Now that they have their own cottage, you will be required to help here; especially when I return to work. Benita and Harold will want to have their meals together. Only, every once in a while we will still share meals together." *At least I think this is the way it will be.*

"Aw, Mom do I have to?" Susan just gave her a look, without a word. Tara turned away to get interested in something else.

"Sounds good to me, you can start tomorrow." Percy put in with a big smile, but knew it wouldn't be that soon.

"I couldn't believe you caught the bouquet, Missy. What's with that?" Tara asked.

"I didn't even try to catch it; it was more like it hit me."

Tara looked at her sister with a smirk. "Yeah right."

Susan did not look at her girls, but listened with a furrow on her brow. She then looked at Missy's man resting on the floor snoring away like he owned the place. *She can't get married, she's got to finish law school, and then she'll probably go to grad school. No, no, she can't get married. I know how he feels about her but I don't think she's ready.*

Tracy watched Susan. Leaning in to her she whispered, "You can't hold on to them forever. Life goes on."

"Do I show it that much?"

"It's only natural to feel protective, but Missy will do what she wants. You've taught her to be very independent. Look, I don't think she'll be getting married for a good long while, but she is not coming home as often. So that means there's more to this relationship, than you considered."

"I admit I just seemed to be in la-la land without thinking about too much of anything. It's taken so much energy for me to come back to the real world. I really can't explain it; except living with all my fears each and every day; I just listened fearing the sound of his voice, or to hear how his feet sounded coming down the hall, wondering if I would be beaten, sexually abused or even fed was my world for so long. At first I felt I'd get away, but as the days dragged on into months ... ah," looking away then back, "I never thought I'd come home. But I never gave up the need to see my family again. I prayed every day, maybe twenty times a day."

"Your mind needed to rest after you came home, and to adjust to the changes that took place while you were away, that didn't help you either. When we are away, it seems hard to remember children grow, people gain or lose weight, look different, take on new values, but you catch my drift. Missy and Tara have done a marvelous job of caring for FJ while you were away. Not many kids would take on such a responsibility so well. And the Higher Power blessed you with Benita and Harold. We were both blessed with Percy and Jim."

A comfort silence lingered between them. "You know, just sitting here watching and listening to the kids brings me back to an evening when we had them doing 'community service' for their friends once a month."

"Yes, that was when I told everyone I was getting engaged to Nick. It seems like a century ago. And now look what's come about. Lives sure don't journey the way we plan them to. I just hope Nick can forgive me. He lies in so much self-pity. His blindness is a hereditary problem. You know, sort of what your father went through, but at least your father hasn't wallowed in self-pity."

She too has so much to get out, so she can deal with everyday living. I wonder if she's seen Tom yet. "Have you made any decisions

166

yet on whether to try and make your marriage work?"

"Yeah, Aunt Tracy, where is Uncle Nick and why didn't he come to the wedding?" Frank asked out of the blue. They both jumped, unaware the kids could overhear them and wondering how much had been heard.

Tracy's face turned crimson right through her tan. Fidgeting in her seat, she was saved by Val, Staci, Irma and Matt all came in from the cottage together, "We sure had good naps; don't know about the rest of you." Staci announced. "Now we're hungry." The intrusion aroused Percy, Jeff, and James.

FJ forgot his question with the two dogs wanting his attention.

"I'm so hungry, we haven't eaten much today and this youngster in his incubator, is letting me know how hungry he is," Val said with a smile.

"You did one great job as ring bearer, FJ. You know, like you've done the job before." Tara teased.

Embarrassed, FJ smiled then snuggled into Blazer's head, trying to deflect the compliment, then pulled hard on the ball to release it from Blazer's mouth. Happily Blazer held fast, enjoying the tug of war.

"There's plenty of food left, just re-heat what you want in the micro." Susan stated. *I sure didn't want to interrupt Tracy, she too needs to vent.* "True enough, my father has been a real trooper, but Mother seems to use it as a way to distance herself from the family. She uses him as an excuse. Mother doesn't mingle, but really she's just not social."

"No kidding, they sure weren't here for the wedding." Staci piped in.

"That's just the way it is. Always has been." Susan added.

"I really don't understand that way of thinking, do you Matt?" Val asked.

"No," finally got out around a bite full of tamale, and beer chasing it.

"Let's change this subject, it's getting dreary here and this is the wedding eve of Benita and Harold. Ok, I'll start; I thought Benita's dress was gorgeous. I agree with you, Tara, she really can sew a great seam and the lilac color looked beautiful with her salt and pepper hair." Percy smiled, remembering.

"You know, wife, we should have Benita do a couple ties for me. His tie matched her dress. Did you notice?" James queried.

"I'm sure Benita would love to make ties for you, dear."

"Oh, Staci, where did you find those lilies? You sure didn't find them for my wedding." Tracy dramatically complained.

"Now you know I tried to find you lilies, but, they were out of season when you got married. I can never understand why everyone wants lilies. There are so many other beautiful flowers and lilies cost so much more."

My kids sure are quiet. They haven't had the attention they so desperately need. I'll make sure to be with them one on one and one on three tomorrow. Missy and Jeff do look happy together; like comfortable. Think Tracy's right; there is a lot more going on there with the two of them. So much happening right here in front of me and I've been so unaware. Higher Power, why did you let me sit mesmerized all this time? Will I ever get an answer to that query? Time will tell, time will tell.

* * *

Four hours later

"It's been such an enjoyable day and evening, but we all need to go to bed. It's about three in the morning." Percy stated. "I think we ought to go home, my love." This was said as they both were rising from their seats and went to the door. Tara let them out, and reset the alarm.

No one else seemed in a hurry to end the evening. "Are all you kids spending the night here on the floor?" Staci asked.

"Un-huh," came from around the area.

Val and Matt rose, "We're heading for the cottage; night everyone. Missy, will you re-set the alarm please?" Missy rose and did as requested, knowing her sister would be watching. After setting the alarm she turned and stuck her tongue out at Tara.

Staci and Irma were kissing their kids and all the other ones good night. "Night all," Irma added as they headed for Benita's bedroom.

"Night, love ya," came from Tracy going down the hall to FJ's room.

Tara came over to her mother, held out her hand, "Come, Mom," she whispered walking her to their rooms. Stopping at her bedroom, she drew her mother inside and closed the door. "Mom, what's wrong with Missy, she hasn't spoken all day or all night?"

Susan smiled. "I was about to ask you the same question. You haven't been talking much either.

"But I am compared to Missy. Are she and Jeff fighting?" Now Tara started to pace. *Whoa, that's something Missy does, not Tara. Guess it's being handed down.* Pulling Tara into her, she hugged her close. "Oh I've missed you so. I'm glad to be able to hold you and kiss you all and laugh, and…."

"Mom, don't get carried away."

Susan couldn't help but giggle, "Let's just let it ride tonight or should I say what's left of it anyway, and then we can really have a family gab session and get to the bottom of things."

"Ah yeah right, Mom, like that's going to happen with Jeff boy here! And is he staying the entire week? I'd like time alone with her too, you know." Tears welled in Tara's eyes. *She is feeling her sister's change coming, such as moving out and getting her own place. She isn't the only one. This is hard on all of us.*

Again, Susan hugged her daughter, letting the tears come. "It hasn't been easy for you girls, but I am very proud of how the two of you have handled things here while I was gone. Now for the family time, it's worth a try, don't you think?"

"Yeah." Tara did let her mother hug her until she hurt. "I've missed you too, Mom." Straightening herself and wiping her face with her sleeve, "I better get back out there. Can't let anything go wrong out there now, can we."

Susan smiled at her daughter leaving her bedroom to spend the night on the floor with everyone else. "No, no we can't." Susan whispered to Tara on her way to her own room, also spying Missy's heading for her room.

FOUR WEEKS LATER

"Welcome back Ms. Susan," chimed from her staff throughout the main school.

"Thank you, it's good to be back."

Susan switched on the light. Looking around the office she spied to see what changes had been made while she was away. *My goodness everything seems to be the same. I guess the last director liked the way I laid it out, or they really didn't care what it was like. It does feel good to have my mind occupied again with work and family. I feel the best place to start is the files. That is probably in a very different state of affairs.* Susan browsed through the files trying to make sense of what the other director had accomplished; *mostly this is trash. Glad Tracy got in to see her cancer specialist so soon. I'll place her on a light schedule especially for the treatments. She already has her school in order; didn't take her long to do that. Glad I added her as assistant director. If anything should happen to me ever again, she can just step into the position. She knows the layout as well as I.*

"Knock, knock. May we come in?"

Susan turned to see who was at her door. Standing before her were Percy and Chief Pierce Daniels. *This is not a social call, body language tells me, also the scowls on their faces.* "Ah, of course, what dare I ask brings the two of you here so bright and early and on my first day back?" as Susan queried, she gestured for them to take a seat. Percy of course took her old director's chair. This made Susan and Pierce smile, "How about a cup of coffee?" Susan inquired.

"Never turn a cup down." Pierce volunteered to pour for all before he seated himself. "Susan, I'm sorry to inform you, they've let Drew out on bail." He could not look her in the eye.

Susan was quieted by this jarring information. "Who would put up bail for him? He has no true friends and his family couldn't put up the money."

"I truly don't know other than the party is from Tucson. That is his old stomping grounds."

"I still can't believe the judge let him out. Anyway Pierce and I want to post guards with you day and night, also with the kids. Jim and I have already set it up so, there is no worry for you. He's so schizoid; we just can't take the chance."

"Percy, you know he's claiming accidental death with Caroline. It's still under investigation," Pierce added.

"Percy that is a costly undertaking and no one knows how long this will take." Now getting up, Susan paced the floor, "No, I can't let you do this." *We may have to move. This is not going to go over well with any of the family.*

"Really? Think about it; there isn't a way you could not let us do it! The schools are under siege over this, your lives are at stake and we can deduct it at the end of the year. So that's that. Don't make it such a big deal." Percy tried to give a look of triumph.

Percy's trying to make light of this, but she's as scared as I am.

"She's got a very practical point. But the main reason I want to talk with you, is I do want you to seek counsel. They will call you in as a witness. So it is best you protect yourself," The Chief said frankly and with rationality.

Susan again walked the floor, as fast as her limp would let her. "Oh God! They could possibly think I actually had something to do with this murder?" Looking at Pierce, "Remember, I was the one kidnapped, beaten, starved, raped, mentally abused, not by one man, but two all that time." Stopping in front of Pierce, "Seriously, I don't think the jury will be in favor of Drew in anyway."

Pierce looked directly at Susan. "In your statement, you did say, Drew accidentally killed Caroline." Not taking her eyes from his, Susan began to shake uncontrollably. Pierce jumped up and caught her, holding her close. Susan froze. Pierce felt her freeze up, "I'm sorry. I only wanted to keep you from falling. I won't hurt you." Susan then relaxed somewhat. He then gently placed her in a chair. "I believe now you understand my point."

Will I ever be able to have a man near me again without freezing? I know he means well, it's so uncontrollable. It gives me such a sick feeling and I use the good ole safety factor and withdraw. Drew could say I was involved with the accident, even though I wasn't. He'd try and lead the court to believe I was with him by choice all those months.

Surely this can't be, but I can see where Pierce and Percy are only trying to help me see what could happen. Drew would do this especially if he knew he couldn't have me, he would ruin me at the same time for not getting what he desired. He always said 'if he couldn't have me he would make sure no one would.' He continually threatened my children with death. I've felt always he was capable of it. There was never any doubt. That was the only reason I tried making things work. I would go to jail, lose my kids, and I thought all the time he had me chained, dying was bad? That would be the worst kind of death, being in jail and not able to be with my children other than visiting. Would they even come to visit? God, would my children believe I was involved in such a thing? Look at how many innocent people have been convicted. And I thought life was going to be good again... "Yes Pierce, I do understand. Do you know anyone I should contact?"

"Percy, Jim and I already took care of that, too. We have an appointment for you next Monday with Harry Spangler. I can't be present, but Percy and Jim will be." Pierce handed her the card. Her hands were shaking still from the shock, right along with rest of her.

"I don't think you should stay at work today, Susan. Let's just load up anything you may need to look at and you can work from home." Even though Percy said this she didn't believe Susan would get any work done today. "I parked in back and Pierce brought one of his officers, so he can drive your car for you. James and Harold are at the schools getting the kids and bringing them home so we can all talk with them."

Susan was completely numb. She let them handle everything.

LIFE CHANGES

"Does this mean we have to move?" Tara asks.

Pierce didn't answer immediately. "Well I guess that depends on what you as a family decides. Of course the preference of the department would be to place you in protective custody."

Sitting next to his mother on the couch, holding her hand, he looked up to her. "What does that mean?" Frank asked.

Susan could not look at her son, so she looked out to the patio area. "Ah well, this means we would have to sell the house, not let anyone know where we will live and it most likely will be in a different state. Also we would have new names and possibly other changes." *It's not a good time to let them know they would not be able to see any of their family again. This is more than enough, for them to handle right now.* Looking over to Harold and Benita, she could see the horror in their faces, as well as the others in the room.

"But Mom, we made a pact that we would live here forever. I don't want to move."

"Me either," Tara added.

"Nor I," Missy commented via Skype. "We've moved enough! Why should we let that asshole drive us out of our home?"

"I do understand you all not wanting to move. However it's for your safety…"

"Sir, excuse me, for our safety? Can they or you assure us of safety? No they can't!" Missy emphasized to all.

Sitting just behind Missy, Jeff listened. He realized that even though she was staying with him many nights, she's wasn't really there. She planned to move home after graduation. This he did not like. He did not want to lose her. Soon they would get down to discussing this, they would either be together or not. He wondered if he could endure living without her.

"This is something we should take a few days to consider, then have a full discussion. I don't want us to make a rash decision." Susan stated.

Pierce looked around the room to all. "This is not something to take lightly. You can't push this aside. For us to fully protect you, we must know within two days at the most."

"Ok, day after tomorrow we gather here at 6 pm." Staci said firmly with a sigh as she rose. Everyone could see she was shaking and tears streamed her cheeks, "Let's be going, Irma. Night everyone," throwing kisses as they headed for the door. Irma and the kids dutifully followed, knowing they had a long night ahead of them.

Missy went off-line. The rest followed Staci's family, making their way out the door. Tara and Frank retired to their rooms, with Blazer following. He chose to sleep with Frank that night, as if he knew he was needed.

Susan and Tracy remained in the living area, having changed into their nightwear. Susan sprawled on the couch, while Tracy as usual flung one long leg over the chair while the other foot touched the floor. Each sipped a glass of red, quietly enjoying each other's company.

"I can't see changing my identity or moving to another state and starting completely over."

"Damn girl, I knew you were going to say that. Don't you understand what everyone is trying to tell you? This man is out to get you one way or the other and this time I do think it's the other. He's probably already on his way here. He's so good at outsmarting the cops; we best have every one of the guns loaded in this house," Tracy said firmly.

"What do you take me for, a loon? They are, and one's on me right now. I'll make sure you get one to keep with you, and I'll show you where another one is hidden. I don't want the kids to know, of course."

"Well, that's good to hear." Tracy said with a smile. "Also, I think we should take shifts in sleeping. He'll make his move in the wee hours of the morning."

"You do remember some of the things I've told you, eh?" Smiling wanly, showing a gotcha. "I just keep going over how everyone believed him years ago, telling y'all I tried committing suicide and was off my rocker on drugs. Oh and let's see, oh yeah, I was never tied up and raped, or hunted down at Jimbo's. I really do believe he had something to do with my brother's death."

Silence reigned for a while, and then finally Tracy laughed. "And

174

that was an f'n mouthful."

"There is so much in my head, I keep going over it, but I rarely get to talk it out to try to put it all together. Like, where is it getting Drew? He will never truly have me, nor can he have my kids on his side. Sociopath turned schizophrenic is all I can come up with. Both diseases seem to encompass his actions and his way of thinking."

"The man just got himself so caught up in you, he thinks of nothing else, no matter the cost. I really don't think you will have a choice. You will have to move for you and the kids to survive. Obviously they're not going to lock this man up and he will not leave you alone."

They sat in silence for a long time, sipping wine, "Have you heard from Nick?" Susan changed the subject, looking closely at Tracy to gauge the truth of her answer.

"Yeah, he says he wants to come." Tracy let it sit out there.

"Well?"

"I'm not so sure if I want him to come."

"*Does this have to do with Tom?* Have you seen Tom?"

Tracy fidgeted, placed both feet to the floor, leaning forward now with elbows on knees and the wine glass held in both her hands. "Yep and yes we went straight to bed; our usual problem. No he's not going to leave his wife and I don't think it's fair."

"Tracy, he will never leave her. You've always known that."

"You just don't know what it's like to be sexually satisfied. There's nothing like it and it takes one heck of a guy to make that happen. It's all chemistry." Susan sat extremely still and did not look at Tracy. Usually Susan would agree with Tracy, for she had never been truly sexually satisfied. This did make Tracy look at Susan, staring at for a good sixty seconds. "Well I'll be damned! Drew did get you off good, didn't he?"

Susan nodded her head in consent. Taking a large gulp, she finished off her glass; without hesitation Tracy got up and refilled it. "Of all the f'n people he was the one. Now it all makes sense to me. He knows, too."

Taking a sip from her new glass of wine, Susan stumbled, "Um, at first he was the most loving person. He was so kind, considerate, bent over backwards to please me, but little did I know that was his way of breaking me. You were one of them that saw through that, but I was blind to it, because for the first time I felt really loved. I think he thought if he did get that from me, then I would never fight to get away. He started drugging me, I believe, because of his losing jobs, and stealing. He realized I would never put up with a person that could be so evil to another. This also made him realize I would never be his, and I was going to break it off with him. He chose abuse as well as saying I tried to commit suicide and mentally lost it. I did lose it for a while, but keeping quiet then was the best I could do with all of you thinking he was telling it straight. But I know for sure, I would live without ever being sexually satisfied, rather than live with a person who wouldn't let me live with him and love on my own terms and not as his and his alone." This time Tracy didn't bother to pour into her glass, she drank from the bottle. Susan silently waited. *I don't care if she doesn't speak for the rest of the night. Maybe she will come to her senses.*

"Well spoken." Tracy finished the bottle and got up from her chair, going straight to bed.

Susan scooted down to fully lie on the couch. Blazer came from Frank's room, to lie down beside her. Scratching Blazer's head, "I guess we have first watch, but then he won't come tonight."

RETURNS

Coming out of her room, Tracy looked extra special. Susan saw this looking sideways at her.

"Aunt Tracy, you look very pretty this morning. Is that a new dress?" Tara asked. "That color of blue is especially good for you."

"Well thank you, honey. I've been saving this dress for a special occasion." Before anyone could ask, "Susan do you think we could take off a little early to go to the airport? Nick is flying in."

"Gee Mom, can we go?" FJ asked. "I love the airport and the planes."

"I doubt we can do that honey, it would be back tracking, ya' know. Also I'm not sure we won't be running out the door at the last minute from work."

"Awwww Mom," FJ whined.

"I t'ink we meet you at airport. Welcome Nick." Benita offered, looking at Harold for reassurance.

Funny I thought they would be at home together more than they are.

Smiling, he said, "Of course, we'll give Nick a great welcome home. Just give us the flight number and airline and we'll meet you there with the kids."

"Oh boy!" Frank jumped up and down.

"We make special meal, right Tara."

"Ah sure, Benita," Tara did not look pleased.

"I guess that's decided. It's funny you didn't mention it yesterday," Susan stated, while she poured coffee for them both.

"Well Nick and I spoke late last night. After talking, we decided we think we can make things work. So he's jumping a plane early this morning."

"Good, I think we can arrange a ride from the airport for Nick. You guys will stay here until you find a place of your own." Susan smiled turning and handing Tracy coffee. "Glad you came to your senses," she whispered.

Tracy leaned in and gave her a kiss on the cheek and whispered, "Sus, we need to find me a couple wigs, I'm starting to lose my hair from the treatments."

* * *

"What the fuck is she doing letting so many people into our house? She knows I don't like that. Not only the retard is back, but the retard is leading a blind person around. Is she running a fucking hotel? I'm going to have to teach her to mind all over again. She knows I don't like to show her who's boss, but I must, just to get her to listen!" Drew yelled inside the car he had borrowed from his brother, at the same time opening his mug of coffee, some of the coffee spilling out and burning his finger. "God damn it! She's even got that damn Tracy back with her and it looks like she's living there too. God damn it!" swearing as he hit the steering wheel, now spilling coffee onto his Levis. "Owww," he jumped up wiping his hand furiously on his Levis to stop the burning. "It's all those folks in that house that's at fault. They have too much influence on her. They will be out of our lives soon. Susan normally wouldn't let those people be with her and the kids. Probably that Val, Percy and the cops telling her what to do and she's listening to them. I must get in there soon and change all this. We can stay here a couple weeks, but we will have to go to Mexico to live. Can't take the retard though, must take care of him."

Drew still fuming, sipped what was left of his coffee. This seemed to calm him a little. Starting the car he pulled away, driving past the house. "I'll be back later this evening, darling, don't worry, I'm here for you."

* * *

Evening

This waiting around for him to come here is for the birds. Adjusting her pillow, Susan decided to read a little longer. She knew sleep would not come. *I do hope Pierce and his crew are patrolling extra heavy, maybe not patrolling, but having them close enough so they can jump right into the house, should Drew arrive. There's no way of knowing when he will arrive, but I do know he will!* This time she punched the pillow a little harder than normal. Tracy and Nick took first watch this night. She could hear their voices in the living area. *Good, they are talking. This is helping the two of them. Nick is really trying hard to make changes and so is she. They're growing together now instead of being stingy bratty self-indulgent children. Also I think Nick finally realizes how ill she really is. Stage three is very serious. I'm amazed she has the strength to get up and go to work. Tracy has a very strong will.* The doorbell interrupted Susan's thoughts. Automatically she checked the clock on her nightstand, *1 am? What the...* Susan jumped from her bed, opened her door, running down the hall. "What the? Staci, Irma, kids? What are you doing here at this hour?"

"Funny, I just asked the very same question," Nick offered.

"Sorry we woke you. I've been trying to stop Irma from coming over, but the more we talked about the situation here, the more agitated she became. Sid is on his way in also, so wait to set the alarm, Tracy," Staci said.

She noticed Tracy going to reset the alarm. *It makes me wonder if there is something more to this situation. I don't think it's just concern for us. Irma has been agitated for quite some time now. Not sure if Staci noticed, but to bring Sid along, that's something very unusual.*

Just then Sid entered. "Sorry it took so long, there was a lot of stuff to put on the doorstep."

"Hello brother in law," Kissing him on the cheek, "It's been quite a long time since we've seen your face around here." Susan said this as she; Stacy and Irma went to help him bring in their overnight cases.

"I know Susan, sorry, but I've been really busy with trying to find work again." *This seems so foreign coming from Sid's lips, since they used to own restaurants and clubs for years. Now he mainly works car sales.* He pecked Susan on the cheek. "So glad you're on the good side of mend, we really need to talk," he whispered.

Without thinking Susan looked questioningly at Irma and Stacy, but neither would look her way. *Something is very wrong!* Susan's insides began to curl to the point of wanting to vomit, feeling the vomit rise. Instinctively she knew this had something to do with Drew.

A knock came from the back patio door. There through the glass door she saw Benita and Harold in their nightly attire, with wonder on their faces.

FJ came running down the hall. "Mom Chelle and Sid woke me up, what's the matter?" Without thinking Frank went to the patio door and let Benita and Harold in.

"What's going on? Is everything all right? We heard so much commotion, we had to come and check things out." Harold asked.

"Sorry we woke everyone," Staci said. "Well we couldn't sleep, and all of us talked and felt we could help out more here, than over at our place." Staci said this without looking to anyone and fidgeting with her fingernails.

Now that is a definite lie sister dear.

"Hi, Sid, it's been awhile," Harold said, reaching out to shake Sid's hand; it showed he was not enjoying this handshake, especially in the middle of the night. He felt something was seriously amiss.

"Hey, it really has. This must be the wonderful woman who got you settled finally. Hello Benita, I'm Sid. I've heard great things about you, especially what a fantastic cook you are."

Benita blushed, shaking hands with Sid. "Gracias."

Sid made his way around the room talking with the others he had not seen for a very long time.

Susan slowly limped over to Staci, "What gives? I know Sid would not have come willingly. What are you not telling me?"

"Not in front of the kids," Staci murmured softly.

"That terrible hunh? Maybe I better sit down for this." No sooner was this said when Sid made his way back to where Staci and Susan stood.

"Can we talk privately, Susan?" Sid asked.

Without a word Susan in her uneven gait led them out to the patio. Sid followed sheepishly, feeling guilty now seeing the many physical limitations resulting from her kidnapping and abuse. This made him feel more uncomfortable over the matter than he wanted to admit. "Ah. Let's sit down, Susan." Without questioning, Susan sat waiting for what Sid came to say. *He's sweating around the mouth. He is nervous about what he's got to say.*

"I don't know how much you know about our home life now. So I think that is where I'll begin. Well ah, not long after you and Frank divorced, Staci and I stopped sharing our bed. Irma and I just switched rooms."

"Oh? No, Staci never mentioned it and, well, I never asked. It wasn't my business how you chose to live in the same house."

"Things got bad financially for all of us after Frank and I made mistakes in running the clubs and restaurant, and you and Frank getting a divorce. I really don't blame you for making sure everything was sold to keep Carol from getting part of them. You were right, our kids are the most important when it came to looking at that side of things. But I had to think of new avenues to make money since I didn't have you and Frank to help out."

"Thanks for the kudos and admission, but yeah, that's when you went back to selling cars."

"Yes, but that didn't even begin to help financially, so I got into other things. You see I am out of the country most of the time now. I'm rarely at the house and well, Staci and I never talk anymore."

"So you're telling me you've found someone else?"

"No, no, your sister is the only one I'll ever be with. Well, don't get me wrong, there are other women, but it's only your sister I have in my heart. It hurts to think what I've done to her. And I made a promise to you to take care of her. We still have the account overseas, so if anything were to happen, you know what to do." Sid ran his hands through his hair, and fidgeted in his chair. "Ok, ah," again he ran his hands through his hair, taking a deeper breath. "When I got home a few weeks ago, I found out you were kidnapped."

"You just found out? Like, are you talking clear back to the first time?"

"Exactly."

Why is this making him so nervous, unless ... no it couldn't be, could it? Susan began to shake. "Ah Sid, we all know you never read a newspaper let alone watch the news on TV; so yes, I'm used to you getting your information from Staci, the kids and whoever else you're around. I've never been able to figure how you know what's happening in the world. So I guess what I'm saying is it's understandable you didn't know. But what does this have to do with now? *He's not answering me very quickly and he's about to get up and run, I can see it in his eyes. Oh my God* ...Tears came to Sid's eyes, his lips trembled.

This is a different man before me; I've never seen this side of him ever. I feel he's afraid to tell me whatever it is. Ok, it's time for one of us to make a move here. "Sid, what kind of work are you doing? Out of the country? Where? Should I be afraid for Staci and the kids? Right now is not a good time for this to be happening, if it is. I'm really not back to my full capabilities and sometimes..."

"This mainly is about you. I've ... I've not exactly been on the right side of things legally, but now that things are better, I plan to make it right." Susan was getting ready to ask more questions or start nagging about his illegal activities, so he held up his hand to quiet her. He grabbed both her hands from her lap, looking into her eyes. "I will get Drew, I know how to get him and put him away for good."

Susan lost all color, which he could not see in the surrounding darkness, relieved only by the dim lighting from the pool.

* * *

That very same moment

Pulling into the curb Drew's eyes popped. "What the fuck? Why so many cars? They really can't be having a party at this hour?" Looking all the cars over, "Well, the regulars are here, but extras, who? ... Wait a minute, Sid? Something must have happened for him to be here, especially at this hour of the night." Drew slammed his hand into the steering wheel. "Damn, she's making this hard on me. I'll really have to teach her a lesson." Sitting back, he absently rubbed his hand after hitting it on the steering wheel. After ten minutes of great consideration, Drew reached down under his seat, bringing out a knife and gun, and hiding them, he got out of the car, quickly scaling the wall as if it wasn't in his path, moving toward the back of the house. Just as he got to the edge of the house, he heard voices. He couldn't make out who they were or what was being said, but he knew it was both male and female. Slowing, now standing quietly, he did his best to try and eavesdrop. In listening mode, he gazed out and saw the new addition and pool, thinking how gorgeous his new home looked. He and Susan and the girls would be very happy here; at least for a while. Then he would sacrifice it back to the old ones who thought themselves grandparents. Moving slowly he took a look around the corner to the back patio. The surprise jerked him out of his stillness. "Well, well, look at this cozy scenario. I didn't realize you cared so much for my wife, brother-in-law and oh yeah, boss."

Sid and Susan both jumped in their seats, but Sid stood almost immediately. "Drew, what are you doing here? Get out of here now, before anyone sees you."

Drew moved further onto the patio, but not far enough for anyone to see him from inside the house. "Why not, I'm the one who has every right to be here. But I never figured you had something going with my wife. So you best be the one to move on out of here right now."

"Be careful, he has a knife in his hand," Susan whispered to Sid. *Did the guards see him? Now I know why Blazer was at the door pawing, whimpering, growling and now barking.*

"Yes, Susan, I do have a knife. You see, I still have excellent hearing. I guess I will have to give you lessons again about having so many guests, and also exactly who will be able to be here to visit. It's time now for you to tell your guests to leave. We have much to talk over, we've been apart too long." Drew moved in closer, but stayed in the outer part of the patio trying to avoid the lighted areas so that he could not be seen.

Sid wanted to make sure to keep facing Drew, so he continued turning as Drew moved. "Aren't the cops looking for you?"

"Hell, I don't know nor do I care. They can hunt all they want, but they won't catch me. I always get away from those assholes. It's so easy, but then you know that don't you, boss? They never saw me the other morning." Drew said maliciously.

"Why are you here? Shouldn't you be on the run then? Don't you have work to do? Yuri told me you were to go on your usual run, so you best get going, man."

"Haven't spoken with Yuri, I have too many things to take care of since getting out of jail; no thanks to you or Yuri. Why is that, boss?"

"Man, you know me; I didn't have that kind of money to get you out. I didn't know if Yuri did either. All my money goes to making sure Staci and the kids are set. Something very strange about you tonight, I just can't put my finger on it."

"Strange? Like what? You know you should be worrying about

Irma being in your home. She's probably doing things with your wife you don't know about. Now it looks like you're here doing cozy things with my wife."

"Aw no, man, I don't do family. You've been around me enough to know that. I just came here to talk with Susan about some details we still had to settle from our old business relationship, right Susan?"

"That's very true. Even though the monies are gone…"

"No way, I saw the two of you holding hands. I'm not blind."

"Yes, you saw right, Drew. Sid felt sorry for me for what I endured when I was taken by you against my will. He was trying to assure me he wouldn't let that happen again, but here you are in front of us. I suppose you're here to take me away again?" *I must get between Drew and Sid.* Susan started to rise, using the arm of the chair to lever herself up.

"What the hell is wrong with you? Why are you moving like a gimp?"

Susan fell back into the chair again, losing her balance. Whether from surprise at Drew's dramatics, or to help her and Sid's situation by taking up time, *I do hope someone inside is watching and will notify the cops.* Susan couldn't help it; she started to laugh, making sure to laugh loud enough to draw attention from inside the house.

* * *

Irma and Staci were sitting on the couch to make sure they had a good view of the patio; awaiting the outcome of the conversation outside. Staci whispered, "Irma, do you think she'll ever speak to me again?"

"Of course she will. It will be hard at first, but she'll come around. It's not like you knew what was happening. It's just a good thing I found out and confronted that so-called hubby of yours." Irma said.

"Oh look, Sid's holding her hands, isn't that good. It's got to be good." There was a low growl from Irma's side of the couch. "What's wrong with Blazer?"

"What you talk so low about?" Benita asked.

"Ah, we were just wondering what Sid and Sus are talking about." Irma countered. "Do you know, Benita, or does anyone for that

184

matter?" Staci kept her head down, for fear deception would show.

Blazer was now moving toward the patio door, growling deeply.

"No. I'm sleepy, think I go to bed; you coming dear?" Benita proceeded to rise, but stopped after taking two steps, causing Harold to run into her.

In order to keep Benita from falling Harold grabbed her around the waist. Giggling, "Wow, I've always wanted a woman to fall for me, but this is diff..." Benita elbowed Harold in the gut, "Ow, what is wrong with you?"

Benita slowly turned around in his arms. "Look at patio, someti'ng muy wrong. Blazer whimper, growl, paw door, and I think policia; call."

"Something isn't right!" Staci said way too loud. "Look, Susan's laughing, what the heck is going on?" Staci rose from the couch like lightning. "Blazer what is wrong with ... Oh God, no, it's ...," Blazer barked, instead of finishing her sentence she raced to the patio door, and threw it open. "Sid, what's going on?" Blazer took his body and fully pushed past her, throwing her into the door, going straight to his mistress, stooping beside her in action ready to pounce. Susan quickly reached out and fingered his fur with commands. Blazer went to the ground with a growl, now a whine beside himself but at the ready to attack on her command. This drew everyone's attention to the patio.

Harold was making the call. Benita followed to shield him with her body, fearing that Drew would notice.

Those within the house saw Susan laughing, almost convulsively, quickly grabbing into Blazers fur. Sid stood with his back to the house. They now realized someone was there standing on the other side of Sid. No one could make an identity; due to Sid in the way and no light. Staci stepped closer to get a better view, fearing who it might be.

Sid did not turn around, almost screaming, "Staci, get back in the house now!"

This abruptly made Susan stop laughing. She turned in her chair, "Ah, oh my, ah Staci honey, you shouldn't be out here. Please go back inside!" Blazer became more agitated pawing the ground, giving low growls and looking to Susan to let him be released.

"No, if anything you shouldn't be laughing, like you know, crying would be the better conclusion. And who the heck is that with you, Sid?

It looks like that scum Drew, but how would he be able to get in here? I really thought you'd be crying by now Sis. I don't get it. I'm not going back in until you explain yourselves." Staci declared, putting her hands to her hips, moving sideways from Susan toward Sid, she then saw around him. "Oh? Good God! You're out of jail? How the hell did you get in here, Drew?"

Not bothering to explain how he got into the patio area, "I was just wondering what's going on with your hubby and my wife. Yes, please do explain yourselves."

"Drew, nothing is going on between them. Now, how did you get in here?"

"Do I really have to explain it to you Staci? If so you are really dumb."

"Oh, please do explain."

Drew smiled, "Scaled the wall, idiot. So many of you here, I guess you didn't need the alarms reset.

The advantage was Sid's. He jumped Drew, to keep the rest safe from a knife attack. He knew Staci had not seen the knife that Drew was wielding towards them. Drew, who overpowered Sid in height, weight, and muscle power, plunged one arm into Sid's shoulder and the other into his gut; Sid was on the ground in seconds, blood immediately showing on his shirt. The blood began to flow fast.

Harold, seeing this and still holding the phone, relayed the need for an ambulance. Benita went running for linens to help staunch the bleeding, praying that Drew would allow her to help Sid.

Staci ran to Sid, dropping down to him, she realized the wound was major. She reached down and hugged him to her. "Oh God, Sid, don't you die on me!"

Drew backed up a little, observing the scene and realizing the effect of his actions. Calculating quickly, he grabbed Staci behind the neck, using her shirt to pull her up. Staci started flailing her appendages, along with screaming and crying, "No, no look what you've done. I must stay with Sid, he needs me. Please let me go." His right arm went around her neck, holding the bloody knife in his left hand, pointed out so everyone could see it.

Oh no not my sister, you don't. Susan signaled Blazer to stay. Standing up from her chair with difficulty, "Drew, it's me you want, not my sister. Let her go; please. I'll go with you! Just let Staci go!" Susan moved toward Drew and Staci, while she spoke.

Chelle and Sid Jr. began crying for their mother, and Frank also. Moans and groans came from the rest, but no one made a move, only Blazer's agitation made him keep looking up and out, back and forth, looking back up and whining to Susan.

Sirens of all kinds were in the background. This made Drew more panicked. His eyes seemed to double in size, glaring wildly.

Susan realized from his eyes he was about to do something rash, so again she started to slowly limping toward him. "You know I'm right. Let Staci go, and then we can get away from here. You know, an ambulance is here is for Sid. So we must hurry. I know you don't want him to die."

"Susan that's not just an ambulance; sounds like fire and cops. Don't try and play games with me; one of your dear fucking family members or whatever contacted them."

Benita interrupted, standing in the doorway, holding towels in front of her. "Please let me care for him," surprising everyone by speaking perfect English. The entire group was suddenly so quiet it was unsettling. All were in the kind of staring shock as in a scene, watching a roadside accident.

"You want he die?" Benita asked.

"Shit, doesn't matter to me. He's a snake of a boss, like most. So if he dies so what?"

"Then you up for murder? No?"

"Lady, I'm up for murder now, which wasn't murder by the way, right Susan? Why do you think I came to get Susan? She can tell them, they'll believe me then. Besides Sid jumped me, so it won't be murder, just a blessed accident. The world will be better off without him."

"No, that isn't quite right about it being an accident; you drew your knife long before and I'm sure even though I don't have sight, from the way it sounds, you used the knife on him deliberately," Nick said. "But if he does die, then it could all change. So much has happened you aren't thinking very straight, so I advise you to let Benita care for him."

Without waiting any longer, with guarded determination Benita moved toward Sid. Drew did not stop her. She then called Tracy and Tara in to help her.

Susan was now in front of Staci and Drew. Tears quietly rolled down Staci's face. "Drew, let…"

"Let Staci go, Drew!" Irma yelled at the top of her lungs. Everyone looked to the patio doors. Irma was there holding a gun in her hand, pointing it at Drew. "I said let her go!"

"Sure Irma, sure; just don't get trigger happy now, cause you know, I'm going to let her go." He moved his arm from Staci's throat and pushed her aside, where she fell into the lounge head first. He then grabbed Susan, turning her quickly so that now his arm was around her neck. Blazer was up, barking, Susan gave him more signals. He did not move a muscle, but was ready. "I'll kill that dog if you don't shut it up" he whispered in her ear. Again Susan signaled her dog. Drew started to back away, somehow realizing they were too near the edge of the pool, so he moved them sideways seriously wanting them to round the house and leave. "Don't anyone try and follow us. I suggest you all clear out of this house, take what you need. Don't ever come back, this is our house, not yours. The girls can stay, but not FJ."

"No Drew, I will not live without all my children under one roof." Susan struggled to say this with his arm squeezing her larynx.

"You can't have my Mother! I'll shoot you first!" FJ yelled loudly, standing in the doorway with a gun in hand. His hands shook badly as he pointed the gun toward Drew and Susan.

God no, where did he get a gun? No, dear God, please don't let this child shoot him.

Drew started laughing, "You really think you have the balls to shoot me kid? More likely you'll shoot your mother. Then who'll take care of you?" Drew dropped the knife, reached behind him and showed his gun, pointing it straight at FJ. "I've waited for this day."

"I am a great shot, so let Susan go." Irma let herself be heard. "FJ, leave this to me, now put the gun away." Irma moved to put herself in front of FJ, her back to him, blocking FJ and the gun he held. "He's messed up too many families; it's time I take him down."

"Oh shit, this is really getting out of hand. All of you put away the guns. The cops will take Drew in, there will be a trial and we can get on with our lives." Harold stated matter-of-factly.

Does he really think he can get them to put their guns away? Does Frank have that gun loaded? Irma? Yes, she has been acting too strange lately. Part of that lies on the ground here with a big hole in him. What webs we weave. I feel like this is surreal. The sirens have stopped. Am I the only one who seems to have noticed? Should I let Blazer go for Drew? I feel Blazer would cause Drew to kill me first, but I don't want this family injured any more than it already is.

Drew started moving them sideways again. Irma did not take her gun off him. Her hand did not shake, so he sensed her aim was dead on him. "Irma, come on now. I let your woman go, so you can put your gun away, we'll just be on our way." *He's buying time. He's also afraid she will shoot him.*

FJ's hand shook so hard he would hit one of many other potential targets, if he did shoot.

Tracy whispered into Nick's ear, and then moved away, coming behind Frank. She reached around pulling Frank into her quickly, at the same time removing the gun from his hand. "No, he can't have my MOM!" Frank now cried openly with Tracy wrapping herself strongly around him, hugging him closely to her.

"Tracy where are you? Are you and Frank all right?"

"Over here Nick, FJ is with me." Nick slowly felt his way over to them.

Tara moved in next to Harold. "I'm so glad Missy isn't here. She wouldn't be able to handle this." Speaking from behind Tracy, Frank and Nick, "I'm glad you no longer have a gun, bro, but I feel like shooting him too. I wish somebody would. You don't think Irma will, do you Aunt Tracy?"

Tracy didn't say a thing, just gave Tara a wary look.

Drew and Susan were almost to the corner of the house. "Stop right there, Drew. Let Susan go!" this voice came from the side of the house. *That must be Pierce. So the fence wasn't charged. With so many coming in and out tonight, it's no wonder Drew got in.*

"I don't think so. Susan is mine and she's coming with me. If you shoot me, I will shoot her. I will NEVER let another man have her. She belongs to me!"

"Way I hear it; you're no longer married, Drew. But we can talk about that later." *No longer married? How did you get his signature?*

"Man, you got that wrong. I would never sign a paper agreeing to a divorce."

"Really? That's odd, the screen on my pc the other day. It showed divorce filed and granted to Susan. You do have a very strange file, I must say." *Oh, the auto time limit for non-contesting, just by my placing the ad in the paper? Forgot about that Drew! I your precious Susan outsmarted you.*

"I don't care about a piece of paper; she's my wife and will stay my wife forever. Now move out of our way, Susan is coming with me."

"Now you know I can't do that, Drew. You'll have to go through me and the twenty others like me around here. We have this place surrounded and I suggest you let the EMT's in to take care of the man you shot."

"I didn't shoot him, he ran into a knife. It's his fault."

* * *

Inside the house

The five EMT's entered the house with a stretcher and equipment. Ozark and two other cops were with them carrying heavy guns and decked in SWAT gear from head to toe. Ozark boldly moved immediately in front, of the group, setting up with a high powered rifle pointed directly at Drew. He let himself be fully seen. "Ozark at the ready!" he yelled.

Drew jumped slightly, directing his attention back to the patio door, spying for the authoritative voice. Sure enough, there was an assault weapon pointed directly at his head. His eyes grew larger. "Hey man, you aren't going to take a shot while I have this beautiful redhead in front of me, are you?"

There was no response, just the rifle aiming at his head.

The Chief is using time to let his other officers get set up outside and inside. I must wait and watch this Ozark for a sign to try and move out of range. I must. He wouldn't shoot otherwise would he? He does look as if he's very sure of himself. I don't want to die. I just got myself to a saner place. My kids need me. Tracy needs our help. She and Irma both helped keep Frank from committing a violent crime. I can never thank them enough. My entire family is here and now I'm possibly leaving them again. I pray Sid lives. God I sure hope this Ozark is a good shot. They wouldn't put someone in that position if he wasn't, would they?

"Everyone, please move inside out of the way so we can give this man the care he needs." This was said calmly but with authority. Neither Staci nor Benita moved. They were still on the ground holding towels against the wound. Both women were covered heavily in blood. "Please, ladies let us get to this man to give him the aid he needs." It was as though neither woman heard a thing; the EMT's patted them on the shoulder and then proceeded pulling them up from the cement. "He's barely conscious, get his vitals quick, and bring the gurney now." Another EMT was on the phone, while another was setting up an IV drip. What seemed like potential mass confusion, moved efficiently before them. There passed mere seconds and they were out the door with Sid.

Benita began to take over caring for Staci, who was desperately trying to get to Sid through the EMT's before her. Benita pulled her back, "Come, let them do job, we go inside." Slowly Benita turned Staci toward the door. Chelle and Sid Jr. came out to help get their Mother inside.

Irma was still at the outside door with gun pointed at Drew and Susan. Staci was in such a state she did not realize she passed Irma nor did she notice Irma blatantly holding a gun.

"Call your fucking man off Chief, Sus and I are leaving now." Again Drew started moving sideways; forcefully he moved them too quickly, causing Susan to lose her balance. Reaching down, Drew regained his hold by picking her up by her hair ... she yelped ... and then wrapped his arm again around her throat again, causing her to gasp and gag. Pierce's position did not allow him to move fast enough to bring down Drew before he regained his grasp on Susan. Amongst trying to ease the pressure on her larynx, Susan signaled Blazer to stay; she saw he was crouched ready to attack Drew. *Its ok Blazer please boy, I don't want you dead.*

The Chief knew Ozark could have shot Drew at this point, but he was waiting on orders. "Now you know I can't let you leave here with Susan. If you try you won't get out alive. So you may as well let her go." Pierce reestablished his position, making sure his gun pointed to Drew's temple. "Ozark is one great shot. He never misses. Doesn't talk much either, but he's firm about his business. I do suggest you let Susan go now, for his fingers are getting mighty tired on that trigger. You just never know what might happen if he decides to take his shot."

Is this Pierce's way of telling Ozark to take his shot when ready? Susan kept her eyes on the gunman. *Drew's shaking, I can feel it, and he's damn scared. God Irma put your gun down. Funny I don't feel the least bit afraid. What comes, comes, just want my kids and everyone else safe. Gee Frank, you may have to take responsibility for your kids. How will you handle that? Good thing he's divorced Carol. But the new dingbat he's got right now is just as bad. What a weird thing to think about right now.*

"Let's go!" Drew started moving again, trying to move fast in his sideways advance. Susan again started to lose her balance, but this time on purpose. An automatic reaction came from Drew, "You fuck'n handicap." Forgetting his situation, he dropped his arm from around her throat and raised the gun up in a gesture to reach out and strike Susan. Susan was falling to the ground. She let herself go limp so the fall would not hurt too badly.

The cracking sound of one shot rang through the air, a dot of blood suddenly blossoming on Drew's temple. Drew's eyes seemed to get large, and then close again quickly; he did not fall hard, but crumpled to the ground. He was dead before he hit the ground. It was quiet now and everything moved in a ballet of slow motion.

Susan was still lying on the ground, afraid to move. In seconds, Blazer changed all that by bouncing to his mistress' side, licking every part of her bare skin he could find. He caused her to laugh.

Irma's shaking hand dropped the gun to the patio. She walked away from it and Ozark moved quickly picking it up. When she got to the patio door, she turned and slid to the cement using her back to glide down the glass. Tears flowed from her eyes as she repeated over and over again, "He can't hurt anyone anymore."

Pierce left his position, gun in both hands, moving toward the main scene. He kicked Drew, then knelt checking his neck for a pulse. Quickly he turned to Susan, "Are you ok?"

"Yes, I think I'm fine." As she sat up, Blazer at her side, she looked over to Drew. "He looks so at peace. He's finally not going to suffer any more in his mind, nor make anyone else suffer. I feel only pity for him."

FJ ran from the house, trying to get to his mother. Ozark caught him in mid stride. "No son, you have to wait."

"But my Mom? Is she…"

"Aw no, she's fine, just shook up." Ozark assured him, "See the Chief is taking good care of her; looks like her dog is too."

"Oh, thank you Mr. Ozark. You saved my Mom. I'll never forget what you did for us."

Ozark did not know exactly how to react. He had never had anyone say something so nice to him right after having to take someone out. This made quite an impact on the officer. "You … you are very welcome. It was my duty to help keep you and your family safe. You sure have a big family in this house, are there more of you?"

"Just my sister Missy, she's at the U of A. She's in pre-law. But I sure do have a lot of aunts and uncles."

"Is it hard to remember them all?"

"Aw naw, I memorize them with pictures."

"Oh, now that's smart." This really took Ozark aback. "You know there's something different, but really kinda special about you. What's your name?"

"Frank sir; they also call me FJ. Can you show me how to shoot a gun?"

"I think we should save it for another time. I'm on duty and I have things to take care of." Ozark moved toward Irma where she sat against the sliding door. "I'll speak with you in a few minutes; ma'am, please don't move."

Irma nodded her head in compliance.

Tracy looked to Nick as he grasped her hand tighter, wanting to know if she just heard what this officer said to Irma. She squeezed in turn. "Now wouldn't they normally cuff her?" Tracy inquired.

The EMT'S had removed Sid long before, taking him by ambulance to the hospital, where he was probably already receiving care. Benita and Harold took Staci, Chelle and Sid Jr. to the hospital, to be there to help in any capacity they could.

The officers took finger prints and statements from each and every one left in the house. It was an exceptionally long night, no one getting to bed until just before sunrise. Needless to say, no one worried about getting children off to school or reporting in to jobs; messages were left where needed.

FACTUAL CHANGES

Our story must abruptly stop here to keep with the true story of our Susan, who is actually a composite of three women:

Two of the Susan's; are somewhere in our great world under the Witness Protection program.

Yes, all the husbands were shot in abusive home situations, but the husbands in two cases survived.

Recently one was released from prison.

Both women are undergoing weekly counseling and still suffer severe nightmares.

The children suffer severe nightmares as well. Also they do not mingle well with other children.

One Susan never went into the Witness Protection.

She is doing extremely well in the business world.

Her friend Tracy is now in remission and doing very well in her marriage.

Staci and Irma are still together.

Sid recovered and worked with the sheriff department to break the illegal drug ring.

Benita and Harold are happily married enjoying the new additions to their family.

Percy and Jim have passed.

Val and Matt are happy with three children.

One Susan's children; are doing very well in school and one is now engaged to be married.

Susan claims it was the love and support of family and friends that kept her 'sane', whatever that means.

"The most important thing in life is the love of family and friends, giving help and direction. "They are the only ones who will stand by you and tell you the truth, even if it hurts, to make you stronger." (Her words)

Recently dating, Susan has rejoined the lifecycle.